FOUR
FAULTLESS
FELONS

FOUR FAULTLESS FELONS

by

G. K. Chesterton

WITH A NEW INTRODUCTION BY
MARTIN GARDNER
Editor of *The Annotated
Innocence of Father Brown*

⊠ ⊠

DOVER PUBLICATIONS, INC.
NEW YORK

Introduction copyright © 1989 by Dover Publications, Inc.
All rights reserved under Pan American and International Copyright
Conventions.

Published in Canada by General Publishing Company, Ltd., 30 Lesmill
Road, Don Mills, Toronto, Ontario.
Published in the United Kingdom by Constable and Company, Ltd.

This Dover edition, first published in 1989, is an unabridged republication of the work as originally published by Cassell and Company, Ltd,
London, 1930. A few obvious typographical errors have been silently
corrected and the chapter numbers changed from Roman to Arabic to agree
with those in the table of contents. Further bibliographical details are given
in the introduction, which has been written specially for the Dover edition
by Martin Gardner.

Manufactured in the United States of America
Dover Publications, Inc., 31 East 2nd Street, Mineola, N.Y. 11501

Library of Congress Cataloging-in-Publication Data

Chesterton, G. K. (Gilbert Keith), 1874–1936.
    Four faultless felons / by G. K. Chesterton ; with a new introduction by
Martin Gardner.
        p.   cm.
    ISBN 0-486-25852-1 (pbk.)
    1. Detective and mystery stories, English. I. Title. II. Title: 4 faultless
felons.
PR4453.C4F6 1989
823'.912—dc19   88-17684
                                                                              CIP

INTRODUCTION TO THE DOVER EDITION

FATHER IAN BOYD, in his book *The Novels of G. K. Chesterton* (1975), aptly describes *Four Faultless Felons* as an "unusual blend" of *The Club of Queer Trades* and Chesterton's greatest novel, *The Man Who Was Thursday.** "Instead of a club made up of men who have invented eccentric trades, we have a club made up of men who have invented eccentric crimes; and instead of detectives who look like anarchists, we have heroes who look like four different kinds of criminals."

The four novellas that make up the book were first published in two British periodicals: "The Moderate Murderer" and "The Ecstatic Thief" in *Cassell's Magazine* (April and September 1929) and "The Honest Quack" and "The Loyal Traitor" in *Storyteller* (July 1929 and May 1930). "The Moderate Murderer" had four pictures by an artist whose signature, as I can best make out, was Arthur or Albert Bailey. He also illustrated the story in color on the magazine's cover. "The Ecstatic Thief" had three sketches by Fred W. Purvis. The other two stories were not illustrated. The four tales were reprinted as a book in 1930 (by Cassell and Company in England; Dodd, Mead and Company in the United States). Each story is a mystery to be solved, and each involves a delicately handled romance between a young man

---

*Both currently available as Dover reprints, nos. 25534-4 and 25121-7, respectively. (Original publication dates are 1905 and 1908.)

and woman. For the book, Chesterton added a prologue and epilogue to tie together the four otherwise unrelated stories.

We learn from the prologue that Asa Lee Pinion, a Chicago newspaper reporter, has gone to London to interview Count Raoul de Marillac, a man with a worldwide reputation as a dashing epicure. It turns out that he only pretends to be a man of pleasure. The Count is actually an austere ascetic who has invented a bizarre "Penance of Boredom"—forcing himself to dine on expensive food he secretly hates, and to attend immoral plays he secretly detests. He is like the Scotsman in an old joke who gives huge sums to charity so people will not know how stingy he is.

The Count introduces Pinion to four members of the Club of Men Misunderstood, of which he is president. The four have been accused, respectively, of attempted murder, fraud, theft, and treason. "I betrayed the four companions of my party," says the fourth felon, "and gave them up to the Government for a bribe." Pinion is too stunned to speak. After a moment of silence, the four men "burst out into a great uproar of laughter."

That roar of laughter is also Chesterton's, laughing at the farcical side of his narratives. It is often said that G. K.'s mystery tales are much too improbable to be believed, and of course this is true. Chesterton did not take his whimsical plots seriously. He saw his fiction, especially his mystery fiction, as a form of ingenious play, written primarily for entertainment, though often with theological themes and metaphysical asides. No one was more aware than he that his stories were humorous fantasies.

In the epilogue, after the four felons have told their wild tales to Pinion, the reporter reveals that he too is misunderstood. I suspect that Chesterton saw himself as another prospective member of the club. Throughout his life he cultivated the reputation of an absent-minded journalist with slovenly writing habits. The truth is that he was a careful writer who took great pride in his craft. Behind his endless jests, paradoxes, and verbal fireworks, there was deadly seriousness of intent, primarily theological, but also moral and political.

The political side of Chesterton tends to be ignored these days, especially by Catholic conservatives who admire his religious rhetoric. Although G. K. had no use for Marxism in any form, he also had little respect for unregulated capitalism. The heart of what he and his friends called "distributism" was the conviction that capitalism had widened the gulf between rich and poor, and that a capitalist state should use its powers to narrow the gulf by redistributing property. William F. Buckley, Jr., a Catholic conservative and an admirer of Chesterton, will concede that free-market excesses should be curbed, but his concessions are always grudging and muted. Whenever the Pope sides with Chesterton by denouncing the chasm between rich and poor, a chasm widened in the U.S. by Reaganomics, Buckley has nothing but contempt for the Vatican's ignorance.

A recent instance was the reaction of both Catholic and non-Catholic conservatives to Pope John Paul's 1988 encyclical *Sollicitudo Rei Socialis*, in which he blasted both "liberal capitalism" and "Marxist collectivism" as sins against the poor: "on the one hand, the all-consuming desire for profit, and on the other the thirst for power." This set off howls of rage from our two leading conservative columnists. William Safire found the Pope "wrongheaded" and "out of date." Buckley, the other William, called the encyclical "heart-tearingly misbegotten . . . the kind of historical revisionism generally associated with modern nihilists."

In his first book, *God and Man at Yale* (1951), Buckley borrowed from Chesterton's *The Ball and the Cross* (1909) by writing that he too saw our age as featuring a sword duel to the death between the free world, presumably founded on Christianity, and the godless Soviet Union. But when the Pope adopts Chesterton's condemnation of both communism and capitalism, Buckley banishes both Pope and G. K. into regions of naïveté. Let me add that I think both Safire and Buckley are right in deploring the 1988 encyclical for implying moral equivalence between the two systems. Chesterton surely would have agreed. But the Pope's condemnation by conservatives would carry more weight if they shared Chesterton's perception of the evils that flow from free markets when they are not bridled by governments sensitive to social injustice.

Father Boyd, in his book cited earlier, says that distributism plays "no obvious part" in *Four Faultless Felons*. This depends on what he means by "obvious." Consider some of the attacks on capitalism's excrescencies in "The Ecstatic Thief." Sir Jacob Nadoway is a wealthy businessman who has made a fortune selling a small biscuit called Nadoway's Nubs ("nubs" is an old English word for lumps). To Alan, one of his sons, the name of Nadoway "stinks to the ends of the earth" because the company that makes the biscuits was "founded on every sort of swindling and sweating and grinding the faces of the poor and cheating the widow and orphan. And above all, on robbery—on robbing rivals and partners and everybody else. . . ."

Later on, Alan calls his father's firm "one great ghastly whited sepulchre of human hypocrisy . . . full of dead men's bones, of men who had died of drink or starvation or despair, in prisons and workhouses and asylums, because this hateful thing had ruined a hundred businesses to build one. Horrible robbery, horrible tyranny, horrible triumph. And most horrible of all, to add to all the horrors, that I loved my father."

Hardly the rhetoric of any contributor to Buckley's *National Review,* though it was common bombast in *G. K.'s Weekly,* the organ of distributism. It is not inappropriate to describe Chesterton's economic and political opinions by a term that conservatives today abhor—democratic socialism. G. K. may have been poorly informed about many things—for a brief period he was an admirer of Mussolini!—but in no way can he be called a passionate disciple of Adam Smith.

People who appear to be what they are not fall roughly into two classes. One group consists of those who seem to possess an admirable trait when in fact they do not. With respect to piety, such pretensions aroused the anger of Jesus more than anything else. It was gentle Jesus, remember, who flung the word "hypocrites" at the religious leaders of his day and likened them to whitewashed graves. One thinks of our Elmer Gantrys who thunder against sins they themselves commit; of political leaders who pose as Christians and good family men when the truth is that they lost their faith early in life and see nothing wrong in endless adulteries; of television evangelists who pretend to be poor but indulge in lavish life styles made possible by donations from poor and gullible followers. Can you imagine how Jesus would react, perhaps whip in hand, if he could tour the mansions of our top televangelists or, for that matter, tour the Vatican?

The other kind of mask that some people wear—the one that most fascinated Chesterton—is the evil mask that hides a good person. It is a common device in romantic fiction and the cinema: the double agent or undercover cop who seems to work for the enemy; the tough detective who appears capable of taking any bribe if the price is right, but who is incorruptible; the happy hooker with the heart of gold. We all enjoy plots that turn on revelations that masks are false, even when good and evil are not involved: the homely-seeming girl with no makeup and dowdy clothes who later proves to have a gorgeous face and body; the mild-mannered reporter who is really Superman; the poor suitor who turns out to be wealthy; the mistreated clerk who secretly owns the business; the shy cowboy who orders milk at the bar but actually is the fastest gun in the West.

In planning this introduction I found in my files a forgotten outline of a story I never wrote. I called it "The Ultimate Saint." My hero was a man so troubled by the notion that perhaps his altruism was motivated by wanting the reputation of a saint that he devised all sorts of clever ways to seem evil. Of course his bad deeds were not really bad. Unfortunately, his friends discover his dark secret and revere him all the more. This makes him furious. In his old age, having learned he has incurable cancer, he plans one last attempt to blacken his name.

A Catholic friend commits suicide. Knowing that the Church considers this a mortal sin, and that the man's death is a terrible blow to his wife and children, my hero invents a set of false clues suggesting that the friend was murdered. Following up on these clues, a detective pins the murder on the saint. He is arrested, convicted, and sent to prison where he dies awaiting execution, happy at finally obliterating his saintly reputation.

I doubt if Chesterton would have liked this crazy plot, even though I intended it to imply a startling conjecture. Could it be that God permits evil so we won't know, at least in this life, how good He really is? There also would have been the suggestion that Jesus himself could have been a member of the Club of Men Misunderstood.

To Chesterton, Jesus was of course the supreme example of a faultless felon, executed as a common criminal between two authentic thieves. "You go through the worst to the best," says Millicent Milton in the third story, "as you go through the west to the east, and there really is a place, at the back of the world, where the east and the west are one. Can't you feel there is something so frightfully and frantically good that it *must* seem bad? . . . A blaze in the sky makes a blot on the eyesight. And after all, . . . the sun was blotted out, because one man was too good to live."

There are many passages in *Four Faultless Felons* that touch on incidents in Chesterton's life and on ideas expressed in his earlier books. Barbara Traill, for example, in the first story, thinks she is going mad. "But she was not in the least mad; she was only young; and thousands of young people go through such a phase of nightmare; and nobody knows or helps." We learn from Chesterton's autobiography that as a youth he went through an agonizing morbid phase in which he was tormented by fears that the outside world was only a projection of his own consciousness, a malady that afflicts some of today's New Age junkies.

In the second tale, the eccentric poet and painter Walter Windrush and the scientist Dr. John Judson represent two sides of the healthy human mind. Chesterton relished this kind of art-versus-science counterpoint, and similar pairs figure in many of his earlier stories. One thinks also of Auberon Quin and Adam Wayne in *The Napoleon of Notting Hill* (1904), symbols of love versus laughter, "two lobes of the brain of a ploughman." One thinks of the Catholic and the atheist who cross swords in *The Ball and the Cross.* One thinks of Sunday in *The Man Who Was Thursday* (1908), both the head of the secret police and the leader of the anarchists.

I have on the wall of my den an engraving of the Garden of Eden's forbidden tree. It has the shape of an atom bomb's mushroom cloud. I think Chesterton, for whom the Tree figures in many a story, would have appreciated this symbolism. Here, in "The Honest Quack," the grotesque tree in Windrush's secret garden is explicitly regarded by the poet as symbolic of the forbidden tree, in turn a metaphor for the good and evil that spring from scientific progress. The gasoline motor makes it easy for us to move about, but (as Windrush points out) the automobile can also kill. Are there regions of knowledge that science should never explore? "I still think that even monkeys would have been wise to leave one taboo tree; one sacred tree they did not climb. But evolution only means. . . ." Chesterton was wise not to finish what would have been a foolish sentence. It was one of his failings that to the end of his life he managed to keep himself from comprehending the overwhelming evidence for evolution.

Chesterton admired good thieves who steal from the rich, like Robin Hood, and like Flambeau, who became Father Brown's best friend. "We want more theft, house-breaking and highway robbery," says distributist Alan to Millicent, "to shift and rearrange the furniture of society; to regroup—if you follow me—its goods and chattels, as if after a spring-cleaning. . . ." Here again we encounter ideas often expressed in G. K.'s earlier books, and even in an amusing incident told in his autobiography. A lady friend had left her parasol in the waiting room of a railway station. Passing the station late that night, Chesterton climbed up the steep embankment, crawled under the platform, entered the waiting room, and recovered the parasol. "I committed," he writes, "my first and last crime, which was burglary, and very enjoyable."

As a young man Chesterton belonged to a debating club called the

I. D. K. When asked what the initials stood for, members would shrug their shoulders and say "I Don't Know." This whimsical dodge reappears in "The Loyal Traitor" at the end of the jingle that was the motto of the Brotherhood of The Word:

> As Aaron's serpent swallowed snakes and rods,
> As God alone is greater than the gods,
> As all stars shrivel in the single sun,
> The words are many, but The Word is one.

"Word" in the last line has at least three levels of significance: the unity of the story's four revolutionaries, the virtue of keeping one's word, and the unity of the Trinity. "In the beginning was the Word, and the Word was with God, and the Word was God" (John 1:1). The book's second tale has a hint of this theological unity when Enid sees her poet father and the man of science apparently fighting on a sunlit road "like two living letters of an alphabet struggling to spell out a word." Father Boyd is right in saying that doctrines peculiar to Roman Catholicism do not enter into the book, but G. K. was almost incapable of writing fiction in which doctrines peculiar to Christianity did not enter.

As much as I regret saying it, Chesterton also found it difficult to write fiction in which anti-Semitism (which he never recognized as such) did not enter. I suspect that one reason, if not the main reason, why *Four Faultless Felons* was allowed to go out of print in the U.S., and its copyright was never renewed, is the anti-Semitism that mars so many pages. In the first tale we are told that Barbara "had no Anti-Semitic prejudice in particular," but that she finds "something sinister in a fair Jew, as in a white negro." In the second story Isaac Morse is a wicked moneylender. In the third tale Isidor Green and his wife are comic characters. Isidor Simon, a banker in the final tale, remarks: "Greed is the Jewish vice: greed for luxury; greed for vulgarity; greed for gambling; greed for throwing away other people's money and their own on a harem or a theatre or a grand hotel or some harlotry—or possibly on a grand revolution."

"But there's something blood-curdling about these cultured Jews," declares Colonel Grimm, head of the police in the imaginary country of Pavonia, "with their delicate and cautious art of pleasure. Some say it's because they don't believe in a future life." Later in the same story we learn that a Jewish usurer had underground tunnels built from his house to the yard so that harlots could secretly come and go.

In the first story, where the locale is near the Great Pyramid of Egypt, the vegetation seems to Barbara

> not like the green growths of home, springing on light stalks to lovely flowers like butterflies captured out of air. It was more like the dead blind bubbling of some green squalid slime: a world of plants that were as plain and flat as stones. She hated the hairy surface of some of the squat and swollen trees of that grotesque garden; the tufts here and there irritated her fancy as they might have tickled her face. She felt that even the big folded flowers, if they opened, would have a foul fragrance. She had a latent sense of the savour of faint horror, lying over all as lightly as the faint moonshine.

Barbara's reaction to Egyptian flora was precisely how Chesterton reacted to the great religions of the East, especially to the Muslim faith, which he saw as a loathsome parody of Christianity.

Nothing is gained by trying to excuse these prejudices. On the other hand, Chesterton's blindnesses should not prevent us from enjoying his insights, his humor, and his swashbuckling style. The absurd trial of Alan Nadoway is Chesterton at his funniest. Chapter 4 of "The Moderate Murderer" includes a moving defense of loving and educating emotionally handicapped children, as well as one of Chesterton's many defenses of the value of riddles and nonsense in teaching all children. The same story includes an amusing description of something we have all experienced, though I have never seen it described before in a work of fiction. Barbara is trying desperately to overhear a conversation across a crowded room while pretending to listen to the boring remarks of a man (in this case a Pyramid crank) who had that habit "so unkind to the inattentive listener" of suddenly asking a question.

Four Faultless Felons is written in Chesterton's familiar style, rich in rhythms, alliteration, unusual figures of speech, and the colorful imagery of a man who had studied painting and once planned to be an artist. Sunsets, sunrises, and moonlight, as in all G. K.'s fiction, are pictured in vivid lines that are very close to poetry. "The afternoon had already reddened into evening, and the sunset lay in long bands of burning crimson across the purple desolation of that dry inland sea." Barbara has just remarked that England has a glorious empire. "England had a glorious empire," she is corrected. "So had Egypt. . . . An Empire on which the sun never sets.

Look . . . the sun is setting in blood.''
Here are two other sunsets from the same story:

> The whole hung under him like a vast coloured cloud in the brief afterglow of the Eastern sunset; then it was rapidly rolled in the purple gloom in which the strong stars stood out over his head and seemed nearer than the things of earth.
>
> *   *   *
>
> The sky behind the green pergolas of foliage was a vivid violet or some sort of blue that seemed warmer than any red; and the furry filaments of the great tree-trunks seemed like the quaint sea-beasts of childhood, which could be stroked and which unfolded their fingers.

In the second story the "small white rim of what was obviously a colossal white cloud barely showed above the ridge; producing one of those rare effects that almost persuade the natural man, in spite of all the proofs adduced for it, that the world is round." Later in the tale "a great morning wind from the south rushed upon the garden, bending all its shrubs and bushes and seeming, as does the air when it passes over sunlit foliage, to drive the sunshine before it in mighty waves." Not by accident is this rushing wind in the garden of a man named Windrush.

Chesterton's notorious alliteration is everywhere. I count myself among those who relish it, even though at times it can be excessive. In the second sentence of the second chapter of "The Loyal Traitor" the "P" of Pavonia is repeated as an initial letter no less than eight times!

A passage in the sixth chapter of "The Ecstatic Thief" seems to me unusually timely for an America where Protestants and Catholics alike have become curiously bifurcated. On the one hand are the fundamentalists, evangelicals, charismatics, and orthodox Catholics who take seriously all the doctrines formulated by Saint Paul. On the other hand are the liberal Protestants and Catholics for whom doctrines no longer matter. They attend mainline churches where they listen to vapid sermons and (if Protestant) sing tuneless hymns and recite creeds they don't believe. Ask for their opinion on any basic Christian dogma, and their eyes go blank and they stammer evasions. They are the Laodiceans of the book of Revelation, neither cold nor hot, living by the splashes of a lukewarm faith which they no longer think about and which they are incapable of putting at the center of their lives.

Pagan savages, Alan tells Millicent, often "have really got hold of religion," whereas "lots of people with a high moral code don't know what religion means. They would run screaming with terror, if they got so much as a glimpse of Religion. It's an awful thing."

MARTIN GARDNER

Hendersonville, North Carolina

CONTENTS

THE ECSTATIC THIEF

THE LOYAL TRAITOR

FOUR
FAULTLESS
FELONS

PROLOGUE OF
THE PRESSMAN

M R. ASA LEE PINION, of the *Chicago Comet,* had crossed half of America, the whole of the Atlantic, and eventually even Piccadilly Circus, in pursuit of the notable, if not notorious figure of Count Raoul de Marillac. Mr. Pinion wanted to get what is called "a story"; a story to put in his paper. He did get a story; but he did not put it in his paper. It was too tall a story, even for the *Comet.* Perhaps the metaphor is true in more ways than one; and the fable was tall like a church-spire or a tower among the stars: beyond comprehension as well as belief. Anyhow, Mr. Pinion decided not to risk his readers' comments. But that is no reason why the present writer, writing for more exalted, spiritual and divinely credulous readers, should imitate his silence.

Really, the anecdote he heard was quite incredible: and Mr. Pinion was not intolerant. While the Count was painting the town red and himself black, it was quite possible to believe that he was not so black as he was painted. After all, his extravagance, and luxury, however ostentatious, did no particular harm to anybody but himself; and if he associated with the dissipated and degraded, he had never been known to interfere with the innocent or the reputable. But while it was credible enough that the nobleman was not so black as he was painted, he certainly could not be quite so white as he was painted, in the wild story that was told that evening. The story came from a friend of the Count's; much too friendly a friend, thought Mr. Pinion;

friendly to the point of feeble-mindedness. He supposed it must be a delusion or a hoax; anyhow he did not put it into his paper. Yet it is because of this highly improbable anecdote that the Count de Marillac stands at the opening of this book, to introduce the four stories which were put forth as parallels to his own.

But there was one fact which struck the journalist as odd even at the beginning. He understood well enough that it would be difficult to catch the Count anywhere, as he whirled from one social engagement to another, in the manner appropriately called "fast." And he was not offended when Marillac said he could only spare ten minutes at his London club before going on to a theatrical first-night and other ensuing festivities. During that ten minutes, however, Marillac was quite polite; answered the rather superficial society questions which the *Comet* wanted answered, and very genially introduced the journalist to three or four club companions or cronies, who were standing about him in the lounge; and who continued to stand about after the Count himself had made his beaming and flashing exit.

"I suppose," said one of them, "that the naughty old man has gone to see the naughty new play with all the naughty new people."

"Yes," grunted a big man standing in front of the fire. "He's gone with the naughtiest person of all, the author, Mrs. Prague. Authoress, I suppose she'd call herself—being only cultured and not educated."

"He always goes to the first night of those plays," assented the other. "P'raps he thinks there won't be a second night, if the police raid the place."

"What play is it?" asked the American in a gentle voice. He was a quiet little man with a very long head and a refined falcon profile; he was much less loud and casual than the Englishmen.

"*Naked Souls,*" said the first man with a faint groan. "Dramatized version of the world-shaking novel 'Pan's Pipes.' Grapples grimly with the facts of life."

"Also bold, breezy and back to Nature," said the man by the fire. "We hear a lot just now about Pan's Pipes. They seem to me a little too like drain-pipes."

"You see," said the other, "Mrs. Prague is so very Modern, she has to go back to Pan. She says she cannot bear to believe that Pan is dead."

"I think," said the large man, with a touch of heavy violence, "that Pan is not only dead but rotting and stinking in the street."

It was the four friends of Marillac who puzzled Mr. Pinion. They were obviously rather intimate friends; and yet they were not, on the whole, of the sort likely to be even acquaintances. Marillac himself was much what might have been expected; rather more restless and haggard than his handsome portraits might have implied; a thing likely enough with his late hours and his advancing years. His curly hair was still dark and thick, but his pointed grey beard was whitening fast; his eyes were a little hollow, and had a more anxious expression than could be inferred, at a distance, from his buoyant gestures and rapid walk. All that was quite in character; but the tone of the group was different. One figure alone out of the four seemed in some sense of Marillac's world; having something of the carriage of a military officer, with that fine shade that suggests a foreign officer. He had a clean-shaven, regular and very impassive face; he was sitting down when he bowed politely to the stranger; but something in the bow suggested that, standing up, he would have clicked his heels. The others were quite English and quite different. One of them was the very big man, with big shoulders bowed but powerful and a big head not yet bald but striped with rather thin brown hair. But the arresting thing about him was that indescribable suggestion of dust or cobwebs that belongs to a strong man leading a sedentary life; possibly scientific or scholarly, but certainly obscure, in its method if not its effect; the sort of middle-class man with a hobby, who seems to have been dug out of it with a spade. It was hard to imagine a more complete contradiction to such a meteor of fashion as the Count. The man next him, though more alert, was equally solid and respectable and free from fashionable pretensions; a short square man with a square face and spectacles; who looked like what he was, an ordinary busy suburban general practitioner. The fourth of Marillac's incongruous intimates was quite frankly shabby. Grey seedy clothes hung limply on his lean figure; and his dark hair and rather ragged beard could, at the best, be only excused as Bohemian. He had very remarkable eyes; sunk very deep in his head and yet, by a paradox, standing out like signals. The visitor found himself continually drawn to them, as if they were magnets.

But, all together, the group bothered and bewildered him. It was not merely a difference of social class; it was an atmosphere of sobriety and even of solid work and worth, which seemed to belong to another world. The four men in question were friendly in a modest and even embarrassed manner, they fell into conversation with the journalist as with any ordinary equal in a tram or a tube; and when, about an hour later, they asked him to share their dinner at the club, he had no such sense of strain as he might have felt in facing one of the fabulous

Luculline banquets of their friend the Count de Marillac.

For however seriously Marillac might or might not be taking the serious drama of Sex and Science, there was no doubt that he would take the dinner even more seriously. He was famous as an epicure of almost the classic and legendary sort; and all the *gourmets* of Europe reverenced his reputation. The little man with the spectacles glanced at this fact, indeed, as they sat down to dinner:

"Hope you can put up with our simple fare, Mr. Pinion," he said. "You'd have had a much more carefully selected menu if Marillac had been here."

The American reassured him with polite expressions about the club dinner; but added:

"I suppose it is true that he does make rather an art of dining."

"Oh, yes," said the man in spectacles. "Always has all the right things at the wrong times. That's the ideal, I suppose."

"I suppose he takes a lot of trouble," said Pinion.

"Yes," said the other. "He chooses his meals very carefully. Not carefully from my point of view. But then I'm a doctor."

Pinion could not keep his eyes off the magnetic eyes of the man with the shabby clothes and shaggy hair. Just now the man was gazing across the table with a curious intentness; and in the ensuing silence, he suddenly intervened.

"Everybody knows he's very particular in choosing his dinner. But I bet not one man in a million knows the principle on which he chooses it."

"You must remember," said Pinion, with his soft accent, "that I am a journalist; and I should like to be the one man in a million."

The man opposite looked at him steadily and rather strangely for a moment, and then said:

"I have half a mind. . . . Look here, have you any human curiosity as well as journalistic curiosity? I mean, would the one man like to know, even if the million never knew?"

"Oh, yes," replied the journalist, "I have plenty of curiosity, even about things I am told in confidence. But I can't quite see why Marillac's taste in champagne and ortolans should be so very confidential."

"Well," answered the other gravely, "why do you think he chooses them?"

"I guess I've got a bromide mind," said the American, "but I should rather suspect him of choosing the things he likes."

"*Au contraire;* as the other *gourmet* said when asked if he lunched on the boat."

The man with the peculiar eyes broke off from his flippant speech, plunged for a few moments into profound silence, and then resumed in so different a tone that it was like another man suddenly speaking at the table.

"Every age has its bigotry, which is blind to some particular need of human nature; the Puritans to the need for merriment, the Manchester School to the need for beauty; and so on. There is a need in man, or at least in many men, which it is not fashionable to admit or allow for in these days. Most people have had a touch of it in the more serious emotions of youth; in a few men it burns like a flame to the last, as it does here. Christianity, especially Catholic Christianity, has been blamed for imposing it; but in fact, it rather regulated and even restrained the passion than forced it. It exists in all religions; to a wild and frantic extent in some of the religions of Asia. There men hack themselves with knives or hang themselves on hooks; or walk through life with withered arms rigidly uplifted, crucified upon empty air. It is the appetite for what one does not like. Marillac has it."

"What on earth——" began the startled journalist; but the other continued:

"In short, it is what people call Asceticism; and one of the modern mistakes is not allowing for its real existence in rare but quite real people. To live a life of incessant austerity and self-denial, as Marillac does, is surrounded with extraordinary difficulties and misunderstandings in modern society. Society can understand some particular Puritan fad, like Prohibition, especially if it is imposed on other people; above all, on poor people. But a man like Marillac, imposing on himself, not abstinence from wine, but abstinence from worldly pleasures of every sort . . . ."

"Excuse me," said Pinion in his most courteous tones, "I trust I'd never have the incivility to suggest that you have gone mad; so I must ask you to tell me candidly whether I have."

"Most people," replied the other, "would answer that it is Marillac who has gone mad. Perhaps he has; anyhow, if the truth were known, he would certainly be thought so. But it isn't only to avoid being put in a lunatic asylum that he hides his hermit's ideal by pretending to be a man of pleasure. It's part of the whole idea, in its only tolerable form. The worst of those Eastern fakirs hung on hooks is that they are too conspicuous. It may make them just a little vain. I don't deny that Stylites and some of the first hermits may have been touched with the same danger. But our friend is a Christian anchorite; and understands the advice, 'When you fast, anoint your head and wash your face.' He is not seen of men to fast. On the contrary, he is seen of men to feast. Only, don't you see, he has invented a new kind of fasting."

Mr. Pinion of the *Comet* suddenly laughed; a curt and startled laugh; for he was very quick and had already guessed the joke.

"You don't really mean——" he began.

"Well, it's quite simple, isn't it?" replied his informant. "He feasts on all the most luxurious and expensive things that he doesn't like. Especially on the things that he simply detests. Under that cover, nobody can possibly accuse him of virtue. He remains impenetrably protected behind a rampart of repulsive oysters and unwelcome *aperitifs*. In short, the hermit must now hide anywhere but in the hermitage. He generally hides in the latest luxurious gilded hotels; because that's where they have the worst cooking."

"This is a very extraordinary tale," said the American, arching his eyebrows.

"You begin to see the idea?" said the other. "If he has twenty different *hors d'œuvre* brought to him and takes the olives, who is to know that he hates olives? If he thoughtfully scans the whole wine-list and eventually selects a rather recondite Hock, who will guess that his whole soul rises in disgust at the very thought of Hock: and that he knows that's the nastiest—even of Hocks? Whereas, if he were to demand dried peas or a mouldy crust at the Ritz, he would probably attract attention."

"I never can quite see," said the man in spectacles restlessly, "what is the good of it all."

The other man lowered his magnetic eyes and looked down with some embarrassment. At last he said:

"I think I can see it, but I don't think I can say it. I had a touch of it myself once; only in one special direction; and I found it almost impossible to explain to anybody. Only there is one mark of the real mystic and ascetic of this sort; that he only wants to do it to himself. He wants everybody else to have what wine or smokes they want and will ransack the Ritz for it. The moment he wants to dragoon the others, the mystic sinks into a mire of degradation and becomes the moral reformer."

There was a pause; and then the journalist said suddenly:

"But, look here, this won't do. It isn't only wasting his money on wining and dining that has got Marillac a bad name. It's the whole thing. Why is he such a fan for these rotten erotic plays and things? Why does he go about with a woman like Mrs. Prague? That doesn't seem like a hermit, anyhow."

The man facing Pinion smiled and the heavier man on his right half turned with a sort of grunt of laughter.

"Well," he said, "it's pretty plain you've never been about with Mrs. Prague."

"Why, what do you mean?" asked Pinion; and this time there was something like a general laugh.

"Some day she's his Maiden Aunt and it's his duty to be kind to her," began the first man; but the second man interrupted him gruffly:

"Why do you call her a Maiden Aunt when she looks like a——"

"Quite so, quite so," said the first man rather hastily, "and why 'looks like'—if it comes to that?"

"But her conversation!" groaned his friend. "And Marillac stands it for hours on end!"

"And her play!" assented the other. "Marillac sits through five mortal acts of it. If that isn't being a martyr——"

"Don't you see?" cried the shabby man with something like excitement. "The Count is a cultivated and even learned man; also he is a Latin and logical to the point of impatience. And yet he sticks it. He endures five or six acts of a Really Modern Intellectual Incisive Drama. The First Act in which she says that Woman will no longer be put on a pedestal; the Second Act in which Woman will no longer be put under a glass case; the Third Act in which Woman will no longer be a plaything for man, and the Fourth in which she will no longer be a chattel; all the *clichés*. And he still has two acts before him, in which she will not be something else; will not be a slave in the home or an outcast flung from the home. He's seen it six times without turning a hair; you can't even see him grind his teeth. And Mrs. Prague's conversation! How her first husband could never understand, and her second husband seemed as if he might understand, only her third husband carried her off as if there was real understanding—and so on, as if there were anything to be understood. You know what an utterly egotistical fool is like. And he suffers even those fools gladly."

"In fact," put in the big man in his brooding manner, "you might say he has invented the Modern Penance. The Penance of Boredom.

Hair-shirts and hermits' caves in a howling wilderness would not be so horrible to modern nerves as that."

"By your account," ruminated Pinion, "I've been chasing a pleasure-seeker tripping on the light fantastic toe and only found a hermit standing on his head." After a silence he said abruptly, "Is this really true? How did you find it out?"

"That's rather a long story," replied the man opposite. "The truth is that Marillac allows himself one feast in the year; on Christmas Day, and eats and drinks what he really likes. I found him drinking beer and eating tripe and onions in a quiet pub in Hoxton; and somehow we were forced into confidential conversation. You will understand, of course, that this is a confidential conversation."

"I certainly shan't print it," answered the journalist. "I should be regarded as a lunatic if I did. People don't understand that sort of lunacy nowadays; and I rather wonder you take to it so much yourself."

"Well, I put my own case before him, you see," answered the other. "In a small way it was a little like his own. And then I introduced him to my friends; and so he became a sort of President of our little club."

"Oh," said Pinion rather blankly, "I didn't know you were a club."

"Well, we are four men with a common bond at least. We have all had occasion, like Marillac, to look rather worse than we were."

"Yes," grunted the large man rather sourly, "we've all been Misunderstood. Like Mrs. Prague."

"The Club of Men Misunderstood is rather more cheerful than that, however," continued his friend. "We are all pretty jolly here, considering that our reputations have been blasted by black and revolting crimes. The truth is we have devoted ourselves to a new sort of detective story—or detective service if you like. We do not hunt for crimes but for concealed virtues. Sometimes, as in Marillac's case, they are very artfully concealed. As you will doubtless be justified in retorting, we conceal our own virtues with brilliant success."

The journalist's head began to go round a little, though he thought himself pretty well accustomed both to crazy and criminal surroundings. "But I thought you said," he objected, "that your reputations were blasted with crime. What sort of crime?"

"Well, mine was murder," said the man next to him. "The people who blasted me did it because they disapproved of murder, apparently. It's true I was rather a failure at murder, as at everything else."

Pinion's gaze wandered in some bewilderment to the next man who answered cheerfully:

"Mine was only a common fraud. A professional fraud, too, the sort that gets you kicked out of your profession sometimes. Rather like Dr. Cook's sham discovery of the North Pole."

"What does all this mean?" asked Pinion; and he looked inquiringly at the man opposite, who had done so much of the explaining so far.

"Oh, theft," said the man opposite indifferently; "the charge on which I was actually arrested was petty larceny."

There was a profound silence, which seemed to settle in a mysterious manner, like a gathering cloud, on the figure of the fourth member; who had not spoken so far a single word. He sat erect in his rather stiff foreign fashion; his wooden handsome face was unchanged and his lips had never moved even for so much as a murmur. But now, when the sudden and deep silence seemed to challenge him, his face seemed to harden from wood to stone and when he spoke at last, his foreign accent seemed something more than alien, as if it were almost inhuman.

"I have committed the Unpardonable Sin," he said. "For what sin did Dante reserve the last and lowest hell; the Circle of Ice?"

Still no one spoke; and he answered his own question in the same hollow tone:

"Treason. I betrayed the four companions of my party, and gave them up to the Government for a bribe."

Something turned cold inside the sensitive stranger, and for the first time he really felt the air around him sinister and strange. The stillness continued for another half minute; and then all the four men burst out into a great uproar of laughter.

The stories they told, to justify their boasts or confessions, are here retold in a different fashion, as they appeared to those on the outskirts rather than the centre of the events. But the journalist, who liked to collect all the odd things of life, was interested enough to record them, and then afterwards recast them. He felt he had really got something, if not exactly what he had expected, out of his pursuit of the dashing and extravagant Count Raoul de Marillac.

THE MODERATE
MURDERER

1

THE MAN WITH THE
GREEN UMBRELLA

HE NEW GOVERNOR was Lord Tallboys, commonly called Top-hat
Tallboys, because of his attachment to that uncanny erection,
which he continued to carry balanced on his head as calmly among
the palm-trees of Egypt as among the lamp-posts of Westminster.
Certainly he carried it calmly enough in lands where few crowns were
safe from toppling. The district he had come out to govern may here
be described, with diplomatic vagueness, as a strip on the edge of
Egypt and called for our convenience Polybia. It is an old story now;
but one which many people had reason to remember for many years;
and at the time it was an imperial event. One Governor was killed,
another Governor was nearly killed; but in this story we are concerned
only with one catastrophe; and that was rather a personal and even
private catastrophe.

Top-hat Tallboys was a bachelor and yet he brought a family with
him. He had a nephew and two nieces of whom one, as it happened,
had married the Deputy Governor of Polybia, the man who had been
called to rule during the interregnum after the murder of the previous
ruler. The other niece was unmarried; her name was Barbara Traill;
and she may well be the first figure to cross the stage of this story.

For indeed she was rather a solitary and striking figure, raven dark
and rich in colouring with a very beautiful but rather sullen profile,
as she crossed the sandy spaces and came under the cover of one long
low wall which alone threw a strip of shadow from the sun, which

was sloping towards the desert horizon. The wall itself was a quaint example of the patchwork character of that borderland of East and West. It was actually a line of little villas, built for clerks and small officials, and thrown out as by a speculative builder whose speculations spread to the ends of the earth. It was a strip of Streatham amid the ruins of Heliopolis. Such oddities are not unknown, when the oldest countries are turned into the newest colonies. But in this case the young woman, who was not without imagination, was conscious of a quite fantastic contrast. Each of these dolls' houses had its toy shrubs and plants and its narrow oblong of back garden running down to the common and continuous garden wall; and it was just outside this wall that there ran the rough path, fringed with a few hoary and wrinkled olives. Outside the fringe there faded away into infinity the monstrous solitude of sand. Only there could still be detected on that last line of distance a faint triangular shape; a sort of mathematical symbol whose unnatural simplicity has moved all poets and pilgrims for five thousand years. Anyone seeing it really for the first time, as the girl did, can hardly avoid uttering a cry: "The Pyramids!"

Almost as she said it a voice said in her ear, not loud but with alarming clearness and very exact articulation: "The foundations were traced in blood and in blood shall they be traced anew. These things are written for our instruction."

It has been said that Barbara Traill was not without imagination; it would be truer to say that she had rather too much. But she was quite certain she had not imagined the voice; though she certainly could not imagine where it came from. She appeared to be absolutely alone on the little path which ran along the wall and led to the gardens round the Governorate. Then she remembered the wall itself, and looking sharply over her shoulder, she fancied she saw for one moment a head peering out of the shadow of a sycamore, which was the only tree of any size for some distance; since she had left the last of the low sprawling olives two hundred yards behind. Whatever it was, it had instantly vanished; and somehow she suddenly felt frightened; more frightened at its disappearance than its appearance. She began to hurry along the path to her uncle's residence at a pace that was a little like a run. It was probably through this sudden acceleration of movement that she seemed to become aware, rather abruptly, that a man was marching steadily in front of her along the same track towards the gates of the Governorate.

He was a very large man; and seemed to take up the whole of the narrow path. She had something of the sensation, with which she was already slightly acquainted, of walking behind a camel through the narrow and crooked cracks of the Eastern town. But this man planted his feet as firmly as an elephant; he walked, one might say, even with a certain pomp, as if he were in a procession. He wore a long frock-coat and his head was surmounted by a tower of scarlet, a very tall red fez, rather taller than the top-hat of Lord Tallboys. The combination of the red Eastern cap and the black Western clothes is common enough among the *Effendi* class in those countries. But somehow it seemed novel and incongruous in this case, for the man was very fair and had a big blonde beard blown about in the breeze. He might have been a model for the idiots who talk of the Nordic type of European; but somehow he did not look like an Englishman. He carried hooked on one finger a rather grotesque green umbrella or parasol, which he twirled idly like a trinket. As he was walking slower and slower and Barbara was walking fast and wanted to walk faster, she could hardly repress an exclamation of impatience and something like a request for room to pass. The large man with the beard immediately faced round and stared at her; then he lifted a monocle and fixed it in his eye and instantly smiled his apologies. She realized that he must be short-sighted and that she had been a mere blur to him a moment before; but there was something else in the change of his face and manner, something that she had seen before, but to which she could not put a name.

He explained, with the most formal courtesy, that he was going to leave a note for an official at the Governorate; and there was really no reason for her to refuse him credence or conversation. They walked a little way together, talking of things in general; and she had not exchanged more than a few sentences before she realized that she was talking to a remarkable man.

We hear much in these days about the dangers of innocence; much that is false and a little that is true. But the argument is almost exclusively applied to sexual innocence. There is a great deal that ought to be said about the dangers of political innocence. That most necessary and most noble virtue of patriotism is very often brought to despair and destruction, quite needlessly and prematurely, by the folly of educating the comfortable classes in a false optimism about the record and security of the Empire. Young people like Barbara Traill have often never heard a word about the other side of the story, as it would be told by Irishmen or Indians or even French Canadians; and it is the fault of their parents and their papers if they often pass abruptly from a stupid Britishism to an equally stupid Bolshevism. The hour of Barbara Traill was come; though she probably did not know it.

"If England keeps her promises," said the man with the beard, frowning, "there is still a chance that things may be quiet."

And Barbara had answered, like a schoolboy:

"England always keeps her promises."

"The Waba have not noticed it," he answered with an air of triumph.

The omniscient are often ignorant. They are often especially ignorant of ignorance. The stranger imagined that he was uttering a very crushing repartee; as perhaps he was, to anybody who knew what he meant. But Barbara had never heard of the Waba. The newspapers had seen to that.

"The British Government," he was saying, "definitely pledged itself two years ago to a complete scheme of local autonomy. If it is a complete scheme, all will be well. If Lord Tallboys has come out here with an incomplete scheme, a compromise, it will be very far from well. I shall be very sorry for everybody, but especially for my English friends."

She answered with a young and innocent sneer, "Oh yes—I suppose you are a great friend of the English."

"Yes," he replied calmly. "A friend: but a candid friend."

"Oh, I know all about that sort," she said with hot sincerity. "I know what they mean by a candid friend. I've always found it meant a nasty, sneering, sneaking, treacherous friend."

He seemed stung for an instant and answered, "Your politicians have no need to learn treachery from the Egyptians." Then he added abruptly: "Do you know on Lord Jaffray's raid they shot a child? Do you know anything at all? Do you even know how England tacked on Egypt to her Empire?"

"England has a glorious Empire," said the patriot stoutly.

"England had a glorious Empire," he said. "So had Egypt."

They had come, somewhat symbolically, to the end of their common path and she turned away indignantly to the gate that led into the private gardens of the Governor. As she did so he lifted his green umbrella and pointed with a momentary gesture at the dark line of the desert and the distant Pyramid. The afternoon had already reddened into evening, and the sunset lay in long bands of burning crimson across the purple desolation of that dry inland sea.

"A glorious Empire," he said, "An Empire on which the sun never sets. Look . . . the sun is setting in blood.''

She went through the iron gate like the wind and let it clang behind her. As she went up the avenue towards the inner gardens, she lost a little of her impatient movement and began to trail along in the rather moody manner which was more normal to her. The colours and shadows of that quieter scene seemed to close about her; this place was for the present her nearest approach to home; and at the end of the long perspective of gaily coloured garden walks, she could see her sister Olive picking flowers.

The sight soothed her; but she was a little puzzled about why she should need any soothing. She had a deeply disquieting sense of having touched something alien and terrible, something fierce and utterly foreign, as if she had stroked some strange wild beast of the desert. But the gardens about her and the house beyond had already taken on a tone or tint indescribably English, in spite of the recent settlement and the African sky. And Olive was so obviously choosing flowers to put into English vases or to decorate English dinner-tables, with decanters and salted almonds.

But as she drew nearer to that distant figure, it grew more puzzling. The blossoms grasped in her sister's hand looked like mere ragged and random handfuls, torn away as a man lying on the turf would idly tear out grass, when he is abstracted or angry. A few loose stalks lay littered on the path; it seemed as if the heads had been merely broken off as if by a child. Barbara did not know why she took in all these details with a slow and dazed eye, before she looked at the central figure they surrounded. Then Olive looked up and her face was ghastly. It might have been the face of Medea in the garden, gathering the poisonous flowers.

2

THE BOY WHO
MADE A SCENE

BARBARA TRAILL WAS a girl with a good deal of the boy about her. This is very commonly said about modern heroines. None the less, the present heroine would be a very disappointing modern heroine. For, unfortunately, the novelists who call their heroines boyish obviously know nothing whatever about boys. The girl they depict, whether we happen to regard her as a bright young thing or a brazen little idiot, is at any rate in every respect the complete contrary of a boy. She is sublimely candid; she is slightly shallow; she is uniformly cheerful; she is entirely unembarrassed; she is everything that a boy is not. But Barbara really was rather like a boy. That is, she was rather shy, obscurely imaginative, capable of intellectual friendships and at the same time of emotional brooding over them; capable of being morbid and by no means incapable of being secretive. She had that sense of misfit which embarrasses so many boys; the sense of the soul being too big to be seen or confessed, and the tendency to cover the undeveloped emotions with a convention. One effect of it was that she was of the sort troubled by Doubt. It might have been religious doubt; at the moment it was a sort of patriotic doubt; though she would have furiously denied that there was any doubt about the matter. She had been upset by her glimpse of the alleged grievances of Egypt or the alleged crimes of England; and the face of the stranger, the white face with the golden beard and the glaring monocle, had come to stand for the tempter or the spirit that denies. But the face of her sister suddenly banished all such merely political problems. It brought her back with a shock to much more private problems; indeed to much more secret problems; for she had never admitted them to anyone but herself.

The Traills had a tragedy; or rather, perhaps, something that Barbara's brooding spirit had come to regard as the dawn of a tragedy. Her younger brother was still a boy; it might more truly be said that he was still a child. His mind had never come to a normal maturity; and though opinions differed about the nature of the deficiency, she was prone in her black moods to take the darkest view and let it darken the whole house of Tallboys. Thus it happened that she said quickly, at the sight of her sister's strange expression:

"Is anything wrong about Tom?"

Olive started slightly, and then said, rather crossly than otherwise: "No, not particularly. . . . Uncle has put him with a tutor here, and they say he's getting on better. . . . Why do you ask? There's nothing special the matter with him."

"Then I suppose," said Barbara, "that there is something special the matter with you."

"Well," answered the other, "isn't there something the matter with all of us?"

With that she turned abruptly and went back towards the house, dropping the flowers she had been making a pretence of gathering; and her sister followed, still deeply disturbed in mind.

As they came near the portico and veranda, she heard the high voice of her uncle Tallboys, who was leaning back in a garden chair and talking to Olive's husband, the Deputy Governor. Tallboys was a lean figure with a large nose and ears standing out from his stalk of a head; like many men of that type he had a prominent Adam's apple and talked in a full-throated gobbling fashion. But what he said was worth listening to; though he had a trick of balancing one clause against another, with alternate gestures of his large loose hands, which some found a trifle irritating. He was also annoyingly deaf. The Deputy Governor, Sir Harry Smythe, was an amusing contrast; a square man with a rather congested face, the colour high under the eyes, which were very light and clear, and two parallel black bars of brow and moustache; which gave him rather a look of Kitchener, until he stood up and looked stunted by the comparison. It also gave him a rather misleading look of bad temper; for he was an affectionate husband and a good-humoured comrade, if a rather stubborn party man. For the rest the conversation was enough to show that he had a military point of view, which is sufficiently common and even commonplace.

"In short," the Governor was saying, "I believe the Government scheme is admirably adapted to meet a somewhat difficult situation. Extremists of both types will object to it; but extremists object to everything."

"Quite so," answered the other; "the question isn't so much whether they object as whether they can make themselves objectionable."

Barbara, with her new and nervous political interests, found herself interrupted in her attempt to listen to the political conversation by the unwelcome discovery that there were other people present. There was a very beautifully dressed young gentleman, with hair like black satin, who seemed to be the local secretary of the Governor; his name was Arthur Meade. There was an old man with a very obvious chestnut wig and a very unobvious, not to say inscrutable yellow face; who was an eminent financier known by the name of Morse. There were various ladies of the official circle who were duly scattered among these gentlemen. It seemed to be the tail end of a sort of afternoon tea; which made all the more odd and suspicious the strange behaviour of the only hostess, in straying to the other garden and tearing up the flowers. Barbara found herself set down beside a pleasant old clergyman with smooth silver hair, and an equally smooth silver voice, who talked to her about the Bible and the Pyramids. She found herself committed to the highly uncomfortable experience of pretending to conduct one conversation while trying to listen to another.

This was the more difficult because the Rev. Ernest Snow, the clergyman in question, had (for all his mildness) not a little gentle pertinacity. She received a confused impression that he held very strong views on the meaning of certain Prophecies in connection with the end of the world and especially with the destiny of the British Empire. He had that habit of suddenly asking questions which is so unkind to the inattentive listener. Thus, she would manage to hear a scrap of the talk between the two rulers of the province; the Governor would say, balancing his sentences with his swaying hands:

"There are two considerations and by this method we meet them both. On the one hand, it is impossible entirely to repudiate our pledge. On the other hand, it is absurd to suppose that the recent atrocious crime does not necessarily modify the nature of that pledge. We can still make sure that our proclamation is a proclamation of a reasonable liberty. We have therefore decided——"

And then, at that particular moment, the poor clergyman would pierce her consciousness with the pathetic question:

"Now how many cubits do you think that would be?"

A little while later she managed to hear Smythe, who talked much less than his companion, say curtly: "For my part, I don't believe it makes much difference what proclamations you make. There are rows here when we haven't got sufficient forces; and there are no rows when we have got sufficient forces. That's all."

"And what is our position at present?" asked the Governor gravely.

"Our position is damned bad, if you ask me," grumbled the other in a low voice. "Nothing has been done to train the men; why, I found the rifle practice consisted of a sort of parlour game with a pea-shooter about twice a year. I've put up proper rifle butts beyond the olive walk there now; but there are other things. The munitions are not——"

"But in that case," came the mild but penetrating voice of Mr. Snow, "in that case what becomes of the Shunamites?"

Barbara had not the least idea what became of them; but in this case she felt she could treat it as a rhetorical question. She forced herself to listen a little more closely to the views of the venerable mystic; and she only heard one more fragment of the political conversation.

"Shall we really want all these military preparations?" asked Lord Tallboys rather anxiously. "When do you think we shall want them?"

"I can tell you," said Smythe with a certain grimness. "We shall want them when you publish your proclamation of reasonable liberty."

Lord Tallboys made an abrupt movement in the garden chair, like one breaking up a conference in some irritation; then he made a diversion by lifting a finger and signalling to his secretary Mr. Meade, who slid up to him and after a brief colloquy slid into the house. Released from the strain of State affairs, Barbara fell once more under the spell of the Church and the Prophetical Office. She still had only a confused idea of what the old clergyman was saying, but she began to feel a vague element of poetry in it. At least it was full of things that pleased her fancy like the dark drawings of Blake; prehistoric cities and blind and stony seers and kings who seemed clad in stone like their sepulchres the Pyramids. In a dim way she understood why all that stony and starry wilderness has been the playground of so many cranks. She softened a little towards the clerical crank and even accepted an invitation to his house on the day after the following, to see the documents and the definite proof about the Shunamites. But she was still very vague about what it was supposed to prove.

He thanked her and said gravely: "If the prophecy is fulfilled now, there will be a grave calamity."

"I suppose," she said with a rather dreary flippancy, "if the prophecy were not fulfilled, it would be an even greater calamity."

Even as she spoke there was a stir behind some of the garden palms and the pale and slightly gaping face of her brother appeared above the palm-leaves. The next moment she saw just behind him the secretary and the tutor; it was evident that his uncle had sent for him. Tom Traill had the look of being too big for his clothes, which is not uncommon in the otherwise undeveloped; the gloomy good looks which he would otherwise have shared with his branch of the family were marred by his dark straight hair being brushed crooked and his habit of looking out of the corner of his eye at the corner of the carpet. His tutor was a big man of a dull and dusty exterior, apparently having the name of Hume. His broad shoulders were a little bowed like those of a drudge; though he was as yet hardly middle-aged. His plain and rugged face had a rather tired expression, as well it might. Teaching the defective is not always a hilarious parlour game.

Lord Tallboys had a brief and kindly conversation with the tutor. Lord Tallboys asked a few simple questions. Lord Tallboys gave a little lecture on education; still very kindly; but accompanied by the waving of the hands in rotation. On the one hand, the power to work was a necessity of life and could never be wholly evaded. On the other hand, without a reasonable proportion of pleasure and repose even work would suffer. On the one hand . . . it was at this point that the Prophecy was apparently fulfilled and a highly regrettable Calamity occurred at the Governor's tea-party.

For the boy burst out abruptly into a sort of high gurgling crow and began to flap his hands about like the wings of a penguin; repeating over and over again, "On the one hand. On the other hand. On the one hand. On the other hand. On the one hand. On the other hand. . . . Golly!"

"Tom!" cried Olive on a sharp accent of agony and there was a ghastly silence over all the garden.

"Well," said the tutor in a reasonable undertone, which was as clear as a bell in that stillness, "you can't expect to have three hands, can you?"

"Three hands?" repeated the boy, and then after a long silence, "Why, how could you?"

"One would have to be in the middle, like an elephant's trunk," went on the tutor in the same colourless conversational tone. "Wouldn't it be nice to have a long nose like an elephant so that you could turn it this way and that and pick up things on the breakfast table, and never let go of your knife and fork?"

"Oh, you're *mad!*" ejaculated Tom with a sort of explosion that had a queer touch of exultation.

"I'm not the only mad person in the world, old boy," said Mr. Hume.

Barbara stood staring as she listened to this extraordinary conversation in that deadly silence and that highly unsuitable social setting. The most extraordinary thing about it was that the tutor said these crazy and incongruous things with an absolutely blank face.

"Didn't I ever tell you," he said in the same heavy and indifferent voice, "about the clever dentist who could pull out his own teeth with his own nose? I'll tell you to-morrow."

He was still quite dull and serious; but he had done the trick. The boy was distracted from his dislike of his uncle by the absurd image, just as a child in a temper is distracted by a new toy. Tom was now only looking at the tutor and followed him everywhere with his eyes. Perhaps he was not the only member of his family who did so. For the tutor, Barbara thought, was certainly a very odd person.

There was no more political talk that day; but there was not a little political news on the next. On the following morning proclamations were posted everywhere announcing the just, reasonable and even generous compromise which His Majesty's Government was now offering as a fair and final settlement of the serious social problems of Polybia and Eastern Egypt. And on the following evening the news went through the town in one blast, like the wind of the desert, that Viscount Tallboys, Governor of Polybia, had been shot down by the last of the line of olives, at the corner of the wall.

3

THE MAN WHO
COULD NOT HATE

I MMEDIATELY AFTER LEAVING the little garden party, Tom and his tutor
parted for the evening; for the former lived at the Governorate,
while the latter had a sort of lodge or little bungalow higher up on the
hill behind amid the taller trees. The tutor said in private what
everybody had indignantly expected him to say in public; and
remonstrated with the youth for his display of imitative drama.

"Well, I won't like him," said Tom warningly, "I'd like to kill him.
His nose sticks out."

"You can hardly expect it to stick in," said Mr. Hume mildly. "I
wonder whether there's an old story about the man whose nose stuck
in."

"Is there?" demanded the other in the literal spirit of infancy.

"There may be to-morrow," replied the tutor and began to climb
the steep path to his abode.

It was a lodge built mostly of bamboo and light timber with a
gallery running round outside, from which could be seen the whole
district spread out like a map; the grey and green squares of the
Governorate building and grounds; the path running straight under
the low garden wall and parallel to the line of villas; the solitary
sycamore breaking the line at one point and further along the closer
rank of the olive trees, like a broken cloister, and then another gap and
then the corner of the wall, beyond which spread brown slopes of
desert, patched here and there with green, where the ground was

being turfed as part of some new public works or the Deputy Governor's rapid reforms in military organization. The whole hung under him like a vast coloured cloud in the brief afterglow of the Eastern sunset; then it was rapidly rolled in the purple gloom in which the strong stars stood out over his head and seemed nearer than the things of earth.

He stood for some moments on the gallery looking down on the darkening landscape, his blunt features knotted in a frown of curious reflection. Then he went back into the room where he and his pupil had worked all day, or where he had worked to induce his pupil to consider the idea of working. It was a rather bare room and the few objects in it rather odd and varied. A few bookshelves showed very large and gaily coloured books containing the verses of Mr. Edward Lear and very small and shabby books containing the verses of the principal French and Latin poets. A rack of pipes, all hanging crooked, gave the inevitable touch of the bachelor; a fishing-rod and an old double-barrelled gun leaned dusty and disused in a corner; for it was long ago that this man, in other ways so remote from the sports of his countrymen, had indulged those two hobbies, chiefly because they were unsociable. But what was perhaps most curious of all, the desk and the floor were littered with geometrical diagrams treated in a manner unusual among geometers; for the figures were adorned with absurd faces or capering legs, such as a schoolboy adds to the squares and triangles on the blackboard. But the diagrams were drawn very precisely; as if the draughtsman had an exact eye and excelled in anything depending on that organ.

John Hume sat down at his desk and began to draw more diagrams. A little later he lit a pipe, and began to study those he had drawn; but he did not leave his desk or his preoccupations. So the hours went by amid an unfathomable stillness around that hillside hermitage; until the distant strains of a more or less lively band floated up from below, as a signal that a dance at the Governorate was already in progress. He knew there was a dance that night and took no notice of it; he was not sentimental, but some of the tunes stirred almost mechanical memories. The Tallboys family was a little old-fashioned, even for this rather earlier time. They were old-fashioned in not pretending to be any more democratic than they were. Their dependents were dependents, decently treated; they did not call themselves liberal because they dragged their sycophants into society. It had therefore never crossed the mind of the secretary or the tutor that the dance at the Governorate was any concern of theirs. They were also old-fashioned in the arrangements of the dance itself; and the date must also be allowed for. The new dances had only just begun to pierce; and nobody had dreamed of the wild and varied freedom of our new fashion, by which a person has to walk about all night with the same partner to the same tune. All this sense of distance, material and moral, in the old swaying waltzes moved through his subconsciousness and must be allowed for in estimating what he suddenly looked up and saw.

It seemed for one instant as if, in rising through the mist, the tune had taken outline and colour and burst into his room with the bodily presence of a song; for the blues and greens of her patterned dress were like notes of music and her amazing face came to him like a cry; a cry out of the old youth he had lost or never known. A princess flying out of fairyland would not have seemed more impossible than that girl from the ballroom, though he knew her well enough as the younger sister of his charge; and the ball was a few hundred yards away. Her face was like a pale face burning through a dream and itself as unconscious as a dreamer's; for Barbara Traill was curiously unconscious of that mask of beauty fixed on her brooding boyish soul. She had been counted less attractive than her sisters and her sulks had marked her almost as the ugly duckling. Nothing in the solid man before her told of the shock of realization in his mind. She did not even smile. It was also characteristic of her that she blurted out what she had to say at once, almost as crudely as her brother:

"I'm afraid Tom is very rude to you," she said. "I'm very sorry. How do you think he is getting on?"

"I think most people would say," he said slowly at last, "that I ought to apologize for his schooling more than you for his family. I'm sorry about his uncle; but it's always a choice of evils. Tallboys is a very distinguished man and can look after his own dignity, but I've got to look after my charge. And I know that is the right way with him. Don't you be worried about him. He's perfectly all right if you understand him; and it's only a matter of making up for lost time."

She was listening, or not listening, with her characteristic frown of abstraction; she had taken the chair he offered her apparently without noticing it and was staring at the comical diagrams apparently without seeing them. Indeed, it might well have been supposed that she was not listening at all; for the next remark she made appeared to be about a totally different subject. But she often had a habit of thus showing fragments of her mind; and there was more plan in the jig-saw puzzle than many people understood. Anyhow, she said suddenly, without lifting her eyes from the ludicrous drawing in front of her:

"I met a man going to the Governorate to-day. A big man with a long fair beard and a single eyeglass. Do you know who he is? He said all sorts of horrid things against England."

Hume got to his feet with his hands in his pockets and the expression of one about to whistle. He stared at the girl and said softly:

"Hullo! Has he turned up again? I thought there was some trouble coming. Yes, I know him—they call him Dr. Gregory, but I believe he comes from Germany, though he often passes for English. He is a stormy petrel, anyhow; and wherever he goes there's a row. Some say we ought to have used him ourselves; I believe he once offered his talents to our Government. He's a very clever fellow and knows a frightful lot of the facts about these parts."

"Do you mean," she said sharply, "that I'm to believe that man and all the things he said?"

"No," said Hume. "I shouldn't believe that man; not even if you believe all the things he said."

"What do you mean?" she demanded.

"Frankly, I think he is a thoroughly bad egg," said the tutor. "He's got a pretty rotten reputation about women; I won't go into details, but he'd have gone to prison twice but for suborning perjury. I only say, whatever you may come to believe, don't believe in him."

"He dared to say that our Government broke its word," said Barbara indignantly.

John Hume was silent. Something in his silence affected her like a strain; and she said quite irrationally:

"Oh, for the Lord's sake say something! Do you know he dared to say that somebody on Lord Jaffray's expedition shot a child? I don't mind their saying England's cold and hard and all that; I suppose that's natural prejudice. But can't we stop these wild, wicked lies?"

"Well," replied Hume rather wearily, "nobody can say that Jaffray is cold and hard. The excuse for the whole thing was that he was blind drunk."

"Then I am to take the word of that liar!" she said fiercely.

"He's a liar all right," said the tutor gloomily. "And it's a very dangerous condition of the press and the public, when only the liars tell the truth."

Something of a massive gravity in his grim humour for the moment overpowered her breathless resentment; and she said in a quieter tone:

"Do you believe in this demand for self-government?"

"I'm not very good at believing," he said. "I find it very hard to believe that these people cannot live or breathe without votes, when they lived contentedly without them for fifty centuries when they had the whole country in their own hands. A Parliament may be a good thing; a top-hat may be a good thing; your uncle certainly thinks so. We may like or dislike our top-hats. But if a wild Turk tells me he has a natural born right to a top-hat, I can't help answering: 'Then why the devil didn't you make one for yourself?' "

"You don't seem to care much for the Nationalists either," she said.

"Their politicians are often frauds; but they're not alone in that. That's why I find myself forced into an intermediate position; a sort of benevolent neutrality. It simply seems to be a choice between a lot of blasted blackguards and a lot of damned drivelling, doddering idiots. You see I'm a Moderate."

He laughed a little for the first time; and his plain face was suddenly altered for the better. She was moved to say in a more friendly tone:

"Well, we must prevent a real outbreak. You don't want all our people murdered."

"Only a little murdered," he said, still smiling. "Yes, I think I should like some of them *rather* murdered. Not too much, of course; it's a question of a sense of proportion."

"Now you're talking nonsense," she said, "and people in our position can't stand any nonsense. Harry says we may have to make an example."

"I know," he said. "He made several examples when he was in command here, before Lord Tallboys came out. It was vigorous—very vigorous. But I think I know what would be better than making an example."

"And what is that?"

"Setting an example," said Hume. "What about our own politicians?"

She said suddenly: "Well, why don't you do something yourself?"

There was a silence. Then he drew a deep breath. "Ah, there you have me. I can't do anything myself. I am futile; naturally and inevitably futile. I suffer from a deadly weakness."

She felt suddenly rather frightened; she had encountered his blank and empty eyes.

"I cannot hate," he said. "I cannot be angry."

Something in his heavy voice seemed full of quality, like the fall of a slab of stone on a sarcophagus; she did not protest, and in her subconsciousness yawned a disappointment. She half realized the depth of her strange reliance and felt like one who had dug in the desert and found a very deep well; and found it dry.

When she went out on to the veranda the steep garden and plantation were grey in the moon; and a certain greyness spread over her own spirit; a mood of fatalism and of dull fear. For the first time she realized something of what strikes a Western eye in Eastern places as the unnaturalness of nature. The squat, limbless growth of the prickly pear was not like the green growths of home, springing on light stalks to lovely flowers like butterflies captured out of air. It was more like the dead blind bubbling of some green squalid slime: a world of plants that were as plain and flat as stones. She hated the hairy surface of some of the squat and swollen trees of that grotesque garden; the tufts here and there irritated her fancy as they might have tickled her face. She felt that even the big folded flowers, if they opened, would have a foul fragrance. She had a latent sense of the savour of faint horror, lying over all as lightly as the faint moonshine. Just as it had chilled her most deeply, she looked up and saw something that was neither plant nor tree, though it hung as still in the stillness; but it had the unique horror of a human face. It was a very white face, but bearded with gold like the Greek statues of gold and ivory; and at the temples were two golden curls, that might have been the horns of Pan.

For the moment that motionless head might indeed have been that of some terminal god of gardens. But the next moment it had found legs and came to life, springing out upon the pathway behind her. She had already gone some distance from the hut and was not far from the illuminated grounds of the Governorate, whence the music swelled louder as she went. Nevertheless, she swung round and faced the other way, looking desperately at the figure she recognized. He had abandoned his red fez and black frock-coat and was clad completely in white, like many tropical trippers; but it gave him in the moonlight something of the silver touch of a spectral harlequin. As he advanced he screwed the shining disk into his eye and it revealed in a flash the faint memory that had always escaped her. His face in repose was calm and classic and might have been the stone mask of Jove rather than Pan. But the monocle gathered up his features into a sneer and seemed to draw his eyes closer together; and she suddenly saw that he was no more a German than an Englishman. And though she had no Anti-Semitic prejudice in particular, she felt somehow that in that scene there was something sinister in a fair Jew, as in a white negro.

"We meet under a yet more beautiful sky," he said; she hardly heard what else he said. Broken phrases from what she had heard recently tumbled through her mind, mere words like "reputation" and "prison"; and she stepped back to increase the distance, but moving in the opposite direction from which she had come. Afterwards she hardly remembered what had happened; he had said other things; he had tried to stop her; and an instantaneous impression of crushing and startling strength, like a chimpanzee, surprised her into a cry. Then she stumbled and ran; but not in the direction of the house of her own people.

Mr. John Hume got out of his chair more quickly than was his wont and went to meet someone who stumbled up the stair without.

"My dear child," he said, and put a hand on her shaking shoulder, giving and receiving a queer thrill like a dull electric shock. Then he went; moving quickly past her. He had seen something in the moonlight beyond and without descending the steps, sprang over the rail to the ground below, standing waist high in the wild and tangled vegetation. There was a screen of large leaves waving to and fro between Barbara and the rapid drama that followed; but she saw, as in flashes of moonlight, the tutor dart across the path of the figure in white and heard the shock of blows and saw a kick like a catapult. There was a wheel of silver legs like the arms of the Isle of Man; and then out of the dense depth of the lower thicket a spout of curses in a tongue that was not English, nor wholly German, but which shrieked and chattered in all the Ghettoes of the world. But one strange thing remained even in her disordered memory; that when the figure in white had risen tottering and turned to plunge down the hill, the white face and the furious gesture of malediction were turned, not towards the assailant, but towards the house of the Governor.

The tutor was frowning ponderously as he came again up the veranda steps, as if over some of his geometrical problems. She asked him rather wildly what he had done and he answered in his heavy voice:

"I hope I half killed him. You know I am in favour of half measures."

She laughed rather hysterically and cried: "You said you could not be angry."

Then they suddenly became very stiff and silent and it was with an almost fatuous formality that he escorted her down the slope to the very doors of the dancing-rooms. The sky behind the green pergolas of foliage was a vivid violet or some sort of blue that seemed warmer than any red; and the furry filaments of the great tree-trunks seemed like the quaint sea-beasts of childhood, which could be stroked and which unfolded their fingers. There was something upon them both beyond speech or even silence. He even went so far as to say it was a fine night.

"Yes," she answered, "it is a fine night"; and felt instantly as if she had betrayed some secret.

They went through the inner gardens to the gate of the vestibule, which was crowded with people in uniform and evening dress. They parted with the utmost formality; and that night neither of them slept.

4

THE DETECTIVE AND
THE PARSON

IT WAS NOT until the following evening, as already noted, that the news came that the Governor had fallen by a shot from an unknown hand. And Barbara Traill received the news later than most of her friends; because she had departed rather abruptly that morning for a long ramble amid the ruins and plantations of palm, in the immediate neighborhood. She took a sort of picnic basket with her, but light as was her visible luggage, it would be true to say that she went away to unpack upon a large scale. She went to unfold a sort of invisible *impedimenta* which had accumulated in her memories; especially her memories of the night before. This sort of impetuous solitude was characteristic of her; but it had an immediate effect which was rather fortunate in her case. For the first news was the worst; and when she returned the worst had been much modified. It was first reported that her uncle was dead; then that he was dying; finally that he had only been wounded and had every prospect of recovery. She walked with her empty basket straight into the hubbub of discussion about these things; and soon found that the police operations for the discovery and pursuit of the criminal were already far advanced. The inquiry was in the hands of a hard-headed, hatchet-faced officer named Hayter, the chief of the detective force; who was being actively seconded by young Meade, the secretary of the Governor. But she was rather more surprised to find her friend the tutor in the very centre of the group, being questioned about his own recent experiences.

The next moment she felt a strange sort of surge of subconscious annoyance, as she realized the subject-matter of the questions. The questioners were Meade and Hayter; but it was significant that they had just received the news that Sir Harry Smythe, with characteristic energy, had arrested Dr. Paulus Gregory, the dubious foreigner with the big beard. The tutor was being examined about his own last glimpse of that questionable public character; and Barbara felt a secret fury at finding the affair of the night before turned into a public problem of police. She felt as if she had come down in the morning to find the whole breakfast-table talking about some very intimate dream she had had in the middle of the night. For though she had carried that picture with her as she wandered among the tombs and the green thickets, she had felt it as something as much peculiar to herself as if she had had a vision in the wilderness. The bland, black-haired Mr. Meade was especially insinuating in his curiosity. She told herself, in a highly unreasonable fashion, that she had always hated Arthur Meade.

"I gather," the secretary was saying, "that you have excellent reasons of your own for regarding this man as a dangerous character."

"I regard him as a rotter and I always did," replied Hume in a rather sulky and reluctant manner. "I did have a bit of a kick up with him last night, but it didn't make any difference to my views, nor to his either, I should think."

"It seems to me it might make a considerable difference," persisted Meade. "Isn't it true that he went away cursing not only you but especially the Governor? And he went away down the hill towards the place where the Governor was shot. It's true he wasn't shot till a good time after, and nobody seems to have seen his assailant; but he might have hung about in the woods and then crept out along the wall at dusk."

"Having helped himself to a gun from the gun-tree that grows wild in these woods, I suppose," said the tutor sardonically. "I swear he had no gun or pistol on him when I threw him into the prickly pear."

"You seem to be making the speech for the defence," said the secretary with a faint sneer. "But you yourself said he was a pretty doubtful character."

"I don't think he is in the least a doubtful character," replied the tutor in his stolid way. "I haven't the least doubt about him myself. I think he is a loose, lying, vicious braggart and humbug; a selfish, sensual mountebank. So I'm pretty sure that he didn't shoot the Governor, whoever else did."

Colonel Hayter cocked a shrewd eye at the speaker and spoke himself for the first time.

"Ah—and what do you mean by that exactly?"

"I mean what I say," answered Hume. "It's exactly because he's that sort of rascal that he didn't commit that sort of rascality. Agitators of his type never do things themselves; they incite other people; they hold meetings and send round the hat and then vanish, to do the same thing somewhere else. It's a jolly different sort of person that's left to take the risks of playing Brutus or Charlotte Corday. But I confess there are two other little bits of evidence, which I think clear the fellow completely."

He put two fingers in his waistcoat pocket and slowly and thoughtfully drew out a round flat piece of glass with a broken string.

"I picked this up on the spot where we struggled," he said. "It's Gregory's eye-glass; and if you look through it you won't see anything, except the fact that a man who wanted a lens as strong as that could see next to nothing without it. He certainly couldn't see to shoot as far as the end of the wall from the sycamore, which is whereabouts they think the shot must have been fired from."

"There may be something in that," said Hayter, "though the man might have had another glass, of course. You said you had a second reason for thinking him innocent."

"The second reason," said Hume, "is that Sir Harry Smythe has just arrested him."

"What on earth do you mean?" asked Meade sharply. "Why, you brought us the message from Sir Harry yourself."

"I'm afraid I brought it rather imperfectly," said the other, in a dull voice. "It's quite true Sir Harry has arrested the doctor, but he'd arrested him before he heard of the attempt on Lord Tallboys. He had just arrested him for holding a seditious meeting five miles away at Pentapolis, at which he made an eloquent speech, which must have reached its beautiful peroration about the time when Tallboys was being shot at, here at the corner of the road."

"Good Lord!" cried Meade, staring, "you seem to know a lot about this business."

The rather sullen tutor lifted his head and looked straight at the secretary with a steady but rather baffling gaze.

"Perhaps I do know a little about it," he said. "Anyhow, I'm quite sure Gregory's got a good alibi."

Barbara had listened to this curious conversation with a confused and rather painful attention; but as the case against Gregory seemed to be crumbling away, a new emotion of her own began to work its way to the surface. She began to realize that she had wanted Gregory to be made responsible, not out of any particular malice towards him, but because it would explain and dispose of the whole incident; and dismiss it from her mind along with another disturbing but hardly conscious thought. Now that the criminal had again become a nameless shadow, he began to haunt her mind with dreadful hints of identity and she had spasms of fear, in which that shadowy figure was suddenly fitted with a face.

As has been already noted, Barbara Traill was a little morbid about her brother and the tragedy of the Traills. She was an omnivorous reader; she had been the sort of schoolgirl who is always found in a corner with a book. And this means generally, under modern conditions, that she read everything she could not understand some time before she read anything that she could. Her mind was a hotch-potch of popular science about heredity and psycho-analysis; and the whole trend of her culture tended to make her pessimistic about everything. People in this mood never have any difficulty in finding reasons for their worst fears. And it was enough for her that, the very morning before her uncle was shot, he had been publicly insulted, and even crazily threatened, by her brother.

That sort of psychological poison works itself deeper and deeper into the brain. Barbara's broodings branched and thickened like a dark forest; and did not stop with the thought that a dull, un-developed schoolboy was really a maniac and a murderer. The unnatural generalizations of the books she had read pushed her further and further. If her brother, why not her sister? If her sister, why not herself? Her memory exaggerated and distorted the distracted demeanour of her sister in the flower-garden, till she could almost fancy that Olive had torn up the flowers with her teeth. As is always the case in such unbalanced worry, all sorts of accidents took on a terrible significance. Her sister had said, "Is there not something the matter with all of us?" What could that mean but such a family curse? Hume himself had said he was not the only mad person present. What else could that mean? Even Dr. Gregory had declared after talking to her, that her race was degenerate; did he mean that her family was degenerate? After all, he was a doctor, if he was a wicked one. Each of these hateful coincidences gave her a spiritual shock, so that she almost cried aloud when she thought of it. Meanwhile the rest of her mind went round and round in the iron circle of all such logic from hell. She told herself again and again that she was being morbid; and then told herself again and again that she was only morbid because she was mad. But she was not in the least mad; she was only young; and thousands of young people go through such a phase of nightmare; and nobody knows or helps.

But she was moved with a curious impulse in the search for help; and it was the same impulse that had driven her back across the moonlit glade to the wooden hut upon the hill. She was actually mounting that hill again, when she met John Hume coming down.

She poured out all her domestic terrors and suspicions in a flood, as she had poured out all her patriotic doubts and protests, with a confused confidence which rested on no defined reason or relation and yet was sure of itself.

"So there it is," she said at the end of her impetuous monologue. "I began by being quite sure that poor Tom had done it. But by this time I feel as if I might have done it myself."

"Well, that's logical enough," agreed Hume. "It's about as sensible to say that you are guilty as that Tom is. And about as sensible to say the Archbishop of Canterbury is guilty as either of you."

She attempted to explain her highly scientific guesses about heredity; and their effect was more marked. They succeeded at least in arousing this large and slow person to a sort of animation.

"Now the devil take all doctors and scientists," he cried, "or rather the devil take all novelists and newspaper men who talk about what even the doctors don't understand! People abuse the old nurses for frightening children with bogies which pretty soon became a joke. What about the new nurses who let children frighten themselves with all the black bogies they are supposed to take seriously? My dear girl, there is nothing the matter with your brother, any more than with you. He's only what they call a protected neurotic; which is their long-winded way of saying he has an extra skin that the Public School varnish won't stick on, but runs off like water off a duck's back. So much the better for him, as likely as not, in the long run. But even suppose he did remain a little more like a child than the rest of us. Is there anything particularly horrible about a child? Do you shudder when you think of your dog, merely because he's happy and fond of you and yet can't do the forty-eighth proposition of Euclid? Being a dog is not a disease. Being a child is not a disease. Even remaining a child is not a disease; don't you sometimes wish we could all remain children?"

She was of the sort that grapples with notions and suggestions one after another, as they come; and she stood silent; but her mind was busy like a mill. It was he who spoke again, and more lightly.

"It's like what we were saying about making examples. I think the world is much too solemn and severe about punishments; it would be far better if it were ruled like a nursery. People don't want penal servitude and execution and all the rest. What most people want is to have their ears boxed or be sent to bed. What fun it would be to take an unscrupulous millionaire and make him stand in the corner! Such an appropriate penalty."

When she spoke again there was in her tones something of relief and a renewed curiosity.

"What do you do with Tom?" she asked, "and what's the meaning of all those funny triangles?"

"I play the fool," he replied gravely. "What he wants is to have his attention aroused and fixed; and foolery always does that for children; very obvious foolery. Don't you know how they have always liked such images as the cow jumping over the moon? It's the educational effect of riddles. Well, I have to be the riddle. I have to keep him wondering what I mean or what I shall do next. It means being an ass; but it's the only way."

"Yes," she answered slowly, "there's something awfully rousing about riddles . . . all sorts of riddles. Even that old parson with his riddles out of Revelations makes you feel he has something to live for . . . by the way, I believe we promised to go to tea there this afternoon; I've been in a state to forget everything."

Even as she spoke she saw her sister Olive coming up the path attired in the unmistakable insignia of one paying calls, and accompanied by her sturdy husband, the Deputy Governor, who did not often attend these social functions. They all went down the road together and Barbara was vaguely surprised to see ahead of them on the same road, not only the sleek and varnished figure of Mr. Meade the secretary, but also the more angular outline of Colonel Hayter. The clergyman's invitation had evidently been a comprehensive one.

The Rev. Ernest Snow lived in a very modest manner in one of the little houses that had been erected in a row for the minor officials of the Governorate. It was at the back of this line of villas that the path ran along the garden wall and past the sycamore to the bunch of olives and finally to the corner where the Governor had fallen by the mysterious bullet. That path fringed the open desert and had all the character of a rude beaten path for the desert pilgrims. But walking on the other side, in front of the row of houses, a traveller might well have imagined himself in any London suburb, so regular were the ornamental railings and so identical the porticoes and the small

front-garden plots. Nothing but a number distinguished the house of
the clergyman; and the entrance to it was so prim and narrow that the
group of guests from the Governorate had some difficulty in
squeezing through it.

Mr. Snow bowed over Olive's hand with a ceremony that seemed to
make his white hair a ghost of eighteenth century powder, but also
with something else that seemed at first a shade more difficult to
define. It was something that went with the lowered voice and lifted
hand of his profession at certain moments. His face was composed,
but it would almost seem deliberately composed; and in spite of his
grieved tone his eyes were very bright and steady. Barbara suddenly
realized that he was conducting a funeral; and she was not far out.

"I need not tell you, Lady Smythe," he said in the same soft accents,
"what sympathy we all feel in this terrible hour. If only from a public
standpoint, the death of your distinguished uncle——"

Olive Smythe struck in with a rather wild stare.

"But my uncle isn't dead, Mr. Snow. I know they said so at first; but
he only got a shot in his leg and he is trying to limp about already."

A shock of transformation passed over the clergyman's face, too
quick for most eyes to follow; it seemed to Barbara that his jaw
dropped and when it readjusted itself, it was in a grin of utterly
artifical congratulation.

"My dear lady," he breathed, "for this relief——"

He looked round a little vacantly at the furniture. Whether the Rev.
Ernest Snow had remembered to prepare tea at tea-time, was not yet
quite clear; but the preparations he had made seemed to be of a less
assuaging sort. The little tables were loaded with large books, many of
them lying open; and these were mostly traced with sprawling plans
and designs, mostly architectural or generally archæological, in some
cases apparently astronomical or astrological, but giving as a whole a
hazy impression of a magician's spells or a library of the black art.

"Apocalyptic studies," he stammered, "a hobby of mine. I believed
that my calculations . . . . These things are written for our instruction."

And then Barbara felt a final stab of astonishment and alarm. For
two facts became instantly and simultaneously vivid to her consciousness. The first was that the Rev. Ernest Snow had been reposing
upon the fact of the Governor's death with something very like a
solemn satisfaction, and had heard of his recovery with something
quite other than relief. And the second was that he spoke with the
same voice that had once uttered the same words, out of the shadow of
the sycamore, that sounded in her ears like a wild cry for blood.

5

THE THEORY OF
MODERATE MURDER

COLONEL HAYTER, THE Chief of the Police, was moving towards the inner rooms with a motion that was casual but not accidental. Barbara indeed had rather wondered why such an official had accompanied them on a purely social visit; and she now began to entertain dim and rather incredible possibilities. The clergyman had turned away to one of the bookstands and was turning over the leaves of a volume with feverish excitement; it seemed almost that he was muttering to himself. He was a little like a man looking up a quotation on which he has been challenged.

"I hear you have a very nice garden here, Mr. Snow," said Hayter. "I should rather like to look at your garden."

Snow turned a startled face over his shoulder; he seemed at first unable to detach his mind from his preoccupation; then he said sharply but a little shakily, "There's nothing to see in my garden; nothing at all. I was just wondering——"

"Do you mind if I have a squint at it?" asked Hayter indifferently; and shouldered his way to the back-door. There was something resolute about his action that made the others trail vaguely after him, hardly knowing what they did. Hume, who was just behind the detective, said to him in an undertone:

"What do you expect to find growing in the old man's garden?"

Hayter looked over his shoulder with a grim geniality. "Only a particular sort of tree you were talking of lately," he said.

But when they went out into the neat and narrow strip of back garden, the only tree in sight was the sycamore spreading over the desert path; and Barbara remembered with another subconscious thrill that this was the spot from which, as the experts calculated, the bullet had been fired.

Hayter strode across the lawn and was seen stooping over something in the tangle of tropical plants under the wall. When he straightened himself again he was seen to be holding a long and heavy cylindrical object.

"Here is something fallen from the gun-tree you said grew in these parts," he said grimly. "Funny that the gun should be found in Mr. Snow's back-garden, isn't it? Especially as it's a double-barrelled gun with one barrel discharged."

Hume was staring at the big gun in the detective's hand; and for the first time his usually stolid face wore an expression of amazement and even consternation.

"Damn it all!" he said softly, "I forgot about that. What a rotten fool I am!"

Few except Barbara even heard his strange whisper; and nobody could make any sense of it. Suddenly he swung round and addressed the whole company aloud, almost as if they were a public meeting.

"Look here," he said, "do you know what this means? This means that poor old Snow, who is probably still fussing over his hieroglyphics, is going to be charged with attempted murder."

"It's a bit premature," said Hayter, "and some would say you were interfering in our job, Mr. Hume. But I owe you something for putting us right about the other fellow, when I admit we were wrong."

"You were wrong about the other fellow and you are wrong about this fellow," said Hume, frowning savagely. "But I happened to be able to offer you evidence in the other case. What evidence can I give now?"

"Why should you have any evidence to give?" asked the other, very much puzzled.

"Well, I have," said Hume, "and I jolly well don't want to give it." He was silent for a moment and then broke out in a sort of fury: "Blast it all, can't you *see* how silly it is to drag in that silly old man? Don't you see he'd only fallen in love with his own prophesies of disaster, and was a bit put off when they didn't come true after all?"

"There are a good many more suspicious circumstances," cut in Smythe curtly. "There's the gun in the garden and the position of the sycamore."

There was a long silence during which Hume stood with huge hunched shoulders frowning resentfully at his boots. Then he suddenly threw up his head and spoke with a sort of explosive lightness.

"Oh, well then, I must give my evidence," he said, with a smile that was almost gay: "I shot the Governor myself."

There was a stillness as if the place had been full of statues; and for a few seconds nobody moved or spoke. Then Barbara heard her own voice in the silence, crying out:

"Oh, you didn't!"

A moment later the Chief of Police was speaking with a new and much more official voice:

"I should like to know whether you are joking," he said, "or whether you really mean to give yourself up for the attempted murder of Lord Tallboys."

Hume held up one hand in an arresting gesture, almost like a public speaker. He was still smiling slightly, but his manner had grown more grave.

"Pardon me," he said. "Pardon me. Let us distinguish. The distinction is of great value to my self-esteem. I did not try to murder the Governor. I tried to shoot him in the leg and I did shoot him in the leg."

"What is the sense of all this?" cried Smythe with impatience.

"I am sorry to appear punctilious," said Hume calmly. "Imputations on my morals I must bear, like other members of the criminal class. But imputations on my marksmanship I cannot tolerate; it is the only sport in which I excel." He picked up the double-barrelled gun before they could stop him and went on rapidly: "And may I draw attention to one technical point? This gun has two barrels and one is still undischarged. If any fool had shot Tallboys at that distance and not killed him, don't you think even a fool would have shot again, if that was what he wanted to do? Only, you see, it was not what I wanted to do."

"You seem to fancy yourself a lot as a marksman," said the Deputy Governor rudely.

"Ah, you are sceptical," replied the tutor in the same airy tone. "Well, Sir Harry, you have yourself provided the apparatus of demonstration, and it will not take a moment. The targets which we owe to your patriotic efficiency are already set up, I think, on the slope just beyond the end of the wall." Before anybody could move he had hopped up on to the low garden-wall, just under the shadow of the sycamore. From that perch he could see the long line of the butts stretching along the border of the desert.

"Suppose we say," he said pleasantly, in the tone of a popular lecturer, "that I put this bullet about an inch inside the white on the second target."

The group awoke from its paralysis of surprise; Hayter ran forward and Smythe burst out with: "Of all the damned tomfoolery——"

His sentence was drowned in the deafening explosion, and amid the echoes of it the tutor dropped serenely from the wall.

"If anybody cares to go and look," he said, "I think he will find the demonstration of my innocence—not indeed of shooting the Governor, but of wanting to shoot him anywhere else but where I did shoot him."

There was another silence; and then this comedy of unexpected happenings was crowned with another that was still more unexpected; coming from the one person whom everybody had naturally forgotten.

Tom's high crowing voice was suddenly heard above the crowd.

"Who's going to look?" he cried. "Well, why don't you go and look?"

It was almost as if a tree in the garden had spoken. And indeed the excitement of events had worked upon that vegetating brain till it unfolded rapidly, as do some vegetables at the touch of chemistry. Nor was this all; for the next moment the vegetable had taken on a highly animal energy and hurled itself across the garden. They saw a whirl of lanky limbs against the sky as Tom Traill cleared the garden wall and went plunging away through the sand towards the targets.

"Is this place a lunatic asylum?" cried Sir Harry Smythe, his face still more congested with colour and a baleful light in his eyes, as if a big but buried temper was working its way to the surface.

"Come, Mr. Hume," said Hayter in a cooler tone, "everybody regards you as a very sensible man. Do you mean to tell me seriously that you put a bullet in the Governor's leg for no reason at all, not even murder?"

"I did it for an excellent reason," answered the tutor, still beaming at him in a rather baffling manner. "I did it because I am a sensible man. In fact, I am a Moderate Murderer."

"And what the blazes may that be?"

"The philosophy of moderation in murder," continued the tutor blandly, "is one which I have given some little attention. I was saying only the other day that what most people want is to be rather murdered; especially persons in responsible political situations. As it is, the punishments on both sides are far too severe. The merest touch or *soupçon* of murder is all that is required for purposes of reform. The little more and how much it is; the little less and the Governor of Polybia gets clean away, as Browning said."

"Do you really ask me to believe," snorted the Chief of Police, "that you make a practice of potting every public man in the left leg?"

"No, no," said Hume, with a sort of hasty solemnity. "The treatment, I assure you, is marked with much more individual attention. Had it been the Chancellor of the Exchequer, I should perhaps have selected a portion of the left ear. In the case of the Prime Minister the tip of the nose would be indicated. But the point is the general principle that *something* should happen to these people, to arouse their dormant faculties by a little personal problem. Now if ever there was a man," he went on with delicate emphasis, as if it were a scientific demonstration, "if ever there was a man meant and marked out by nature to be rather murdered, it is Lord Tallboys. Other eminent men, very often, are just murdered; and everyone feels that the situation has been adequately met; that the incident is terminated. One just murders them and thinks no more about it. But Tallboys is a remarkable case; he is my employer and I know him pretty well. He is a good fellow, really. He is a gentleman, he is a patriot; what is more, he is really a liberal and reasonable man. But by being perpetually in office he has let that pompous manner get worse and worse, till it seems to grow on him, like his confounded top-hat. What is needed in such a case? A few days in bed, I decided. A few healthful weeks standing on one leg and meditating on that fine shade of distinction between oneself and God Almighty, which is so easily overlooked."

"Don't listen to any more of this rubbish," cried the Deputy-Governor. "If he says he shot Tallboys, we've got to take him up for it, I suppose. He ought to know."

"You've hit it at last, Sir Harry," said Hume heartily, "I'm arousing a lot of dormant intellects this afternoon."

"We won't have any more of your joking," cried Smythe with sudden fury; "I'm arresting you for attempted murder."

"I know," answered the smiling tutor, "that's the joke."

At this moment there was another leap and scurry by the sycamore and the boy Tom hurled himself back into the garden, panting aloud:

"It's quite right. It's just where he said."

For the rest of the interview, and until that strange group had broken up on the lawn, the boy continued to stare at Hume as only a boy can stare at somebody who has done something rather remarkable in a game. But as he and Barbara went back to the Governorate together, the latter indescribably dazed and bewildered, she found her companion curiously convinced of some view of his own, which he was hardly competent to describe. It was not exactly as if he disbelieved Hume or his story. It was rather as if he believed what Hume had not said, rather than what he had.

"It's a riddle," repeated Tom with stubborn solemnity. "He's awfully fond of riddles. He says silly things just to make you think. That's what we've got to do. He doesn't like you to give it up."

"What we've got to do?" repeated Barbara.

"Think what it really means," said Tom.

There was some truth perhaps in the suggestion that Mr. John Hume was fond of riddles; for he fired off one more of them at the Chief of Police, even as that official took him into custody.

"Well," he said cheerfully, "you can only half hang me because I'm only half a murderer. I suppose you have hanged people sometimes?"

"Occasionally, I'm sorry to say," replied Colonel Hayter.

"Did you ever hang somebody to prevent him being hanged?" asked the tutor with interest.

6

THE THING THAT
REALLY HAPPENED

IT IS NOT true that Lord Tallboys wore his top-hat in bed, during his brief indisposition. Nor is it true, as was more moderately alleged, that he sent for it as soon as he could stand upright and wore it as a finishing touch to a costume consisting of a green dressing-gown and red slippers. But it was quite true that he resumed his hat and his high official duties at the earliest possible opportunity; rather to the annoyance, it was said, of his subordinate the Deputy-Governor, who found himself for the second time checked in some of those vigorous military measures which are always more easily effected after the shock of a political outrage. In plain words, the Deputy-Governor was rather sulky. He had relapsed into a red-faced and irritable silence; and when he broke it his friends rather wished he would relapse into it again. At the mention of the eccentric tutor, whom his department had taken into custody, he exploded with a special impatience and disgust. "Oh, for God's sake don't tell me about that beastly madman and mountebank!" he cried, almost in the voice of one tortured and unable to tolerate a moment more of human folly. "Why in the world we are cursed with such filthy fools . . . shooting him in the leg . . . moderate murderer . . . mouldy swine!"

"He's not a mouldy swine," said Barbara Traill emphatically, as if it were an exact point of natural history. "I don't believe a word of what you people are saying against him."

"Do you believe what he is saying against himself?" asked her uncle, looking at her with screwed-up eyes and a quizzical expression. Tallboys was leaning on a crutch; in marked contrast to the sullenness of Sir Harry Smythe, he carried his disablement in a very plucky and pleasant fashion. The necessity of attending to the interrupted rhythm of his legs had apparently arrested the oratorical rotation of his hands. His family felt that they had never liked him so much before. It seemed almost as if there were some truth in the theory of the Moderate Murderer.

On the other hand, Sir Harry Smythe, usually so much more good-humoured with his family, seemed to be in an increasingly bad humour. The dark red of his complexion deepened, until by contrast there was something almost alarming about the light of his pale eyes.

"I tell you of all these measly, meddlesome blighters," he began.

"And I tell you you know nothing about it," retorted his sister-in-law. "He isn't a bit like that; he——"

At this point, for some reason or other, it was Olive who intervened swiftly and quietly; she looked a little wan and worried.

"Don't let's talk about all that now," she said hastily. "Harry has got such a lot of things to do. . . ."

"I know what I'm going to do," said Barbara stubbornly. "I'm going to ask Lord Tallboys, as Governor of this place, if he will let me visit Mr. Hume and see if *I* can find out what it means."

She had become for some reason violently excited and her own voice sounded strangely in her ears. She had a dizzy impression of Harry Smythe's eyes standing out of his head in apoplectic anger and of Olive's face in the background growing more and more unnaturally pale and staring; and hovering over all, with something approaching to an elvish mockery, the benevolent amusement of her uncle. She felt as if she had let out too much, or that he had gained a new subtlety of perception.

Meanwhile John Hume was sitting in his place of detention, staring at a blank wall with an equally blank face. Accustomed as he was to solitude, he soon found something of a strain in two or three days and nights of the dehumanised solitude of imprisonment. Perhaps the fact most vivid to his immediate senses was being deprived of tobacco. But he had other and what some would call graver grounds of depression. He did not know what sort of sentence he would be likely to get for confessing to an attempt to wound the Governor. But he knew enough of political conditions and legal expedients to know that it would be easy to inflict heavy punishment immediately after the public scandal of the crime. He had lived in that outpost of civilization for the last ten years, till Tallboys had picked him up in Cairo; he remembered the violent reaction after the murder of the previous Governor, the way in which the Deputy-Governor had been able to turn himself into a despot and sweep the country with coercion acts and punitive expeditions, until his impulsive militarism had been a little moderated by the arrival of Tallboys with a compromise from the home Government. Tallboys was still alive and even, in a modified manner, kicking. But he was probably still under doctor's orders and could hardly be judge in his own cause; so that the autocratic Smythe would probably have another chance of riding the whirlwind and directing the storm. But the truth is that there was at the back of the prisoner's mind something that he feared much more than prison. The tiny point of panic, which had begun to worry and eat away even his rocky stolidity of mind and body, was the fear that his fantastic explanation had given his enemies another sort of opportunity. What he really feared was their saying he was mad and putting him under more humane and hygienic treatment.

And indeed, anyone watching his demeanour for the next hour or so might be excused for entertaining doubts and fancies on the point. He was still staring before him in a rather strange fashion. But he was no longer staring as if he saw nothing; but rather as if he saw something. It seemed to himself that, like a hermit in his cell, he was seeing visions.

"Well, I suppose I am, after all," he said aloud in a dead and distinct voice. "Didn't St. Paul say something? . . . Wherefore, O King Agrippa, I was not disobedient to the heavenly vision. . . . I have seen that heavenly one coming in at the door like that several times; and rather hoped it was real. But real people can't come through prison doors like that. . . . Once it came so that the room might have been full of trumpets and once with a cry like the wind and there was a fight and I found out that I could hate and that I could love. Two miracles on one night. Don't you think that must have been a dream—that is supposing you weren't a dream and could think anything? But I did rather hope you were real then."

"Don't!" said Barbara Traill, "I am real now."

"Do you mean to tell me in cold blood that I am not mad," asked Hume, still staring at her, "and you are here?"

"You are the only sane person I ever knew," she replied.

"Good Lord," he said, "then I've said a good deal just now that ought only to be said in lunatic asylums—or in heavenly visions."

"You have said so much," she said in a low voice, "that I want you to say much more. I mean about the whole of this trouble. After what you have said . . . don't you think I might be allowed to know?"

He frowned at the table and then said rather more abruptly:

"The trouble was that I thought you were the last person who ought to know. You see, there is your family; and you might be brought into it, and one might have to hold one's tongue for the sake of someone you would care about."

"Well," she said steadily, "I *have* been brought into it for the sake of someone I care about."

She paused a moment and went on: "The others never did anything for me. They would have let me go raving mad in a respectable flat, and so long as I was finished at a fashionable school, they wouldn't have cared if I'd finished myself with laudanum. I never really talked to anybody before. I don't want to talk to anybody else now."

He sprang to his feet; something like an earthquake had shaken him at last out of his long petrified incredulity about happiness. He caught her by both hands and words came out of him he had never dreamed were within. And she, who was younger in years, only stared at him with a steady smile and starry eyes, as if she were older and wiser; and at the end only said:

"You will tell me now."

"You must understand," he said at last more soberly, "that what I said was true. I was not making up fairy-tales to shield my long-lost brother from Australia, or any of that business in the novels. I really did put a bullet in your uncle, and I meant to put it there."

"I know," she said, "but for all that I'm sure I don't know everything. I'm sure there is some extraordinary story behind all this."

"No," he answered. "It isn't an extraordinary story; except an extraordinarily ordinary story."

He paused a moment reflectively and then went on:

"It's really a particularly plain and simple story. I wonder it hasn't happened hundreds of times before. I wonder it hasn't been told in hundreds of stories before. It might so easily happen anywhere, given certain conditions.

"In this case you know some of the conditions. You know that sort of balcony that runs round my bungalow; and how one looks down from it and sees the whole landscape like a map. Well, I was looking down and saw all that flat plan of the place; the row of villas and the wall and path running behind it and the sycamore, and further on the olives and the end of the wall, and so out into the open slopes being laid out with turf and all the rest. But I saw what surprised me; that the rifle-range was already set up. It must have been a rush order; people must have worked all night. And even as I stared, I saw in the distance a dot that was a man standing by the nearest target, as if adding the last touches. Then he made a sort of signal to somebody away on the other side and moved very rapidly away from the place. Tiny as the figure looked, every gesture told me something; he was quite obviously clearing out just before the firing at the target was to begin. And almost at the same moment I saw something else. Well, I saw one thing, anyhow. I saw why Lady Smythe is worried, and wandered distracted in the garden."

Barbara stared; but he went on: "Travelling along the path from the Governorate and towards the sycamore was a familiar shape. It just showed above the long garden wall in sharp outline like a shape in a shadow pantomime. It was the top-hat of Lord Tallboys. Then I remembered that he always went for a constitutional along this path and out on to the slopes beyond; and I felt an overwhelming suspicion that he did not know that the space beyond was already a firing-ground. You know he is very deaf; and I sometimes doubt whether he hears all the things officially told to him; sometimes I fear they are told so that he cannot hear. Anyhow, he had every appearance of marching straight across as usual; and there came over me in a cataract a solid, an overwhelming and a most shocking certainty.

"I will not say much about that now. I will say as little as I can for the rest of my life. But there were things I knew and you probably don't about the politics here and what had led up to that dreadful moment. Enough that I had good reason for my dread. Feeling vaguely that if things were interrupted there might be a fight, I snatched up my own gun and dashed down the slope towards the path, waving wildly and trying to hail or head him off. He didn't see me and couldn't hear me. I pounded along after him along the path, but he had too long a start. By the time I reached the sycamore, I knew I was too late. He was already half-way down the grove of olives and no mortal runner could reach him before he came to the corner.

"I felt a rage against the fool which a man looks against the background of fate. I saw his lean pompous figure with the absurd top-hat riding on top of it; and the large ears standing out from his head . . . the large, useless ears. There was something agonizingly grotesque about that unconscious back outlined against the plains of death. For I was certain that the moment he passed the corner that field would be swept by the fire, which would cut across at right

angles to his progress. I could think of only one thing to do and I did
it. Hayter thought I was mad when I asked him if he had ever hanged a
man to prevent his being hanged. That is the sort of practical joke I
played. I shot a man to prevent his being shot.

"I put a bullet in his calf and he dropped, about two yards from the
corner. I waited a moment and saw that people were coming out of the
last houses to pick him up. I did the only thing I really regret. I had a
vague idea the house by the sycamore was empty, so I threw the gun
over the wall into the garden, and nearly got that poor old ass of a
parson into trouble. Then I went home and waited till they
summoned me to give evidence about Gregory."

He concluded with all his normal composure, but the girl was still
staring at him with an abnormal attention and even alarm.

"But what was it all about," she asked; "who could have——?"

"It was one of the best planned things I ever knew," he said. "I don't
believe I could have proved anything. It would have looked just like
an accident."

"You mean," she said, "that it wouldn't have been."

"As I said before, I don't want to say much about that now,
but . . . Look here, you are the sort of person who likes to think about
things. I'll just ask you to take two things and think about them; and
then you can get used to the idea in your own way.

"The first thing is this. I am a Moderate, as I told you; I really am
against all the Extremists. But when journalists and jolly fellows in
clubs say that, they generally forget that there really are different sorts
of Extremists. In practice they think only of revolutionary Extremists.
Believe me, the reactionary Extremists are quite as likely to go to
extremes. The history of faction fights will show acts of violence by
Patricians as well as Plebeians, by Ghibellines as well as Guelphs, by
Orangemen as well as Fenians, by Fascists as well as Bolshevists, by
the Ku-Klux-Klan as well as the Black Hand. And when a politician
comes from London with a compromise in his pocket—it is not only
Nationalists who see their plans frustrated.

"The other point is more personal, especially to you. You once told
me you feared for the family sanity, merely because you had bad
dreams and brooded over things of your own imagination. Believe
me, it's not the imaginative people who become insane. It's not they
who are mad, even when they are morbid. They can always be woken
up from bad dreams by broader prospects and brighter visions—
because they are imaginative. The men who go mad are the
unimaginative. The stubborn stoical men who have only room for

one idea and take it literally. The sort of man who seems to be silent but stuffed to bursting, congested——"

"I know," she said hastily; "you needn't say it, because I believe I understand everything now. Let me tell you two things also; they are shorter; but they have to do with it. My uncle sent me here with an officer who has an order for your release . . . and the Deputy-Governor is going home . . . resignation on the grounds of ill-health."

"Tallboys is no fool," said John Hume, "he has guessed."

She laughed with a little air of embarrassment.

"I'm afraid he has guessed a good many things," she said.

What the other things were is no necessary part of this story; but Hume proceeded to talk about them at considerable length during the rest of the interview; until the lady herself was moved to a somewhat belated protest. She said she did not believe that he could really be a Moderate after all.

THE HONEST
QUACK

1

THE PROLOGUE
OF THE TREE

M<small>R. WALTER WINDRUSH</small>, the eminent and eccentric painter and poet, lived in London and had a curious tree in his back-garden. This alone would not have provoked the preposterous events narrated here. Many persons, without the excuse of being poets, have planted peculiar vegetables in their back-gardens. The two curious facts about this curiosity were, first that he thought it quite remarkable enough to bring crowds from the ends of the earth to look at it; and, second, that if or when the crowds did come to look at it, he would not let them look.

To begin with, he had not planted it at all. Oddly enough, it looked very much as if he had tried to plant it and failed; or possibly tried to pull it up again, and failed again. Cold classical critics said they could understand the pulling up better than the putting in. For it was a grotesque object; a nondescript thing looking stunted or pollarded in the manner recalling Burnham Beeches, but not easily classifiable as vegetation. It was so squat in the trunk that the boughs seemed to spring out of the roots and the roots out of the boughs. The roots also rose clear of the ground, so that light showed through them as through branches, the earth being washed away by a natural spring just behind. But the girth of the whole was very large; and the thing looked rather like a polyp or cuttle-fish radiating in all directions. Sometimes it looked as if some huge hand out of heaven, like the giant in Jack and the Beanstalk, had tried to haul the tree out of the earth by the hair of its head.

Nobody indeed had ever planted this particular garden tree. It had grown like grass; and even like the wild grass of the wildest prairies. It was, in all probability, by far the oldest thing in those parts: there was nothing to prove it was not older than Stonehenge. It had never been planted in anybody's garden. Everything else had been planted round it. The garden and the garden-wall and the house had been planted round it. The street had been planted round it; the suburb had been planted round it. London, in a manner of speaking, had been planted round it. For though the suburb in question was now sunk so deep in the metropolis that nobody ever thought of it as anything but metropolitan, it belonged to a district where the urban expansion had been relatively recent and rapid; and it was not really so very long ago that the strange tree had stood alone on a windy and pathless heath.

The circumstances of its ultimate preservation or captivity were as follows. Nearly half a lifetime before, it happened that Windrush, who was then an art student, was crossing the open common with two companions, one a student of his own age, but attached to the medical and not the artistic section of his own college, the other a somewhat older friend, a business man whom the young men wished to consult upon a matter of business. They proposed to discuss their business (which was not unconnected with the general incapacity of young students to be business-like) at the inn of the Three Peacocks on the edge of the common; and the elder man especially showed some impatience to reach its shelter, as the wind was rising and dusk was falling over that rather desolate landscape.

It was at this point that their progress was delayed by the highly exasperating conduct of Walter Windrush. He was moving as rapidly as the rest, when the strange outline of the tree seemed to bring him up all standing. He even raised his hands, not only in a pantomime of amazement unusual in the men of his race, but in gestures that might have been taken for some sort of pagan worship. He spoke in a hushed voice, and pointed, as if drawing their attention to a funeral or some occasion of awe. His scientific friend admitted that the way in which the tree straddled out of the earth was something of a botanical curiosity; but he did not need to be very scientific to discover the cause in the brook or fountain, that broke from the upper ground behind it and had forced its way through the crannies of the roots. He had the curiosity to hop up on one of the high roots and hoist himself up by one of the low branches, and then, remarking that the tree seemed to be half hollow, turned as if to resume his march. The commercial gentleman had already been waiting with some impatience to do so.

But Walter Windrush could not be awakened from his trance of admiration. He continued to walk round and round the tree, to stare down into the straggling pools of water and then up to the wide cup or nest formed by the crown of boughs.

"At first," he said at last, "I did not know what had happened to me. Now I understand."

"Can't say I do," said his friend shortly, "unless it's going dotty. How long are you going to hang about here?"

Windrush did not answer immediately; then he said:

"Don't you know that all poets and painters and people like me are naturally Communists? And don't you know that, for the same reason, we're all naturally vagabonds?"

"I confess," said their business adviser rather grimly, "that some of your recent financial antics might appeal to the Communists. But as for vagabonds, I imagine that vagabonds at least have the virtue of getting a move on."

"You don't understand me," said Windrush with a strange sort of dreamy patience; "I mean that I'm not a Communist now. I'm not a vagabond any more."

There was a staring silence and then he said in the same tone:

"I never before in all my life saw anything that I wanted to possess."

"Do you really mean," expostulated the other, "that you would like to possess this one rotten old tree?"

Windrush went on as if the other had not spoken. "I have never before seen, in all my wanderings, any place where I wanted to stop and make my home. There cannot be anywhere in the world anything like that fantasia of earth and sky and water; built upon bridges like Venice, and letting daylight peer through its caverns like hell in Milton's poem; cloven as if by Alph the subterranean river and rising stark and clear of the clinging earth like the dead at the trump of doom. I have never seen anything like it. I do not really want to see anything else."

There was perhaps some excuse for his freak of imagination, in the momentary conditions that added mystery to the freak of nature. The stormy sky above the heath had changed from grey to purple, and from that to a sort of sombre Indian red which only brightened at the horizon in a single scarlet strip of sunset. Against this background the black and bizarre outline of the tree had really the appearance of something more mystical than a natural object; as if a tree were trying to walk or a monster from the waters rising in a wild effort to fly. But even if Windrush's companions had been more sympathetic with such moods than they were, they would hardly have been prepared for the finality with which he flung himself down on a clump of turf beside the brook and took out a pipe and tobacco pouch, rather as if he had just sat down in an arm-chair at the club.

"May I ask what you are doing?" asked his friend.

"I am acquiring squatter's rights," said the other.

They both besieged him with remonstrances; and it became more and more apparent to the others that he was perfectly serious, even if he was not perfectly sane. The business man indicated to him in a brisk manner that, if he was really and truly interested in this absurd scrap of wilderness, he would be wiser to consult the agents of the estate of which it formed a part; as he would not get any "squatter's rights" in half a century. To the extreme astonishment of the adviser, the poet thanked him quite gravely for the advice and took out a piece of paper to note down the agent's name and address.

"Meanwhile," said the commercial gentleman with great decision, "as this does not seem to me at all an agreeable place to squat in, you will have to come and squat in the Three Peacocks if you want to do any further business with me."

"Don't be a fool, Windrush," said his other companion sharply, "you can't really want to be left here all night."

"That happens to be exactly what I do want," replied Windrush. "I have seen the sun sink in my own private pool; and I want to see the moon rise out of it. You can't blame a prospective purchaser for testing the property under all conditions."

The business friend had already turned away, and his dark sturdy figure, expressing scorn in the very line of its back, had disappeared behind the sprawling tree. The other man lingered a moment longer; but in the face of the irrational rationality of the last remark, he also followed in the same path. He had gone about six yards and was also turning round by the tree, when the poet's whole manner suddenly altered. He threw down his pipe with an apologetic word and pursued his friends with an entirely new style and gesture, bowing with sweeping motions of courtesy.

"I beg your pardon," he said magnificently, "I do hope you will come down to my little place again. I fear I have failed in hospitality."

After he had himself lingered a moment or two by the tree and then resumed his seat on the bank, he sat gazing in a fascinated manner at the pools before him which, in the last intensity of sunset, gleamed like lakes of blood. He actually remained thus for many hours, seeing the red pools turn black with night and white with moonlight; as if he were indeed some Hindoo hermit who had gone into a stony ecstasy. But when he first moved on the following morning, he seemed filled with a far more novel and surprising practicality. He betook himself to the agents of the estate; he explained and negotiated for several months; and at length became the actual legal possessor of about two acres of ground surrounding his favourite freak of vegetation; and proceeded to fence it in with the most mathematical rigidity, like a settler staking out a claim in a desert. The rest of his extraordinary enterprise was all the more extraordinary for being comparatively ordinary. He built a small house on the land; he betook himself to habits of literary industry and respectability which soon enabled him to turn it into a very presentable country dwelling. In due course he even completed his social solidification by marrying a wife, who died after presenting him with one child, a daughter. The daughter grew up happily enough in these rustic but not rude conditions; and the life of Mr. Walter Windrush continued in sufficient serenity, until the coming of the great tragedy of his later life.

The name of that tragedy was London. The endless expansion of the city came crawling over those hills and commons like a rising sea; and the rest of his history, or of that part of his history, was entirely concerned with his moods of defiance and measures of defence in the face of so incongruous a deluge. He swore by all the Muses that if this loathsome labyrinth of ugliness and vulgarity must indeed surround his sacred tree and his secret garden, at least it should not touch them. He erected a ridiculously high wall all round the spot; he observed the utmost ceremony about admitting anyone into it; and indeed, towards the end, the ceremony rather hardened into suspicion. Some unwary guests had treated the garden as if it were a garden; nay, even the tree as if it were a tree. And as it was his boast that this his hermitage was the last free space of the earth left in England, and the refuge of a poetry everywhere else conquered by prose, he fell latterly into a habit of locking the door into the garden and putting the key in his pocket. In every other aspect of life he was quite hospitable and humane; he gave his daughter a very good time in every other direction; but he tended more and more to treating this place as sacred to his own solitude; and through long days and nights nothing ever stirred in that strange enclosure but its lonely master walking round and round his tree.

2
THE MAN WITH
THE BLACK BAG

E NID WINDRUSH, A very good-looking young woman with a brilliant
shock of light hair and a profile of the eager and sanguine sort,
had fallen behind her companion in the walk up the steep street and
stopped to make a small purchase at a small confectioner's shop. In
front of her the road rose in an abrupt white curve across a hill and the
open spaces of a suburban park. The small white rim of what was
obviously a colossal white cloud barely showed above the ridge;
producing one of those rare effects that almost persuade the natural
man, in spite of all the proofs adduced for it, that the world is round.
Against that background of blue sky, white road and white rim of
cloud, only two human figures happened at that moment to appear.
They appeared to be totally disconnected and indeed were in every
possible point dissimilar. And yet, a moment afterwards, she stared
and started hastily forward. For she saw enacted, on that high place in
the broad sunlight, what seemed to be one of the most inexplicable
cases of assault and battery in all the annals of crime.

One of the men in question was tall and bearded, with rather long
hair under a wide hat; he wore loose clothes and was walking with
loose strides in the sunny centre of the thoroughfare. Just before he
crested the ridge he turned and looked idly backwards down the road
he had climbed. The other man was moving decorously along the
pavement and appeared to be in every way a more decorous and even
duller sort of person. He wore a top-hat and his compact but not

conspicuous figure was clad neatly in dark clothes; he was walking briskly and rapidly, but very quietly, and he carried a small black bag. He might have been a City clerk who prided himself on being punctual, but feared he was a little late. Anyhow, he seemed to look straight in front of him and to take no interest in anything but his goal.

Quite suddenly he turned at right angles from the pavement, hurled himself, bag and all, into the middle of the road and appeared to pin or throttle the gentleman with the beard and the large hat. He was the shorter man of the two, but his spring was like a black cat's and he had all the advantage of youthful energy and the surprise. The tall man went staggering backwards towards the opposite pavement; but the next moment he had broken away from his mysterious enemy and started hitting back at him with refreshing vigour. At this moment a car coming from over the hill obscured for a moment the girl's view of the conflict, and when the space was clear again, it underwent yet a third change. The man in black, whose top-hat was now stuck somewhat askew on his head, but who still feverishly clasped his bag, appeared to be trying to break contact, in the military phrase; and to be disinclined to continue what he had so wantonly begun. He retreated slightly, waving hand and bag in what, not even a girl, at such a distance, could mistake for motions of pugilism; they appeared to be rather motions of expostulation. As, however, the tall man, now hatless and with hair and beard flying, seemed bent on pursuing his vengeance, the other suddenly hurled away his bag, tucked up his neat cuffs and proceeded to slog into the other in an entirely new, vigorous and scientific manner. All this had taken less than half a minute to happen; but by this time the girl was running up the street as fast as she could, leaving a staring confectioner with a small brown paper parcel dangling from his finger. For, as it happened, Miss Enid Windrush took a certain interest in the tall man with the long beard; an interest which many will rightly rebuke as antiquated and superstitious, but from which she had never been able entirely to emancipate herself. He was her father.

By the time she arrived on the scene, or possibly because she had arrived on the scene, the violence of the pantomime had somewhat abated; but both sides were still panting and snorting with the passions of war. The wearer of the top-hat, on closer inspection, revealed himself as a young man with dark hair, whose square face and square shoulders had a touch of the Napoleonic; for the rest he looked quite respectable and rather reticent than otherwise, and there was certainly nothing about him to explain his antic of attack.

Nor indeed did he appear to think that the explanation was required from him.

"Well!" he said, breathing hard, "of all the blasted old fools! . . . Of all the damned doddering old donkeys. . . ."

"This man," declared Windrush with fiery hauteur, "criminally assaulted me in the middle of the road for no reason whatever and——"

"That's what he says!" cried the young man in a sort of triumphant derision. "For no reason whatever! And in the middle of the road! Oh, my green-eyed grandmother!"

"Well, what reason?" began Miss Windrush, making an attempt to intervene.

"Why, because he was in the middle of the road, of course!" exploded the young man. "He'd have been in the middle of Kensal Green Cemetery pretty soon. And, speaking generally, I should say he ought to be in the middle of Hanwell Asylum now. He must have escaped from there, I should think, to go stravaging up the middle of a modern road like that, and turning his back to admire the landscape, as if he were alone in the Sahara. Why, every reasonably modern village idiot knows that the motorists can't see what's on the other side of this hill when they come over it; and if I hadn't happened to hear the car——"

"The car!" said the artist with a grave and severe astonishment, as one who convicts a child of romancing. "What car?" He turned round in a lordly manner and surveyed the street. "Where is this car?" he said sarcastically.

"By the rate it was going at, I should say it was about seven miles away," said the other.

"Why, of course it's quite true," said Enid, as a light broke upon her. "There was a car that came very fast over the hill, just as you——"

"Just as I committed my criminal assault," said the young man in the top-hat.

Walter Windrush was a gentleman and, what is by no means always the same thing, a man who valued a reputation for handsome behaviour. But he would have been more than human, if he had found it easy to adjust rapidly his relations to a gentleman, who had first flung him across the road and then, on his retaliating, started pommelling him like a pugilist, and to behold instantly in the same being, and veiled in the same face and form, a beloved friend and saviour to whom he must now dedicate his whole life in gratitude.

His acknowledgments were a little dazed and halting; but his daughter was in a position to be more magnanimous and hearty. Upon rational reconsideration, she rather liked the look of the young man; for neatness and respectability do not always displease ladies who have seen a good deal of the sublime liberty of the artistic life. Also, she had not been seized suddenly by the throat in the middle of the road.

Cards and courtesies began to be exchanged; the young man learned with surprise that he had insulted or rescued a distinguished man of letters; and the other learned that his insulter or rescuer was a young doctor, whose brass plate they had seen somewhere in the neighbourhood, inscribed with the name of John Judson.

"Oh, if you're a doctor," said the poet, joking in a rather jerky fashion, "I'm sure you've been guilty of grossly unprofessional conduct. You ought to be reported to the Medical Council for taking the bread out of my doctor's mouth. I thought you medical men only stopped to count the accidents in the street and put them down on the credit side of the ledger. Why, if I had been half killed with the car, you could have finished me off with an operation."

It seemed destined, from the first, that these two somewhat controversial characters should always say the wrong thing to each other. The young doctor smiled grimly; but there was a gleam of battle in his eye as he answered:

"Oh, I think we generally try to save anybody, in the street or the gutter or anywhere. Of course I didn't know I was saving a poet; I thought I was only saving an ordinary useful citizen."

It must be admitted with regret that this was a sample of the common conversations between the two. And, curiously enough, those conversations became rather common. To all appearance, they met only to argue; and yet they were always meeting. For some reason or other, Dr. Judson was continually coming round to the poet's house on one pretext or another; and the poet never failed in hospitality, though it had so strange a ring of hostility. It may be explained in part by the fact that each had met for the first time his complete antithesis and his completely convinced antagonist. Windrush was a man in the old tradition of Shelley or Walt Whitman. He was a poet to whom poetry seemed almost synonymous with liberty. If he had enclosed a wild tree in a tame suburban garden, it was by his account that it might be the last thing really allowed to grow wild. If he walked in a solitary path secluded by high walls, it was apparently by the instinct that has led many a squire to fence in a wilderness and call it a park. He liked loneliness because it was the only perfect form of doing as he liked. He regarded all the mechanical civilization that had spread around him as a mere materialistic slavery, and, as far as possible, treated it as if it were not there; even, as we have seen, to the extent of standing in the middle of a main road with his back to a motor-car.

Dr. Judson was the sort of man of whom his more foolish friends say that he will get on, because he believes in himself. This was probably a slander on him. He did not merely believe in himself; he believed in things requiring far more faith; in things which some think far more incredible and difficult to believe. He believed in modern organization and machinery and the division of labour and the authority of the specialist. Above all, he believed in his job; in his art and science and profession. He was one of an advanced school, propounding many daring theories, especially in the department of psychology and psycho-analysis. Enid Windrush began to notice his name appended to letters in the ordinary papers, and then to articles in the scientific papers. He had the simplicity to carry his highly modern monomanias into private life, and propounded them to her for hours at a time, striding up and down the artistic drawing-room, while Windrush was wandering round his private garden engaged in perennial tree-worship. The walking up and down was characteristic; for the second definite impression which Judson produced, after the impression of professional primness and dullness of attire, was the impression of a bubbling and even restless energy. Sometimes he had, with characteristic directness, broken out in remonstrance against the poet himself upon his own poetical eccentricity: the Tree, which the poet always talked of as the type of radiating energy in the universe.

"But what's the *good* of it?" Judson would cry out of the depths of dark exasperation. "What's the *use* of having a thing like that?"

"Why, no use whatever," replied his host. "I suppose it is quite useless as you understand use. But even if art and poetry have no use, it does not follow that they have no value."

"But look here," the doctor would start in again, scowling painfully. "I don't see the value of it as art and poetry—let alone reason or sense. What's the beauty of one dingy old tree stuck in the middle of bricks and mortar? Why, if you abolished it, you'd have room for a garage and you could go and see all the woods and forests in England—every blessed tree between Cornwall and Caithness."

"Yes," retorted Windrush; "and wherever I went, I should see petrol-pumps instead of trees. That is the logical end of your great progress of science and reason—and a damned illogical end to a damned unreasonable progress. Every spot of England is to be covered with petrol stations, so that people can travel about and see more petrol stations."

"It's only a question of knowing their way about when they travel about," insisted the doctor. "People born in the motoring age have got a new motor-sense, and they don't mind these things so much as you think. I suppose that's the real difference between the generations."

"All right," said the elder gentleman tartly. "Let us say you have all the motor-sense, and we have all the horse-sense."

"Well," said the other, also with a sharpened accent. "If you'd had a little more motor-sense, or any sort of sense, you wouldn't have been so bally near killed the other day."

"If there were no motors at all," answered the poet calmly, "there would have been nothing to kill me."

And then Dr. Judson would lose his temper and say the poet was cracked, and then he would apologize to the poet's daughter and say that of course the poet was a gentleman of the old school and had a right to be rather old-fashioned. But she, he would assert, with more earnest appeal, ought to have more sympathy with the future and the new hopes of the world. Then he would leave the house boiling with protests and arguing with invisible persons all the way home. For he really was a man profoundly convinced of the prospects and prophesies of science. He had a great many theories of his own, which he was only too anxious to throw out to the world in general. He was accused by his more playful friends of inventing diseases that nobody had ever experienced, in order to cure them by discoveries that nobody could ever explain. Superficially, he was indeed one with all the faults of a man of action, including the temptation of ambition. But for all that, there was a dark but busy cell in his inmost brain, where thought for thought's sake went on in an almost dangerous degree of turmoil and intensity. Anyone who could have looked into that dim whirlpool might have guessed that there could arise out of it, in some strange hour of stress, a thing like a monster.

Enid Windrush was a sufficient contrast to this intellectualism and secrecy, and seemed always walking in the sunlight. She was healthy, hearty and athletic; and in her tastes she might have been the shining incarnation of her father's frustrated love of the open country and the tall trees. She was more conscious of her body than her soul, and expressed in the suburban substitutes of tennis and golf and the swimming-bath, what might have been a native love of country sports. And yet it may be that in her also there was, at odd moments, a touch of her father's more transcendental fancy. Anyhow, it is true that long afterwards, when this story was ended, she stood again in the sunlight and looked back at those earlier days through a storm of black and brain-racking mysteries, and of horror truly piled upon horror. And looking back at this beginning of her story, she wondered if there were something in the old notion of omens and prefiguring signs. She wondered whether the whole of her riddle would not have been clear to her, from first to last, if she could have read it in those two dark figures dancing and fighting on the sunlit road against the white cloud; like two living letters of an alphabet struggling to spell out a word.

3

THE TRESPASSER IN
THE GARDEN

FOR VARIOUS CAUSES, which accumulated in his dark and brooding
brain for the next day or two, Dr. Judson eventually summoned
up all his courage and decided to go and consult Doone.

That he referred to him in his mind in this fashion indicated no
familiarity; but rather the reverse of familiarity. The person in
question had, of course, passed at some period through the more or
less human phases of being Mr. Doone and Dr. Doone and then
Professor Doone, before he rose into the higher magnificence of being
Doone. Men said Doone just as men said Darwin. It soon became
something of an affectation, if not an affront, to say Professor Darwin
or Mr. Charles Darwin. And it was now fully twenty years since
Professor Doone had published the great work on the parallel diseases
of anthropoids and men, which had made him the most famous
scientific man in England, and one of the four or five most famous in
Europe. But Judson had been one of his pupils when he was still
practising medicine at the head of a great hospital. And Judson
fancied that the fact might give him a slight advantage in one of those
incessant arguments of his, in which the name of Doone had cropped
up in a disputed point. To explain how it had cropped up, and how it
had come to seem so important, it is necessary to return once more
(after the habit of Dr. Judson) to the house of the poet Windrush.

When last Dr. Judson had paid a call there, he had found the one
thing in the world calculated to annoy him more than he was already

annoyed. He had, in fact, found another young man installed in the family circle, and learned that he was a next-door neighbour who very frequently dropped in for a chat. It may already have been darkly hinted that, whatever were the real sins or virtues of Dr. Judson (and he was full of many rather deep and unexplored possibilities) he did not possess a very good temper. He chose, for some mysterious reason or other, to take a dislike to the other young man. He did not like the way in which two wisps of his long fair hair lay on his cheek in a suggestion of incipient side-whiskers; he did not like the way in which he smiled politely while other people were talking. He did not like the way he talked himself, in a large and indifferent manner, about art, science or sport as if all subjects were equally important or unimportant; or the way in which he apologized alternately to the poet and the doctor for doing so. Lastly, the doctor faintly disapproved of the fact that the visitor was about two-and-a-half inches taller than himself, and also of the (infernally affected) stoop with which he almost redressed the difference. If the doctor had known as much about his own psychology as he did about everybody else's, he might have understood the symptoms better. There is normally only one condition in which a man dislikes another man for all that is repulsive and all that is attractive about him.

The name of the gentleman from next door appeared to be Wilmot, and there was nothing to indicate that he had anything to do in the world except collect impressions of a cultivated sort. He was interested in poetry, which might serve to explain his having found favour with the poet. Unfortunately, he was also interested in science; and this did not by any means find favour with the scientific man. There is nothing that exasperates a passionate specialist and believer in specialism so much as somebody graciously informing him of the elements of his own subject; especially when (as sometimes happens) they are the elements which the specialist himself started to explode and abolish ten years before. The doctor's protest was vehement to the verge of rudeness; and he declared that certain notions about Arboreal Man had been exposed as nonsense when Doone first began to write. It need hardly be said that Doone, being a great man of science, was almost universally praised in the newspapers for saying something very like the opposite of what he actually said in his books and lectures. Judson had attended the lectures; Judson had read the books; but Wilmot had read the newspapers. This naturally gave Wilmot a great advantage in discussion before any modern cultivated audience.

The debate had arisen out of a chance boast of the poet touching his early experiments as a painter. He showed them some old rhythmic designs of a decorative sort; and said he had often practised drawing with both hands simultaneously; and had sometimes begun to detect the beginnings of a difference or independence in the action of the two hands.

"So you might end up, I suppose," said Wilmot smiling, "by drawing a caricature of your publisher with one hand while you worked out the details of a piece of town-planning with the other."

"A new version," said Judson rather grimly, "of not letting your left hand know what your right hand doeth. If you ask me, I should say it was a damned dangerous trick."

"I should have thought," said the strange gentleman languidly, "that your friend Doone would have approved of a man using two hands, since his sacred ancestor the monkey actually uses four."

Judson sprang up in his explosive way. "Doone deals with the brains of men and monkeys, and uses his own like a man," he said. "I can't help it if some men prefer to use theirs like monkeys."

When he had gone, Windrush appeared not a little annoyed with such abrupt manners, though Wilmot was entirely serene.

"That young man is becoming insufferable," said the artist. "He turns every talk into an argument and every argument into a quarrel. What the devil does it matter to anybody what Doone really said?"

To the scowling Dr. Judson, however, it did evidently matter very much what Doone really said. It mattered so much that the doctor (as already indicated) took the trouble to cross the town in order to hear Doone really say it. Perhaps there was something like a touch of morbidity in his concentration in proving himself right on such a point, and certainly he was the sort of man who cannot bear to leave an argument unanswered; perhaps he had other motives or reasons mixed up in his mind. Anyhow, he went off stormily in the direction of that scientific shrine or tribunal, leaving Windrush angry, Wilmot supercilious and Enid puzzled and pained.

The great West End mansion of Dr. Doone, with its classic and pillared portico and rather funereal blinds, did not daunt the younger doctor as he ran resolutely up the steps and rang vigorously at the bell. He was shown into the great man's study and after a few sentences succeeded in recalling himself and receiving a mildly benevolent recognition. The great Dr. Doone was a very handsome old gentleman with curly white hair and a hooked nose, and did not look much older than the numerous portraits that appeared in bookish weeklies illustrating the conflict of Religion and Science. It did not take

Judson long to verify the accuracy of his version of the original Doone Theory. But all the time they were talking, the dark and restless eyes of the young doctor were darting about the room, probing every corner, in endless professional curiosity about the progress of science. He saw the stacks of new books and magazines lying on the table as they had arrived by post; he even automatically turned over the pages of a few of them, while his eye would wander and run along the serried ranks of the book-cases, and Doone went on talking, as old men will, of old friends and of old enemies.

"It was that egregious Grossmark," he was saying with reawakening animation, "who made the same absurd muddle of my meaning. Do you remember Grossmark? Of all the extraordinary examples of what concerted boosting can do——"

"Rather like the way Cubbitt is being boosted now," said Judson.

"I dare say," said Doone rather irritably. "But Grossmark really made a spectacle of himself on the Arboreal question. He did not answer a single one of my points, except with that absurd quibble about the word Eocene. Branders was better; Branders had made some real contribution in his time, though he could not quite see that his time was past. But Grossmark—well, really!"

And Dr. Doone settled himself back in his arm-chair and laughed genially.

"Well," said Judson, "I am much obliged to you. I knew I should learn a great deal if I came here."

"Not at all," said the great man, rising and shaking hands. "You say you have been discussing it with Windrush, the landscape painter, I think. I met him years ago, but he would hardly remember me. An able man; but eccentric, very eccentric."

Dr. John Judson came away from the house with a very thoughtful expression and seemed to be revolving rather more than might have appeared to have passed at the interview. He had no very clear intention of going back in triumph to the Windrush abode, armed with the thunderbolts of Doone; but he had a general and half-conscious tendency to drift in that direction in any case. And before his own intentions were clear, he found himself in front of the house and saw something which brought him to a standstill, staring up at it with a sort of stolid suspicion. For some instants he stood quite motionless; then crossed the road with catlike swiftness and peered round the corner of the house.

Night had fallen and a large moon painted everything with pale colours. The house or bungalow that the landscape-painter had originally built in an open landscape was now wedged in a row of villas, though it retained something of a quaint or uncouth outline of its own. It almost seemed to be, rather awkwardly, turning its back upon the street. Perhaps this hint of secrecy was only suggested by its own absurd secret, for just behind it could be seen the high spiked walls of the garden like the castellated walls of some pantomime prison. Only one crack gave a green glimpse of the enclosed shrubbery; where, on one side of the house, was a high narrow gate of a lattice pattern, which was always kept locked; but through the loopholes the stranger in the street could just see the glimmer of moonlight on the leaves. But the stranger in the street (if Dr. Judson may be so described) could at this moment see something else, and something that surprised him very much.

A long slim figure, dark against the moonshine, was most unmistakably using this sort of lattice as a ladder. He was scaling it swiftly from inside, with long-legged sinuous movements that rather recalled the monkeys that had formed the topic of conversation. He seemed, however, to be an unusually tall monkey and when he came to the top rung of his ladder—towering as if he might tip over into the street—the wind of that high place took two long locks of his hair and waved them fantastically, as if he were a sort of demon with two horns which he could move like ears. But in that last touch, in which some might find the culmination of the uncanny, the common sense of Dr. Judson found reality and recognition. He was well acquainted with those two exceedingly annoying wisps of hair. He had seen them flopping (as he would have illiberally expressed it) like two woman-ish whiskers on the countenance of the condescending Mr. Wilmot. And sure enough, the condescending Mr. Wilmot, alighting with a graceful leap, greeted him with no shade of gloom in his condescension.

"What the devil are you doing there?" asked Judson angrily.

"Why, it's the doctor!" said the other, with an air of pleased surprise. "Do I seem to be a case *de lunatico inquirendo?* I had forgotten that it must be quite a case for a psychologist."

"It seems to me to be a case for a policeman," said Dr. Judson. "May I ask what you are doing in Windrush's garden, which he likes to keep locked up—and anyhow, why you should leave it in that fashion?"

"I might very well ask why you should ask," replied the other pleasantly. "Unless I am curiously misinformed, you are not Mr. Walter Windrush any more than I am. But I assure you I don't want to quarrel, Dr. Judson."

"You are taking a rum way to avoid it," said the doctor in a bellicose manner.

The mysterious Mr. Wilmot drew near in a curious confidential manner that was quite new; his rather foolish airs and graces had fallen from him and he said, lowering his voice to a tone of great earnestness:

"I can assure you, doctor, that I have excellent authority, the best possible authority, for being in Windrush's garden."

And with that the mystic neighbour appeared to melt into the shadows, presumably eventually vanishing into his own house next-door; and Dr. Judson turned abruptly and, walking up to the front-door of the Windrush house, furiously rang the bell.

Mr. Windrush was not at home. He had gone out to some grand banquet of artistic celebrities and would not be home till late. But the conduct of Dr. Judson was certainly rather odd and rude; so much so that the lady who received him had a momentary and horrible feeling that he might have been drinking, incongruous as this was with the hard hygienic routine of his existence. He sat down in the drawing-room, opposite Enid Windrush; he sat down suddenly and resolutely as if resolved to say something and then said nothing. He was as motionless as a dark image and yet he fumed; she could only think of the metaphor that he smouldered. She had never realized before how his broad, round head seemed to bulge at the temples and over the eyebrows; how his clean-shaven jaws and chin seemed to swell implacably and what a glow of dark emotions could look out of his eyes. And all the time he seemed doubly grotesque because his square, strong hands were clasped on the head of an umbrella, the emblem of his precise and prosaic life. She waited, rather as she would have sat watching a round black bomb that was ticking and smoking in the parlour.

At last he said in a harsh voice:

"I wish I could see that tree your father's so fond of."

"I'm afraid that's impossible," she said. "It's really the only point he is very particular about. He says he would like every other man to have a favourite tree; meaning a place of solitude for himself. But he says he won't lend anybody else his tree any more than his tooth-brush."

"This is all nonsense," said the doctor gruffly. "What would he do if I just jumped over a wall, or somehow went into his garden?"

"I'm awfully sorry," she said in a wavering voice, "but if you came into his garden, you wouldn't ever come again into his house."

Judson sprang to his feet and she felt somehow that the last click had sounded before the catch and the detonation.

"And yet he allows Mr. Wilmot to go into his garden. The gentleman seems privileged in many ways."

Enid sat staring at him for a few seconds without speech. "Allows Mr. Wilmot to go into his garden!" she repeated.

"Thank God for that," said the doctor. "you don't seem to know anything about it, anyhow. Wilmot told me he had the very best authority; and I naturally thought of your authority or your father's authority. But, of course, it's just possible. . . . Here, wait a minute. . . . I'll let you know later. . . . Your father will forbid me the house! Will he?"

And with that, this far from soothing medical practitioner bolted from the house as abruptly as he had come into it. It struck her that he must have a remarkable bedside manner.

Enid dined alone, very thoughtfully revolving very complex and even contradictory criticisms of this extraordinary young man. then her thoughts went off to her father and his very different sort of unconventionality; and something led her to make her way to his study and studio at the back of the house, jutting out into the garden. Here were the large scrawled canvases with the unfinished sketches about which the argument had raged the day before; and she looked at them uneasily, remembering the controversial extremes to which such things could give rise. She herself was of a straightforward and very sane type of intelligence; and could no more see anything to quarrel about in such things than she could see metaphysics in a wallpaper or morals in a Turkey carpet. But the atmosphere of debate disturbed her, partly because it disturbed her father; and she looked rather moodily out of the french windows at the extreme end of the studio, into the gloom of the secluded garden.

At first she was subconsciously puzzled that there should be anything like a breeze on that clear moonlit night. She gradually awoke to the realization that nothing was moving in the garden except the one thing in its centre; the uncouth and sprawling outline of the nameless tree. She had an instant of babyish bogey feeling in the notion that it could move of itself like an animal, or create its own wind like a giant fan. Then she saw that its shape was changed, as if a new branch had sprouted, and then saw that a human figure was swinging upon it. The figure swung and dropped in the manner of a monkey and then advanced towards the window in the recognizable outline of a man. As it did so, all lesser thoughts vanished, and she knew it was not her father and not Mr. Wilmot from next door. An increasing but incomprehensible terror took hold of her, as when the faces of friends change in a bad dream. John Judson came close up to the closed window and spoke; but she could not hear what he said. All nightmare was in that soundless moving mouth against that invisible film. It was as if he were dumb like a fish, floating up to a port-hole; and his face was as pale as the underside of the deep-sea fishes.

The windows giving onto the garden were locked, like all such exits; but she knew where her father kept the keys, and in a moment they were open. Her indignant greeting was stopped on her lips; for Judson cried, in a hoarse voice she had never heard from any human being:

"Your father . . . he must be mad."

He stopped and seemed startled at his own words. Then he put his hands to his bulging brows, as if clutching his short dark hair, and after a silence said, but with a different emphasis: "He *must* be mad."

Enid's instinct told her that he had said two quite different things, even in repeating the same words. But it was long before she came to understand the difference between those two exclamations, or what had happened between them.

4

THE DISEASE OF
DUODIAPSYCHOSIS

ENID WINDRUSH WAS a human being; a very human being. She had
several shades and different degrees of indignation; only on the
present occasion she had them all at once. She was angry because a
visitor turned up at that time of night and entered by the window
instead of the door; she was angry that a person for whom she had felt
some regard should behave like a cat-burglar; she was angry that her
father's wishes should be scornfully disregarded; she was angry at
being frightened, and more angry at seeing no sense even in the
occasion of the fright. But she was human, and was perhaps most
angry of all at the fact that the intruder did not even answer or
acknowledge any of her expressions of anger. He sat with his elbows
on his knees and his hands clutching his bursting temples; and it was
long before there came from him even the impatient reply: "Can't you
see I'm thinking?"

Then he jumped up in his energetic way and ran to one of the large
unfinished pictures and peered into it. Then, equally feverishly, he
examined another and then another. Then he turned on her a face
about as reassuring as a skull and cross-bones, and said:

"I am greatly grieved to say it, Miss Windrush. In plain words, your
father is suffering from Duodiapsychosis."

"Is that your notion of plain words?" she asked.

He added in a low hoarse voice: "It began as an example of Arboreal
Atavism."

It is an error for the man of science to lapse into being intelligible. The last two words were sufficiently familiar, in an age of popular science, to cause the lady to leap up like a leaping flame.

"Have you the impudence to suggest," she cried, "that my father ever wanted to live in a tree like a monkey?"

"What other explanation is there?" he said gloomily. "This is a very painful business; but the hypothesis clearly covers the facts. Why should he wish always to be alone with the tree, unless his dealings with it were more grotesque than seemed suitable to his social dignity?—you know what this suburb is like! For that matter, his own horror of the suburb, his own quite exaggerated horror of towns, his quite feverish and fanatical yearning for woodlands and wild country—what can all this mean except the same Arboreal Atavism? For that matter, what else can explain the whole story—the story of how he found the tree and fixed on the tree? What was the nature of that ungovernable craving that first surged up in him at the very sight of the tree? An appetite as powerful as that must have come out of the depths of nature, out of the very roots of the evolutionary origin of man. It can only have been an anthropoid appetite. It is a melancholy but most convincing example of Doone's Law."

"What is all this nonsense?" cried Enid. "Do you imagine my father had never seen a tree before?"

"You must remember," replied the other in the same hollow and hopeless voice, "the peculiar features of the tree. It might have been designed to stimulate these faint memories of the original home of man. It is a tree that seems all branches, of which the very roots are like branches, and invite the climber with a hundred footholds. These primary promptings or fundamental instincts would have been plain enough in any case but unfortunately the case has since grown more complex. It has developed into a case of Semi-Quadrumanous Ambidexterity."

"That's not what you said before," she said suspiciously.

"I admit," he said, with a shudder, "that it is in a sense a discovery of my own."

"And I suppose," she said, "you are so fond of your horrible discoveries that you would sacrifice anybody to them—my father or me."

"Not sacrifice you. Save you," said Judson, and shuddered again. Then he mastered himself with an effort, and went on in the same maddening mechanical tone like that of a lecturer.

"The anthropoid reaction carries with it an attempt to recover the use of all the limbs equally, in the monkey fashion. This leads to experiments in ambidexterity like those he himself admitted. He tried to draw and paint with both hands. At a later stage he would probably attempt also to paint with his feet."

They stared across at each other; it measures the horror of that interview that neither of them laughed.

"The result," went on the doctor, "the really dangerous result lies in a tendency to separation between the functions. Such ambidexterity is not natural to man in his existing evolutionary stage and may lead to a schism between the lobes of the brain. One part of the mind may become unconscious of what is attempted by the other part. Such a person is not responsible . . . and really should be under supervision."

"I will not believe a word of all this," said the lady angrily.

He lifted one finger and pointed in a sombre manner at the sombre canvases and frames of brown paper that hung above them, on which were traced in vortical lines and lurid colours the visions of the ambidextrous artist.

"Look at those pictures," he said. "Look at them long enough and you will see exactly what I mean—and what they mean. The tree-motive is repeated again and again like a monomania; for a tree has a radiating and centrifugal pattern that suggests the waving of both hands at once, with a brush in each. But a tree is not a wheel—there would be less harm in a wheel. Though a tree has branches on each side, they are not the same on each side. And that is where the curse and the creeping peril begins."

This time there was a deadly silence, which he himself broke by going on with the lecture.

"The attempt to render the variation of branches by simultaneous ambidextrous action leads to a dissociation of cerebral unity and continuity, a breach of responsible moral control and co-ordinated consecutive conservation——"

In the black storm of her mind she had a lightning blaze of intuition and said:

"Is this a sort of revenge?"

He stopped in the very middle of a polysyllable and turned pale to the lips.

"Have you come to the end of your long words, you liar and quack and mountebank?" she cried in a tempest of indescribable fury. "Do you think I don't know why you're trying to make out my father isn't responsible? Because I told you he could turn you out of the house . . . because . . . ."

The pale lips seemed to move as if with a grin of agony: "And why should I mind that?"

"Because," she began and then stopped dead. An abyss had opened in herself into which she did not look. For a moment he sat on the sofa stiff as a corpse and then suddenly the corpse came to life.

"Yes!" he cried, leaping up. "You are right! It is you. It is you all the time! How can I leave you alone with him? You must believe me! I tell you the man is mad." He cried out suddenly in a new and ringing voice: "I swear to God I am afraid he will kill you! And how should I live after that?"

She was so astounded at this burst of passion after all the pedantry, that for the first time something broke or wavered in her hard voice and she could only say: "If it is me you are thinking about, you must leave him alone."

And with that a sort of stony detachment suddenly settled back upon him and he said, in a voice that seemed a hundred miles away: "You forget that I am a doctor. I have in any case a duty to the public."

"And now I know you are a skunk and a scoundrel," she said. "They always have a duty to the public."

And then, in the silence that followed, they both heard the sounds which could alone, perhaps, have aroused them from their dumb mutual defiance. A long, light and swinging step was heard down the corridors, and the light humming of some post-prandial song, told Enid with sufficient clearness who had returned; and the next moment Walter Windrush stood in the room, looking festive and rather magnificent in evening dress. He was a tall and handsome old gentleman; and before him the figure of the sullen doctor looked not only square but almost squat. But when the artist looked across his studio, he saw the windows open and the festivity faded from his face.

"I have just walked through your garden," said the doctor in a soft voice.

"Then you will kindly walk out of my house," said the artist.

He had turned pale with anger or some other passion; but he spoke clearly and firmly. After a silence he said: "I must ask you to cease from any communications with me and my family."

Judson started and stepped forward with a violent gesture which he checked as he made it. But his voice broke out of him like something beyond his control.

"You say I am to go out of this house. I say it is you who shall go out of this house!"

Then, as if grinding his teeth, he added with what seemed inconceivable intellectual cruelty: "I am going to have you certified as a lunatic."

He walked furiously out of the room towards the front-door; and Windrush turned to his daughter. She was staring at him with wide eyes; but her colour was such that he thought, for the fraction of an instant, that she was dead.

Of the next frightful forty-eight hours in which the threat was carried out with all its consequences, Enid could never remember many details. But she remembered some nameless hour of night or morning that seemed but a part of a sleepless night, when she stood on the door-step and looked wildly up and down the street, as if expecting her neighbours to rescue her from a house on fire. And there crept upon her the cold certainty, more cruel than any fire, that in this sort of calamity there was no hope from neighbours, nor any appeal against the machine of modern oppression. She saw a policeman standing near the next lamp-post, outside the next house. She thought of calling to the policeman, as if to save her from a burglar; and then she realized that she might as well call to the lamp-post. If two doctors chose to testify that Walter Windrush was mad, they turned the whole modern world with them—police and all. If they chose to testify that it was an emergency case, he could be taken away at once, under the eye of any policeman; and it seemed that he was being taken away at once. Nevertheless, there was something about the policeman planted at that particular spot, where she had never seen one before, that riveted her eye. And even as she gazed, the next-door neighbour, Mr. Wilmot, came out of his front-door with a light suitcase in his hand.

She felt a sudden impulse to consult him; perhaps it was an impulse to consult anybody. But he had always seemed to be a man of many types of information, including the scientific; and she impulsively ran across and asked for a moment's interview. Mr. Wilmot seemed a little hurried, which was far from being his usual demeanour; but he politely bowed her back into his front-parlour. When she got there, a rather inexplicable shyness or evasion overcame her. She felt a new and irrational reluctance to give away somebody or something, she knew not what. Moreover, there was something unfamiliar about the familiar face and form of Mr. Wilmot. He was wearing horn spectacles, through which his glance seemed sharper and more alert than of old. His clothes were the same, but they were buttoned up more neatly and all his movements were more brisk. He still had the wisps that looked like whiskers; but the face underneath had so altered in expression that one might almost fancy the whiskers were part of a wig.

Dazed and doubtful in a new fashion, she felt impelled to put her point in a more impersonal way; and asked whether he could give any advice to a friend of hers, who had been warned of a disease called Duodiapsychosis. Could he tell her if there was such a disease, as she knew he knew a lot about those things?

He admitted that he knew a little about those things. But he still seemed hurried—courteously but convincingly hurried. He looked it up in a work of reference, turning the pages very rapidly; no, he doubted whether there was any such thing.

"It seems to me," he said, looking gravely at her through his spectacles, "that your friend may be the victim of a quack."

With that repetition of her suspicions, she turned homewards and he rather eagerly followed her into the street. The policeman saluted him; there was nothing much in that; policemen saluted her father and other well-known residents. But she did think it odd that he said to the policeman, as he went off: "There's one thing more I must make sure of. Unless I wire, things can go forward here as arranged."

When she came back to her own house, she knew it was something worse than a house of death. There was a black taxicab waiting outside it, which made her think of a funeral, almost with envy. If she had known who was already in the taxicab, she might have stopped and made a scene in the street. As it was, she burst into the house and found two grave, dark-clad doctors sitting in the light of the bow-window in front, with a table between them, covered with official documents and pen and ink. One of the doctors, who was just about to sign one of the documents, was a stately, silver-haired gentleman in a very elegant astrachan overcoat; she gathered from the conversation that his name was Doone. The other doctor was the abominable John Judson.

She had paused an instant just outside the room and heard the tail-end of their scientific talk.

"You and I know, of course," Judson was saying, "how much the mere idea of subconsciousness, or horizontal division of the mind, has been superseded by vertical division of the mind. But the layman has hardly heard yet of the new double or ambidextrous consciousness."

"Quite so," said Dr. Doone in a level and soothing voice.

He had a very soothing voice, and with it he earnestly did his best to soothe Enid Windrush. He really seemed to be profoundly touched with the tragedy of her position.

"I cannot expect you to believe how much I feel for your misfortunes," he said. "I can only say that anything that can soften the shock for anyone involved will be done. I will not disguise from you that your father is already in the cab outside, under the care of tactful and humane attendants. I will not disguise from you that some deception, such as has to be used to the sick, has been employed in prevailing upon him; but I told him no more than the truth in saying that he was going with his best friends. These things are very terrible, my child; but perhaps we may all draw nearer to each other in——"

"Oh, sign the thing and be done," said Dr. Judson rudely.

"Be silent, sir," said Doone with fine dignity and indignation. "If you have neither the manners nor the morals for dealing with people in misfortune, I, at least, have more experience. Miss Windrush, I am sorry."

He held out his hand and Enid stood hesitating and then retreated like one distraught; so distraught that she actually turned to Dr. Judson.

"Send that man away," she cried with the shrillness of hysteria. "Send him away! He is more horrible even than——"

"More horrible than——" repeated Judson, waiting.

She looked at him with a wild inscrutable stare and said:

"More horrible than you."

"Have you signed that damned thing yet?" said Judson, boiling with impatience. But, even as they had turned away from him, Doone had signed the paper and Judson snatched it up with furious haste and ran out of the house.

And then she saw something that finally put him beyond pardon. For as he ran down the steps, he seemed to give a sort of bound of cheerfulness, like a boy on a holiday; like a man who has at last got what he wanted. She felt she could have forgiven him everything except that last little leap of joy.

Some time after—she could not have said how long—she still sat staring out of the bow-window into the empty street. She had reached that state when the soul feels that nothing worse can happen in the world. But she was wrong. For it was only a few minutes later that two policemen and a man in plain clothes came up those steps and, after some apologies and uncomfortable explanations, announced that they had a warrant for the arrest of Walter Windrush on a charge of murder.

5

THE SECRET OF
THE TREE

THE MOTIVES OF the simple are more subtle than those of the subtle. The former do not sort out their own emotions and the result is often more mysterious, especially as they never afterwards attempt to solve the mystery. Enid was a very elemental and unconscious character, who had never before been thrown into such a turmoil of thoughts and feelings. And her first feeling, under her last shock, was a primitive human feeling that for her isolation had come to an end. She had found something more crushing and complicated than she could carry alone; and she must have a friend.

She therefore went straight out of the front-door and down the road to find a friend. She went to find a charlatan, a schemer, a grotesque lying mystagogue, a man who had done her and hers the most abominable wrong; and she found him just going into his own house, with the brass plate outside it. Something not to be formulated in words told her that, in some dark, distorted, undiscoverable way he was on her side, and that he would manage to get whatever he chose to try for. She stopped the villain of her strange story and spoke to him quite naturally, as if he were her brother.

"I wish you would come back to our place a moment," she said. "Another ghastly thing has happened now and I can't make head or tail of anything."

He turned promptly and threw a sharp glance up the street.

"Ah," he said; "then the police have come already."

She stared at him speechless for a moment, as a light gradually began to break upon her rocking brain.

"Did you know they were coming?" she cried; and then in a final universal flash she seemed to take in a thousand things at once. The combined product of them all was perhaps curious. For there broke out of her only the expression of incredulous astonishment: "But aren't you wicked then?"

"Only moderately so," he replied. "But I dare say what I did would be considered indefensible. It was the only thing I could think of to save him. It had to be done in rather a hurry."

She drew a deep breath and there dawned upon her gradually, like something seen in the distance, a memory and a meaning.

"Why, I see now," she said. "It was just like what you did, when you shoved him from under the car."

"I'm afraid I'm impetuous," said Judson; "and perhaps I jump too soon."

"But on both occasions," she said, "you only jumped just in time."

Then she went into the house alone; her mind was still stratified with terror; the notion of her father as a monkey, as a lunatic, as something worse. And yet in a corner of her sunken subconscious soul something was singing, because her friend was not so wicked after all.

Ten minutes later, when Inspector Brandon, a sandy-haired representative of the C.I.D., with a stolid appearance but a lively eye, entered the Windrush parlour, he found himself confronted with a square-faced, square-shouldered medical gentleman, with dark hair and an inscrutable smile. Nobody, who had seen Dr. Judson shaken by the various passions of the late peril and crisis, could have recognized him, in the placid impenetrable friend of the family who now sat facing the policeman.

"I am sure, Inspector, that you agree with me in wishing to spare the unfortunate lady as far as possible," he said smoothly. "I happen to be the family physician, and I shall have to be responsible for her condition in any case. But I am responsible in other ways, too; and you may take it from me that a man in my position will put no obstacles in your way in doing your duty. I hope you have no objection, for the moment, to explaining the general nature of your business to me."

"Well, sir," said the Inspector; "so far as that is concerned, it's generally rather a relief in these cases to be able to talk to a third party. But you'll understand, of course, that I shall expect you to talk straight."

"I'll talk straight enough," answered the doctor coolly. "I understand you have a warrant for the arrest of Mr. Walter Windrush."

The policeman nodded:

"For the murder of Isaac Morse," he said. "Do you know where Windrush is at present?"

"Yes," said Judson gravely, "I know where Windrush is at present."

He looked across the table tranquilly, with level brows, and added:

"I will tell you, if you like. I will take you to him, if you like. I know exactly where he is just now."

"We mustn't have any hiding or hanky-panky, you know," said the Inspector. "You will be taking a serious responsibility, if there's any chance that he will escape."

"He will not escape," said Dr. Judson.

There was a silence, which was broken by a slight scurry outside and a telegraph-boy ran up the steps with a wire for the Inspector. That official read it with a frown of surprise, and then looked across at his companion.

"This comes opportunely in one sense," he said. "It seems to justify our pausing for an explanation, if you're quite sure of what you say."

He handed the telegram to the doctor, who read with his rapid glance the words:

"Don't do anything about W. W. till I come. Shall be round in half an hour.—HARRINGTON."

"That is from my superior officer," said the official. "The chief detective who has been studying this matter on the spot. Indeed, one of the chief detectives in the world to-day, I suppose."

"Yes," said the doctor, dryly. "Didn't Mr. Harrington pursue his studies under the name of Mr. Wilmot? And live next door?"

"You seem to know a thing or two," said Inspector Brandon with a smile.

"Well, your friend behaved so much like a burglar that I guessed he must be a policeman," said Judson, "and he said he had the best authority; I found it wasn't the authority of the family, so I assumed it was probably the authority of the law."

"Whatever he said was pretty sound, you may be certain," said the other. "Harrington is pretty nearly infallible in the long run. And in this case he was certainly justified by what he found, though nobody would ever have guessed it."

"What he found," said the doctor, "was the skeleton of a man, stuffed into the hollow of the tree, evidently having been there for a

long time, marked by an unmistakable injury to the occiput, done by
violence and inflicted with the left hand.''

Brandon stared across at him. "And how do you know that he
found that?" he asked.

"I know because I found it myself," answered Judson.

There was a pause; and then he added: "Yes, Inspector, it is quite
true that I know something about this business; as I told you, I can
take you to Windrush himself if necessary. Of course, I don't claim
any right to bargain with you; but since you are hung up by that
telegram for the moment, and I may be in a position to help, do you
mind doing me a favour in return? Will you tell me the whole story?
Or perhaps I should say the whole theory?"

The face of Brandon of the C.I.D. was not only humorous and
good-humoured; it was also highly intelligent, when the first veneer
of official stolidity had worn off. He looked at the doctor thoughtfully
for a little, and seemed to approve of what he studied. Then he said
with a smile:

"I suppose you are one of those amateur detectives who read
detective stories, or even write them. Well, I don't deny this is a bit of a
detective story. And there is one question that's always turning up in
books and talk of that sort, and it's rather relevant here. You've seen it
twenty times. Suppose a real Man of Genius wanted to commit a
crime?"

He ruminated a little and then went on. "From our point of view,
the great problem in any crime of killing is always what to do with the
body. I expect that fact has saved many a man from being murdered.
The fact that he is more dangerous to his enemy dead than alive. All
sorts of tricks are tried; dismembering and dispersing the body,
throwing it into kilns and furnaces, putting it under concrete floors,
like Dr. Crippen. And in the study of such stories, this story does stand
out as the very extraordinary and yet effective expedient of what I call
a Man of Genius.

"Isaac Morse flourished about twenty years ago as a financial agent
and adviser; I imagine you know what that means. In fact he
flourished as a money-lender, and flourished like the green bay-tree,
otherwise the wicked man. He flourished so very much, and so very
much at other people's expense, that he was probably pretty
unpopular with a good many people whose circumstances were not
so flourishing. Among these were two students; the one, who was a
less interesting person, was a medical student named Duveen. The
other was an art student named Windrush.

"The financial adviser was imprudent enough to leave his car and chauffeur, and walk across a corner of a heath to the hotel where the conference was to be held. In doing so, they passed a very desolate dip in the moorland marked only by this queer hollow tree. . . . What would the ordinary stupid professional killer have done? He would have killed, doubtless when his other companion's back was turned, and if he got away with it, would have skulked back and tried to scratch a shallow grave in the sandy heath. Or tried to cart away the corpse in a box under the eyes of all the servants at the inn. That is the difference between him and a man with imagination—an artist. The artist attempted something perfectly wild and new, and apparently absurd; but something that has succeeded for twenty years. He professed to have a romantic affection for that particular spot, he boasted of his intention of buying it and living on it. He did buy it, and he did live on it, and he did by this method bury from all eyes but his own the secret of what he had left there. For in those few moments, when the other student had gone on ahead and was hidden beyond the sprawling tree, he struck Morse a mortal blow with his left hand and threw his body into the yawning cavern in the tree. It was a solitary spot and naturally nobody actually saw him do the deed. But long after the medical student had gone on to the hotel and caught a train to London, another traveller on the moor saw Windrush sitting staring at the tree and the pools, in a dark reverie doubtless full of his daring scheme. And it is an odd thing that even the passer-by thought his solitary figure looked as tragic as Cain; and the pools under the red sunset looked like blood.

"The rest of his audacious scheme, or artistic pose, worked easily enough. By bragging of being cranky, he escaped all chance of the suspicion of being criminal. He could cage up the tree like a wild animal, without anybody thinking it any sillier than it seemed. You will notice that his caging grew more strict; when people began to touch or examine the tree, he locked everybody out of the garden. Except Harrington—and apparently you."

"I suppose," said Judson, "that Harrington, or Wilmot, or whatever you call him, told you that the artist admitted being ambidextrous—doing things with his left hand as well as his right."

"Quite so," replied the Inspector. "Well, Dr. Judson, I have obliged you and told you practically all I know at present. If there is anything more that you know, and we don't know, I am bound to warn you in any case that you are bound to return the favour. This is a deadly serious business. It is a hanging matter."

"No," said Dr. Judson thoughtfully; "not a hanging matter."

As the other only stared he added, still in a meditative style:

"You will never hang Walter Windrush."

"What do you mean?" demanded the officer, in a new and sharp voice.

"Because," said the doctor, beaming at him, "Walter Windrush has been in a lunatic asylum for some little time. He was certified in the regular old official manner"—he talked of it as of something that happened a hundred years before—"and the medical authorities that certified him noted the symptom of ambidextrous action and a somewhat excessive development of power in the left hand."

Inspector Brandon was staring like one stunned at the brisk and smiling doctor, who rose to his feet as if the interview were over. But even as he stepped towards the door, he found his exit blocked by the presence of a newcomer; and found himself looking once more at the long hair and long smiling visage of the gentleman he had so heartily disliked under the name of Mr. Wilmot.

"Back again," said Wilmot, or Harrington, his smile widening to a grin, "and apparently just in time."

The Inspector had recovered from his stupefaction and his senses and perceptions were quick enough. He got to his feet quickly and said:

"Is anything the matter?"

"No," said the great detective; "nothing is the matter. Except that we are after the wrong man."

And he settled himself comfortably in a chair and smiled at the Inspector.

"The wrong man!" repeated Brandon. "You can't mean that Windrush is the wrong man! I've just been taking the liberty of telling Dr. Judson the real story——"

"Under the impression," said Harrington, "that you knew the real story. For my part, I never knew it till about twenty minutes ago."

His face and manner were eminently cheerful; but as he turned to speak to the doctor, they took on a sort of business-like gravity and he seemed to choose and weigh his words.

"Doctor," he said, "you are a man of science and you understand what hardly anybody in this world does understand. You understand what is really meant by a hypothesis that holds the field. As a man of science, you must have had the experience of building up a very elaborate, a very complete and even a very convincing theory."

"Why, yes," said John Judson, with a grim smile; "I have certainly had the experience of building up a very elaborate, very complete and even convincing theory."

"But," went on the detective thoughtfully, "as a man of science, you were nevertheless ready to entertain the possibility, even if it were the remote possibility, that your theory was after all untrue."

"You are right again," said Judson, and the smile grew grimmer. "I was ready to entertain the remote possibility that my theory was quite untrue."

"Well, I take full responsibility for the unexpected collapse of my theory," said the great detective, with his agreeable smile. "You must not blame the Inspector; the whole of that story of the artist criminal and his original scheme of concealment was my idea, and an infernally intelligent and interesting idea too, though I say it who shouldn't. There's really nothing to be said against it; except that it can't be true. Everything has a little weakness somewhere."

"But why can't it be true?" asked the astonished Brandon.

"Only," answered his commanding officer, "because I have just discovered the real murderer."

Amid the startled silence that followed he added, as in a pleasant abstraction: "That grand and bold artistic crime we dreamed of was, like many great things, too great for this world. Perhaps in Utopia, perhaps in Paradise, we may have murders of that perfect and poetical sort. But the real murderer behaves in a much more ordinary fashion. . . . Brandon, I have found the other student. Naturally, you know rather less about the other student."

"Pardon me," said the Inspector stiffly, "of course, we traced the movements of the other student and of everybody who could be involved. He took the train to London that evening and, a month after, went to New York on business and thence to the Argentine, where he set up a successful and highly respectable practice as a doctor."

"Exactly," said Harrington. "He did the dull ordinary thing that the real criminal does. He bolted."

Dr. Judson seemed to find his voice for the first time since the last turn of events, and it was like the voice of a new man.

"Are you quite certain," he said at last, "that Windrush is innocent after all?"

"I am quite certain," said Harrington seriously. "This is not a hypothesis but a proof. There are a hundred converging proofs; I will only give you a few. The injury to the skull was done with a very unusual surgical instrument; and I have found the instrument in possession of the man who used it. The spot selected would only have been so chosen by a man of special knowledge. The man called Duveen, whom we know to have been present, and to have had a stronger motive than Windrush (for he was ruined and in fear of exposure), was and is a man with exactly that special knowledge. He is a surgeon and a skilful man. He is also a left-handed man."

"If you are certain, sir, the thing is settled," said the Inspector rather regretfully. "As Dr. Judson has explained, the left-handed business was also a part of the disease or aberration of Windrush——"

"You will agree that I never said I was certain about Windrush," said Harrington calmly, "I do say I am certain now."

"Doctor Judson says——" began the Inspector.

"Dr. Judson says," said that physician himself, springing up like a spring released; "Dr. Judson says that everything that Dr. Judson has said for the last forty-eight hours is a pack of lies! Dr. Judson says that Walter Windrush is no more mad than we are. Dr. Judson begs to announce that his celebrated theory of Arboreal Ambidexterity is a blasted mass of balderdash that ought never to have taken in a baby! Duodiapsychosis! Huh!" And he snorted with a violent and indescribable noise.

"This is very extraordinary," said Inspector Brandon.

"I bet it is," said the doctor. "We all seem to have made pretty damned fools of ourselves by being too clever; but I was the damndest. Look here, this has got to be put straight at once! It's bad enough for Miss Windrush that her father should be locked up for a day. I must make out some sort of document admitting a mistake, or announcing a recovery, or some nonsense; and get him out again."

"But," said Harrington gravely, "I understood that no less a person than Dr. Doone also signed the emergency order; and his authority——"

"Doone!" cried Judson with a quite indescribable frenzy of contempt. "Doone! Doone would sign anything! Doone would say anything. Doone is a doddering old fraud! He wrote one book that was boomed when I was a baby, and he's never opened a book since. I saw all the new books on his table with none of the leaves cut. And the way he talked about prehistoric man was more prehistoric than fossils. As if any serious scientific man now believed all his stuff about Arboreal Man! Golly, I didn't have any difficulty with Doone! I only had to flatter him at first by making it all very Arboreal, and then talking about what he didn't understand and dared not question. I had great fun with something newer than Psycho-analysis."

"All the same," said Harrington, "as Dr. Doone has signed the order, he'll have to sign the countermanding of it."

"Oh, very well," cried the impetuous Judson, who had already scribbled something on a page and was already rushing from the room; "I'll cut round and get him to sign it, too."

"I think I should rather like to go with you," said Harrington.

In the track of the headlong Judson, they trailed round with tolerable rapidity to that stately and pillared house in the West End, the house with the sombre blinds, which the doctor had once visited alone. The scene between him and the stately Dr. Doone was rather curious. Now that they had some inner light on the matter, they could appreciate the evasiveness of the great man and the pertinacity of the smaller one. However, Dr. Doone evidently felt it was wiser to join in his colleague's recantation; and, carelessly picking up a quill pen, he signed the paper with his left hand.

6
THE EPILOGUE OF
THE GARDEN

A FORTNIGHT AFTERWARDS, Mr. Walter Windrush was walking round his favourite garden, smiling and smoking as if nothing had happened. He was smoking a small cigarette in a very long cigarette-holder; and he really was doing it as if nothing had happened. For that was the real mystery of Walter Windrush, which neither medical nor legal experts were ever in the least likely to fathom. That was the real Secret; which no detective would ever detect.

He had been turned into a monstrosity in the eyes of his nearest and dearest; he had been described to his own child as a chimpanzee and as a chattering maniac; he had been described again as a pitiless and patient assassin, planning his whole life upon the concealment of a crime; he had been dragged through or threatened by every degrading and hideous experience; he had found that his favourite private paradise had been the scene of a murder and that his friend found it possible to believe him to be a murderer; he had been in the madhouse; he had been near to the gallows. And all these things were of less importance to him than the shape of the great coloured cloud of morning that came sailing up out of the east, or the fact that the birds had begun to sing in the branches of the tragic tree. Some would have said his mood was too shallow for such tragedies. Some, who saw deeper, might have said it was too deep for them. But upon such deep springs of levity he lived; and so he walked, as if in another world. It is possible that Inspector Brandon did not completely comprehend the monster called a Man of Genius.

Indeed, he was much less affected by the morbid memories than the man of common sense. When he had strolled about alone for a few moments, he was joined by his young friend the doctor; but the doctor looked comparatively gloomy and embarrassed; so much so that the artist rallied him about it.

"Well," said Dr. Judson, with something of his old sort of sullen candour; "I ought to be ashamed of it, I suppose, as well as of everything else. But I confess I can't think how you can bear to hang about in the place."

"My dear fellow, and you are the cold and rational man of science," said Windrush lightly. "In what superstitions you wallow! In what mediæval darkness you brood all your days! I am only a poor, impracticable, poetic dreamer; but I assure you I am in broad daylight. In fact, I have never been out of it, not even when you put me in that pleasant little sanatorium for a day or two. I was quite happy there; and as for the lunatics, well I came to the conclusion that they were rather saner than my friends outside."

"There's no need to rub it in," said Judson with a groan. "I won't apologize for thinking you a madman, because I never did think so. But I suppose that, given a fine sense of delicacy, I ought to apologize for thinking you a murderer. But there are murderers and murderers; all I knew was that I had found a murdered man you had hidden in your garden. I didn't know how far you might have been provoked or justified. Indeed, from all I hear of the late lamented Mr. Morse, he was of the sort that won't be missed. But I knew that Wilmot was a detective and was poking round the tree, and I knew that meant your arrest in precious quick time. I had to act pretty quickly myself; I generally do act a good deal too quickly, for that matter. A plea of insanity after arrest is always weak—especially when it's not true. But if you were already certified you couldn't even be arrested. I had to invent an imaginary disease, entirely out of my own head in about five minutes. I put it together somehow out of bits of that talk we had about ambidexterity and bits of Doone's rotten old rubbish about anthropoids. I put that in, partly because I foresaw that I should have to nobble Doone somehow; and partly because it fitted so well into the tale of the tree. But even now I hate to think of the horrors I made up; even though they were horrors that never happened. But what must one feel about the horrors that really have happened?"

"Well," replied the artist cheerfully, "and what do you feel about them?"

"I can't help feeling," said Judson, "that men might avoid the place like a plague-spot."

"The birds perch on the tree," said Windrush, "as if it were the shoulder of St. Francis."

There was a silence and then the brooding Judson said:

"After all, sir, it *is* damned extraordinary that you lived alone with this tree for twenty years and never found what was inside it. I know it rotted to bones pretty quickly, because the stream carried away the decomposition; but you might have been pulling the tree about any day."

Walter Windrush looked at him steadily with his clear glassy eyes.

"I have never even touched the tree," he said. "I have never been within two yards of it."

Something in his manner suggested to the young man that they had come near the nerve of the eccentricity; he was silent and the artist went on:

"You tell us a great deal about Evolution and the Ascent of Man. You scientific men are very superior, of course, and there is nothing legendary about you. You do not believe in the Garden of Eden. You do not believe in Adam and Eve. Above all, you do not believe in the Forbidden Tree."

The doctor shook his head in half-humorous deprecation, but the other went on with the same grave fixity of gaze.

"But I say to you, always have in your garden a Forbidden Tree. Always have in your life something that you may not touch. That is the secret of being young and happy for ever. There was never a story so true as that story you call a fable. But you will evolve and explore and eat of the tree of knowledge, and what comes of it?"

"Well," said the doctor defensively; "a good many things have come of it that are not so bad."

"My friend," said the poet. "You once asked me what was the Use of this tree. I told you I did not wish it to be any Use. And was I wrong? I have got nothing but good out of it, because to me it was useless. What have they got out of it, those to whom it was useful? What did they get who asked, after the manner of that ancient folly, for the Fruit of the tree? It was useful to Duveen, or Doone, or whatever you call him; and what fruit did he gather but the fruit of sin and death? He got murder and suicide out of it; they told me this morning that he had taken poison, leaving a confession of the murder of Morse. It was useful to Wilmot in a way, of course; but what did even Wilmot and Brandon get out of it, but the dreadful duty of dragging a fellow-creature to the gallows? It was useful to you; when you wanted a nonsensical nightmare of some sort, with which to lock me up for life and terrify my family. But it was a nightmare; and you yourself still seem to be a little haunted by the nightmare. But I repeat that it was useless to me; and I am still in the broad daylight."

As he spoke, Judson looked up across the lawn and saw Enid Windrush come out of the shadow of the house into the sun. Something in the golden balance of her figure, with the flushed face and flame-like radiation of her hair, made her look as if she had actually stepped from an allegorical picture of the dawn; and swiftly as she moved, her movements always had the grand gradual curves of great unconscious forces, of the falling waters and the wind. Something of this congruity with the almost cosmic drift of the conversation doubtless rose into the poet's mind, as he said casually enough:

"Well, Enid, I've been boosting the old property again. I've been modestly comparing my own backyard to the Garden of Eden. But it's no good talking to this deplorable materialistic young man. He doesn't believe in Adam and Eve or anything they tell you about on Sundays."

The young man said nothing; at that moment he was wholly occupied with seeing.

"I don't know whether there are any snakes about," she said, laughing.

"Some of us," said Judson, "have been in the sort of delirium in which men see snakes. But I think we are all cured now, and there are other things to see."

"I suppose you would say," said Windrush dreamily, "that we have evolved into a higher condition and can see something nicer. Well, don't misunderstand me; I'm not against anybody evolving, if he does it quietly, in a gentlemanly way, and without all this fuss. It wouldn't matter much, if we had begun by climbing about in trees. But I still think that even monkeys would have been wise to leave one taboo tree; one sacred tree they did not climb. But evolution only means . . . bother, my cigarette's gone out. I think I must go and smoke in the library henceforward."

"Why do you say henceforward?"

They did not hear his answer as he walked away; but he said:

"Because it is The Garden of Eden."

A sudden silence fell between the two who were left facing each other on the lawn. Then John Judson went across to the girl and confronting her with great gravity said:

"In one respect your father underrates my orthodoxy."

Her own smile grew a little graver as she asked him why he said so.

"Because I do believe in Adam and Eve," answered the man of science; and he suddenly seized both her hands.

She left them where they were and continued to gaze at him with an utter stillness and steadiness. Only her eyes had altered.

"I believe in Adam," she said, "though I was once quite firmly convinced that he was the Serpent."

"I never thought you were the Serpent," he answered in the same new tone of musing, that was almost mystical; "but I thought you were the Angel of the Flaming Sword."

"I have thrown away the sword," said Enid Windrush.

"And left only the angel," he answered; and she rejoined: "Left only the woman."

On the top of the once accursed tree a small bird burst into song; and at the same moment a great morning wind from the south rushed upon the garden, bending all its shrubs and bushes and seeming, as does the air when it passes over sunlit foliage, to drive the sunshine before it in mighty waves. And it seemed to both of them that something had broken or been loosened, a last bond with chaos and the night, a last strand of the net of some resisting Nothing that obstructs creation; and God had made a new garden and they stood alive on the first foundations of the world.

THE ECSTATIC
THIEF

1
THE NAME OF NADOWAY

THE NAME OF Nadoway was in one sense famous, and even after a fashion, inspiring and sublime. Alfred the Great had borne it before him like a boon or gift, as he wandered in the woods and awaited the deliverance of Wessex. So at least one would infer from the poster in which he was represented, in flamboyant colours, as repairing the ruin of the Burning Cakes by the offer of Nadoway's Nubs, a superior sort of small biscuit. Shakespeare had heard the name like a trumpet-blast; at least if we may credit the striking picture inscribed "Anne Hathaway Had a Way with Nadoway," and representing the poet lifting a shining morning face on the appearance of these refreshments. Nelson, in the high moment of battle, had seen it written on the sky; at least it is so written on all the gigantic hoardings of the Battle of Trafalgar, with which we are so familiar in the streets; the picture to which are aptly appended the noble lines of Campbell; "Of Nelson and the Nubs, Sing the glorious day's renown." Equally familiar is the more modern patriotic poster representing a British Sailor working a machine-gun, from which a shower of Nubs is perpetually pouring upon the public. This somewhat unjustly exaggerates the deadly character of the Nubs. He who has been privileged to put a Nub to his lips has certainly been somewhat at a loss to distinguish it from other and lesser biscuits. But to have a Nub embedded in the body, by the ordinary process of digestion, has never been known to be actually fatal like a bullet. And, on the whole, many have tended to suspect that the chief difference, between Nadoway's Nubs and anybody else's, lay in the omnipresence of this superb picture-gallery of advertisements; which seemed to surround Nadoway with flamboyant pageantry and splendid heraldic and historic processions.

In the midst of all this encircling blazonry and blowing of trumpets, there was nothing but a little, plain, hard-faced man with a grey goatish beard and spectacles, who never went anywhere except to business and to a brown brick Baptist Chapel. This was Mr. Jacob Nadoway, later of course Sir Jacob Nadoway, and later still Lord Normandale, the original founder of the firm and fountain of all the Nubs. He still lived very simply himself, but he could afford every luxury. He could afford the luxury of having the Honourable Millicent Milton as private secretary. She was the daughter of a decayed aristocratic house, with which he had been on superficially friendly terms, as they lived in the same neighbourhood; and it was natural that the relative importance of the two should have gradually changed. Mr. Nadoway could afford the luxury of being the Honourable Millicent's patron. The Honourable Millicent could not afford the luxury of not being Mr. Nadoway's secretary.

It was, however, a luxury of which she sometimes had golden dreams. Not that old Nadoway treated her badly, or even paid her badly, or would have ventured to be rude to her in any respect. The old chapel-going Radical was much too shrewd for that. He understood well that there was still something like a bargain and a balance between the New Rich and the New Poor. She had been more or less familiar with the Nadoway household, long before she had an official post there; and could hardly be treated otherwise than as a friend of the family, even if it was not exactly the sort of family she would have sought in which to find her friends. And yet she had found friends there; and had once been even in danger of finding not only friends but a friend. Perhaps, at one time, not only a friend.

Nadoway had two sons, who went to school and college, and in the recognized modern manner were unobtrusively manufactured into gentlemen. The manner of the moulding was indeed somewhat different in the two cases; and in both she watched it with a certain curious interest. It was perhaps symbolic that the elder was John Nadoway, dating from the days when his father retained a taste for plain or preferably Scriptural names. The younger was Norman Nadoway, and the name marked a certain softening towards notions of elegance, foreshadowing the awful possibility of Normandale.

There had been a happy time, when John could really be described as Jack. He was a very boyish sort of boy and played cricket and climbed trees with a certain natural grace, like that of a young animal alive and innocent in the sunshine. He was not unattractive and she was not unattracted by him. And yet every time he reappeared, at different stages of his college and early commercial career, she was conscious that something was fading while something was solidifying. He was passing through that mysterious process, by which so many radiant and godlike boys eventually turn into business men. She could not help feeling that there must be something wrong with education—or possibly something wrong with life. It seemed somehow as if he was always growing bigger and growing smaller.

Norman Nadoway, on the other hand, began to be interesting just about the moment when Jack Nadoway began to be uninteresting. He was one that flowered late; if the figure of a flower can be used of one who (throughout his early years) resembled a rather pallid turnip. He had a large head and large ears and a colourless face and expression; and for a time passed for something of a moon-calf. But when he was at school, he worked hard at mathematics; and when he was at Cambridge at economics. From this it was but one wild leap to the study of politics and social reform; and from this came the grand burst-up in the House of Nubs and Jacob's wrath, to Nadoway's the direful spring.

Norman had begun by shaking the brown brick chapel to its foundations by announcing his intention of being a curate in the Church of England—nay, in the High Church party of the Church of England. But his father was less troubled by this than by the reports that reached him of his son's highly successful lectures on Political Economy. It was a very different sort of Political Economy from that which his father had successfully preached and practised. It was so different that his father, in a memorable explosion at the breakfast-table, described it as Socialism.

"Somebody must go down to Cambridge and stop him!" said the elder Mr. Nadoway fidgeting in his chair and rapping restlessly on the table. "You must go and talk to him, John; or you must bring him here and I'll talk to him. Otherwise the business will simply go smash."

Both parts of the alternative programme apparently had to be carried out. John, the junior partner of Nadoway and Son, did go down to Cambridge and talked to him; but apparently did not stop him. John did eventually bring him back to Jacob Nadoway, that

Jacob might talk to him. Jacob was in no way reluctant to do so, and yet the interview did not turn quite as he had intended. Indeed, it was a rather puzzling interview.

It took place in old Jacob's study, which looked out through round bow-windows at 'The Lawns,' after which the house was still named. It was a very Victorian house, of the sort that would have been described at the time as built by Philistines for Philistines. There was a great deal of curved glass about it, in its conservatories and its semicircular windows. There was a great deal of dome and cupola and canopy about it, with all the porches covered as if by escalloped wooden umbrellas. There was a good deal of rather ugly coloured glass and a good deal of not altogether ugly, but very artificial, clipped hedges and Dutch gardening. In short, it was the sort of comfortable Victorian home that was regarded as very vulgar by the æsthetes of that period. Mr. Matthew Arnold would have passed the house with a gentle sigh. Mr. John Ruskin would have recoiled in horror and called down curses from heaven on it, from a neighbouring hill. Even Mr. William Morris would have grumbled as he passed, about the sort of architecture that was only upholstery. But I am not so sure about Mr. Sacheverell Sitwell. We have reached a time when the curved windows and canopied porticoes of that house have begun to take on something of a dreamy glamour of distance. And I am not sure that Mr. Sitwell might not have been found wandering in its inner chambers and composing a poem about its dusty charms; though it would certainly have surprised Mr. Jacob Nadoway to find him so engaged. Whether, after the interview, even Mr. Sitwell could write a poem about Mr. Nadoway, I will not undertake to decide.

Millicent Milton had come through the garden to the study, at about the same moment as the junior partner arrived there. She was tall and fair and her lifted and pointed chin gave her profile a distinction beyond mere good looks. Her eyelids looked at the first glance a littly sleepy and at the second a little haughty; but she was not really either one or the other, but only reasonably resigned. She sat down at her ordinary desk to do her ordinary work; but she very soon rose from it again, as if with a silent offer to withdraw; since the domestic discussion was becoming very domestic. But old Nadoway motioned her back with irritable reassurance and she remained the spectator of the whole scene.

Old Nadoway had barked out rather abruptly, like one bothered for the first time:

"But I thought you two had had a talk."

"Yes, Father," said John Nadoway, looking at the carpet, "we have had a talk."

"I hope you got Norman to see," went on the old man in a milder tone, "that he simply mustn't chalk out all these wild projects so long as we're all really in the business. My business would be ruined in a month if I tried to carry out those crazy ideal schemes about Bonuses and Co-Partnership. And how can I have my son using my name, and shouting everywhere that my methods are not fit for a dog? Is it reasonable? Didn't John explain to you that it's not reasonable?"

The large pale face of the curate, rather to everybody's surprise, wrinkled into a dry smile, and he said: "Yes, Jack explained a great deal of that to me; but I also did a little explaining. I explained, for instance, that I have a business, too."

"What about your father's business?" asked Jacob.

"I am about my Father's business," said the priest in a hard voice.

There was a glaring silence, broken rather nervously.

"The fact is, Father, it won't do," said John Nadoway heavily, and still studying the carpet. "I believe I said everything for you you could have said yourself. But Norman knows the new conditions, and it won't do."

Old Mr. Nadoway made a motion as if swallowing something, and then said: "Do you mean to sit there and tell me you're against me, too? Against me and the whole concern?"

"I'm in favour of the whole concern, and that's the whole point," said John. "I suppose I shall be responsible for it—well, some time. But I'm damned if I'll be responsible for all the old ways of doing things."

"You're glad enough of the money that was got by the old way of doing things," said his father savagely, "and now you come back to me with this nonsensical namby-pamby Socialism."

"My dear Dad," said John Nadoway, staring stolidly. "Do I look like a Socialist?"

Millicent, as an onlooker, took in the whole of his heavy and handsome figure, from its beautifully blacked boots to its beautifully oiled hair; and could hardly repress a laugh.

The voice of Norman Nadoway clove into it with a sudden vibrancy, not without violence.

"We must clear the Nadoway name."

"Do you dare to tell me," cried the old man fiercely, "that my name needs any clearing?"

"By the new standards, yes," said John after a silence.

The old merchant sat down suddenly and silently in his chair and turned to his secretary, as if the interview were ended.

"I find I shall not want you this evening," he said. "You had better take a little time off."

She rose rather waveringly and went towards the french windows that gave upon the garden. The pale evening sky had been suddenly turned to night by the contrast of a large luminous moon coming up behind dark trees and striping the grey-green lawns with dark shadows. She had always been puzzled by the fact that there seemed to be something romantic about the garden and even the grotesque house, which was inhabited by such highly prosaic people. She was already outside the glass doors and in the garden, when she heard old Nadoway speak again.

"The hand of the Lord is heavy upon me," he said. "It seems hard that I have had three sons and they all turned against me."

"There is no question of turning against you, Father," said John rapidly and smoothly. "It is only a question of reconstructing the business so as to suit new conditions and a rather different public opinion. I am sure that neither of your sons intends to show ingratitude or impertinence."

"If either of your sons did that," said Norman in his deep voice, "it would be every bit as wicked as going on in the old way."

"Well," said his father rather wearily, "we will leave it at that just now. I shall not go on much longer."

But Millicent Milton was staring at the dark house in a new fit of mystification. The two brothers had ignored and slurred over, with something resembling skill, a certain phrase used by their father. But she had quite unmistakably heard the old man say: 'Three sons.'

She had never heard of any other son. She remained staring at the rococo outline of that rather ridiculous and yet romantic villa, with its domes and ornamental verandas dark against the moon; with its bulbous windows and plants in bloated pots; its clumsy statues and congested garden-beds and all the swollen outline of the thing made almost monstrous by moonshine and darkness; and she wondered for the first time if it held a secret.

2

THE BURGLAR AND
THE BROOCH

IT WAS THE scare of the burglary that actually started the story towards the discovery of rather strange things. As a burglary it was trivial enough, in the sense that the thief did not apparently succeed in taking anything, being surprised before he could do so. But it was certainly not only the burglar who was surprised.

Jacob Nadoway had provided his secretary with some excellent apartments leading out of the central hall and not far from his own. He had fitted up the suite with every elegant convenience, including an aunt. It was indeed doubtful, at times, whether the aunt was to be classed as a convenience or an inconvenience. She was supposed in a vague way to regularize the Victorian household and add even to the secretary an extra touch of gentility. But there was a difference; because the aunt, who was a Mrs. Milton-Mowbray, was given to suddenly getting back on the high-horse and then sliding off again; while her niece, with a more negative dignity, trod the dusty path of duty as a proud pedestrian. On this occasion Millicent Milton had been engaged all the evening in soothing her aunt, and after that experience, felt she would like to spend a little time in soothing herself. Instead of going to bed, she took up a book and began reading by the dying fire. She read on till it was very late, without realizing that everybody else had presumably retired to rest, when she heard in the utter stillness a new and unmistakable sound from the central hall without, which led into her employer's study. It was a sort of whirring and grinding sound, such as is produced by metal working its way into metal. And she remembered that in the angle between the two rooms stood the safe.

She had the best sort of quite unconscious courage, and she simply walked out into the hall and looked. What she saw astounded her by being so ordinary. She had seen it in so many films and read about it in so many novels, that she could hardly believe that it really looked like that. The safe stood open and a shabby man was kneeling in front of it, with his back to her, so that she could see nothing but his shabbiness, his head being covered by a battered and shapeless broadbrimmed hat. On one side of him on the floor glittered the steel of a centre-bit and some other tools of his art; on the other side glittered even more brilliantly the silver and stones of some ornament, looking like a chain and clasp, presumably a portion of his spoils. There seemed somehow to be nothing sharp or unexpected about the experience; it was almost conventional, in being so like what it was supposed to be. She only spoke as she felt, in a tone entirely cold and commonplace, when she said: "What are you doing here?"

"Well, I'm not climbing the Matterhorn or playing the trombone at present," grunted the man in a gruff and distant voice. "I suppose it's plain enough what I am doing."

Then, after a silence, he resumed in a warning tone:

"Don't you go saying that brooch thing there is yours, because it isn't. I didn't even get it out of this safe; let's say I lifted it off another family earlier in the evening. It's a pretty thing—sort of imitation fourteenth century, with *Amor Vincit Omnia* on it. It's all very well to say that love conquers everything, and force is no remedy and all that. But I've forced this safe: I never found a safe I could open by just loving what was inside."

There was something rather paralysing about the way in which the burglar placidly went on talking without even looking round; and she thought it a little odd that he should know the meaning of the Latin inscription, simple as it was. Nor could she bring herself to scream or run or stop him in any way, when he went on with the same conversational composure.

"Must be meant for a model of the big clasp that Chaucer's Prioress wore; that had the same motto on it. Don't you think Chaucer was a corker in the way he hit off social types—even social types that are there still? Why, the Prioress is an immortal portrait in a few lines of a most extraordinary creature called the English Lady. You can pick her out in foreign hotels and pensions. The Prioress was nicer than most of those; but she's got all the marks; fussing about her little dogs; being particular about table-manners; not liking mice killed; the whole darned thing even down to talking French, but talking it so that Frenchmen can't understand."

He turned very slowly and stared at her.

"Why, *you're* an English Lady!" he cried as if astonished. "Do you know they are getting rare?"

Miss Millicent Milton probably did possess, like the Prioress of Chaucer, the more gracious virtues of the English Lady. But it must in honesty be admitted that she also possessed some of the vices of the type. One of the crimes of the English Lady is an unconscious class-consciousness. Nothing could alter the fact that, the moment the shabby criminal had begun to talk about English literature in the tones of her own class, her whole judgment was turned upside down, and she had a chaotic idea that he could not really be a criminal at all. In abstract logic, she would have been obliged to admit that it ought not to make any difference. In theory, she would concede that a student of mediæval English has no more business to break open other people's safes than anybody else. In principle she might confess that a man does not purchase a right to steal silver brooches, even by showing an intelligent interest in the "Canterbury Tales." But something of uncontrollable custom in her mind made her feel that the case was altered. Her feeling could only have been conveyed by the very vague colloquialisms which such people employ; as that he wasn't exactly a *real* burglar, or that it was "Quite Different"; or that there was "some mistake." What she really meant (to the grave disadvantage of all her culture and her world) was that there were some people, criminals or no, whom she could see from the inside; and all other people she saw from the outside, whether they were burglars or bricklayers.

The young man who was staring at her was dark, shaggy and unshaven; but the neglect of shaving had passed its most repellent stage of transition and might be regarded as a rather imperfect beard. Its patchiness reminded her of the quaintly divided beards of certain foreigners; and gave him something of the general look of a cultivated Italian organ-grinder. There was something else that was abnormal about his face, which she could not immediately define; but she thought it was the fact that his mouth was always twisting with mockery, rather as if it had taught itself always to mock; and yet his dark sunken eyes were not only grave but, in some sort of mad way, enthusiastic. If the grotesque beard could have completely covered the

mouth like a mask, they might have been the eyes of a fanatic in the
desert shouting a battle-cry of belief. He must be deeply indignant
with society to have turned to this lawless life; or perhaps he had had a
tragedy with a woman or something. She wondered what the real
story was, and what the woman was like.

While she was forming these confused impressions, the remarkable
burglar went on talking; whatever else he felt, he seemed to feel no
embarrassment about talking.

"It's jolly fine of you to stand there like that—well, that's another
trait. The English Lady is brave; Edith Cavell was a type of the tribe.
But there are other tribes now; and that sort of brooch generally
belongs to the last sort of person for whom it was made. That alone
would be a justification for the trade of burglary, which keeps things
briskly in circulation, doesn't allow them to stagnate in incongruous
surroundings. If that brooch had really been worn by Chaucer's
Prioress at the moment, you don't imagine I'd have taken it, do you?
On the contrary, if I really met anybody as nice as the Prioress, I might
be tempted to give it to her straight away, at the expense of my
professional profits. But why should some vulgar cockatoo of a sham
Countess own a thing like that? We want more theft, house-breaking
and highway robbery to shift and rearrange the furniture of society; to
regroup—if you follow me—its goods and chattels, as if after a
spring-cleaning; to——"

At this important point in the social programme, it was interrupted
by a gasp and snort as startling as a trumpet-blast. And Millicent,
looking across, saw her employer, the aged Nadoway, standing
framed in the doorway, and looking a very small and shrunken figure
in an enormous purple dressing-gown. It was not until that moment
that she awoke to astonishment at her own silence and composure; or
saw anything odd in the fact that she had stood listening to the
criminal in front of the safe, as if he had been talking to her over the
tea-table.

"*What!* A burglar?" gasped Mr. Nadoway.

Almost at the same moment there was a scurry of running and the
big breathless figure of the Junior Partner, John Nadoway, dressed in
his shirt and trousers, also burst into the room, with a revolver in his
hand. But he almost instantly lowered the weapon he had lifted and
said, in the same incredulous and curiously emphatic voice: "Damn it
all! A *burglar!*"

The Rev. Norman Nadoway was not long behind his brother—he
was respectably muffled in a great-coat and looked very pale and

solemn. But perhaps the most curious thing about him was that he also confined himself to saying, with the same inscrutable intensity: "A *burglar!*"

Millicent thought there was, on the face of it, something singularly inept about this triple emphasis. It was about as obvious that the burglar was a burglar as that the safe was a safe. She could not imagine why the three men should all talk as if a burglar were a griffin, or something they had never heard of before, until it suddenly dawned on her that their surprise was not at a burglar paying them a particular visit, but rather at this particular visitor being a burglar.

"Yes," said the visitor, looking round at them with a smile, "it's quite true I'm a burglar now. I think I was only a begging-letter writer when we last met. Thus do we rise on our dead selves to higher things; it was a very paltry little misdemeanour compared to this, wasn't it, for which Father first turned me out?"

"Alan," said Norman Nadoway very gravely, "why do you come back here like this? Why here, of all places?"

"Why, to tell you the truth," said the other, "I thought that our respected papa might want a little moral support."

"What the devil do you mean?" asked John Nadoway irritably. "A nice sort of moral support you are!"

"I am a very moral support," observed the stranger with proper pride. "Don't you realize it? I am the only real son and heir. I am the only man who is really carrying on the business. I am an example of atavism; I am a reversion to type."

"I don't know what you're talking about," cried old Nadoway with sudden fury.

"Jack and Norman know," said the burglar grimly. "They know what I'm talking about. They know what I mean when I say I'm the real representative of Nadoway and Son. It's the fact they've been trying to cover up, poor old chaps, for the last five or six years."

"You were born to disgrace me," said the old man, trembling with anger; "you would have dragged my name in the dirt, if I hadn't sent you to Australia and got rid of you, and now you come back as a common thief."

"And the real representative," said the other, "of the methods that made Nadoway's Nubs." Then he said with sudden scorn:

"You say you're ashamed of me. Good Lord, my dear Dad! Haven't you discovered yet that both your other sons are ashamed of you? Look at their faces!"

It was enough that the other two sons involuntarily turned their faces away, and even as it was, turned them too late.

"They are ashamed of you. But I am not ashamed of you. We are the Adventurers of the family."

Norman Nadoway raised a protesting hand, but the other went on with a sweep of spontaneous satire.

"Do you think I don't know? Do you think everybody doesn't know? Don't I know that's why Norman and Jack are announcing new industrial methods and preaching new social ideals and all the rest? Cleansing the Name of Nadoway—because the Name of Nadoway stinks to the ends of the earth! Because the business was founded on every sort of swindling and sweating and grinding the faces of the poor and cheating the widow and orphan. And above all, on robbery—on robbing rivals and partners and everybody else, exactly as I have robbed that safe!"

"Do you think it decent," asked his brother angrily, "to come here and not only rob your father's safe, but insult and attack your father before his face?"

"I am not attacking my father," said Alan Nadoway; "I am defending my father. And I am the only man here who can defend him. For I am a criminal, too."

He let loose the next few words with an energy that made everybody jump. "What do you know about it? You go to college with his money; you get a partnership in his firm; you live on the money he made and are ashamed of the way he made it. But *he* didn't begin like that, any more than I did. He was thrown out into the gutter, just as I was thrown out into the gutter. You try it, and see what sort of dirt you will eat! You don't know anything about the way men are turned into criminals; the shifts and the delays and the despair; and the hopes that an honest job may turn up, that end by taking a dishonest one. You've no right to be so damned superior to the Two Thieves of the family."

Old Nadoway made an abrupt movement, adjusting his spectacles; and Millicent, who was an acute observer, suspected that for one instant he was not only staggered but strongly moved.

"All this," said John Nadoway after a silence, "doesn't explain what you're doing here. As you probably know, there's practically nothing in that safe; and the thing you've got there certainly doesn't come out of it. I can't quite make out what you're up to, in any case."

"Well," said Alan, with his ironical smile, "you can examine the safe and the rest of the premises after I've gone. Perhaps you may make a few discoveries. And perhaps on the whole I——"

In the middle of his words there arose, faint but shrill and unmistakable, upon Millicent's ear, the sound of something at once alarming and amusing; something she had been subconsciously expecting for a long time past. In the room beyond, her aunt had awakened; probably she had awakened to all the melodramatic possibilities of an interruption in the middle of the night. The Victorian tradition had still its living witness. Millicent herself had been frozen into a cool acceptance of the adventure—an acceptance she could not fully explain even to herself. But somebody at least had shrieked, in a respectable manner, on hearing a house-breaker.

The five people looked at each other and realized that, after that shriek, the extraordinary family situation could no longer be kept in the family. The only chance was for the burglar to bolt with the promptitude of any other burglar. He turned and darted through the apartments on his left, which happened to be the apartments of Miss Milton and Mrs. Mowbray, so that shriek after shriek now rent the air. But a crash of glass from a remote window told the rest that the intruder had managed to burst out of the house and disappear in the darkness of the garden, and they all, for varied and rather complex reasons, heaved their separate sighs of relief.

Millicent, needless to say, had to resume in a serious manner the duties of soothing an aunt; so that the shriek faded into shrill questions. Then she went into her own room, beyond which the hole in the burst window showed a black star in the slate-green of the glass. Then she realized that, right in the path of the disappearing robber, there was deliberately spread out for inspection, on her own dressing-table, as crown jewels are spread out upon velvet, the silver chain and studded clasp which had been fancifully dedicated to the Prioress, and on which was written in Latin "Love Conquers All."

3

A QUEER REFORMATION

MILLICENT MILTON COULD not help wondering a good deal, especially when walking about the garden in her off hours, whether she would ever see the burglar again. In the ordinary way, it would seem improbable. But then, nobody could say that this criminal was connected with the household in an ordinary way. As a burglar, he would presumably vanish; as a brother, he would not improbably turn up again. Especially as he was a rather disreputable brother, for they always turn up again. She tentatively asked questions of the other two brothers, but could get very little light on the situation. The acquisitive Alan had mockingly advised them to examine the house for the traces of his depredations. But he must have conducted them with great secrecy and selection, for nobody seemed sure of how much he had taken. It was one of the many problems in the story that she could not solve, and could not see any particular probability that she ever would solve, when she looked up idly and saw him standing quite calmly on the top of the garden wall and looking down into the garden. The wind plucked the plumes of his dark hair one by one and turned them over as he was turning the leaves of the tree nearest his perch.

"Another way to burgle a house," he said, in a clear distant voice like a popular lecturer, "is to get over the garden wall. It sounds simple, but stealing things is generally simple. Only, in this case, I can't quite make up my mind what to steal.

"I think," he added calmly, "that I shall begin by stealing a little of your time. But don't be alarmed, in any secretarial sense. I assure you I have an appointment."

He jumped from the wall and alighted on the turf beside her, but without in any way disturbing the flow of his remarks.

"Yes; it is really true that I am summoned to quite a family council; an inquiry into the possibility of rehabilitating my affairs. But, thank God, I can't be rehabilitated for another hour or so. While I am still in a completely criminal state of mind, I should rather like to have a talk with you."

She said nothing but gazed at the distant line of rather grotesque palm-trees planted as a frontier in the garden and felt returning upon her that irrational sense that this place had always been rather romantic, in spite of the people who lived in it.

"I suppose you know," said Alan Nadoway, "that my father flew into a frightful rage with me when I was only eighteen, and flung me bodily all the way to Australia. Looking back on it now, I can see that there was something to be said for his business standards in the matter. I had given one of my boon companions a handful of money which I really regarded as my own, but which my father regarded rigidly as belonging to the firm. From his point of view, it was stealing. But I didn't really know much about stealing then, compared with the close and conscientious study I have given to it since. But what I want to tell you is what happened to me on my way back from Australia."

"Wouldn't your family like to hear about it?" she could not help asking, with a touch of experimental irony.

"I dare say they would," he said. "But I am not sure they'd understand the story, even if they did hear it." Then after a brief reflective silence he said:

"You see, my story is too simple to be understood. Too simple to be believed. It sounds exactly like a parable; that is, it sounds like a fable and not a fact. There's my brother Norman now—he's a sincere man and very serious. He reads the parables in the New Testament every Sunday. But he could hardly believe in anything so simple as one of those parables, if it happened in real life."

"Do you mean that you are the Prodigal Son?" she asked; "and he is the Elder Brother?"

"Rather hard if the Australians had to be the Swine," said Alan Nadoway. "But I don't mean that at all. On the one hand, it underrates the magnanimity of my brother Norman. On the other hand, it perhaps slightly exaggerates the leaping and ecstatic hospitality of my father."

She could not repress a smile; but, filled with the loftiest secretarial traditions, refrained from comment.

"No; what I mean," he said, "is that stories told in that simple way, for the sake of illustration, always sound as if they weren't true. It's just the same with the parables of political economy. Norman has read a lot of political economy too, if you come to that. He must often have read those text-books that begin with the statement: 'There is a man on an island.' Somehow the student or the schoolboy always feels inclined to say there never was any man on any island. All the same, there was."

She began to feel a little bewildered. "Was what?" she asked.

"There was me," said Alan. "You can't believe this story because there's a desert island in it. It's like telling a story with a dragon in it. All the same, there's a moral to the dragon."

"Do you mean," she asked, growing rather impatient, "that you have been on a desert island?"

"Yes, and on one or two other odd things. But the extraordinary thing was that everything was all right till I came to an inhabited island. Well, I spent several years, to start with, in a pretty uninhabited part of a more or less inhabited island. I mean, of course, the one marked on the map as Australia. I was trying to farm in a very remote part of the Bush, till a run of bad luck forced me to crawl as best I could back to the towns. I was going to say back to civilization, but that sounds odd, if you know the towns. By the final stroke of luck my transport animals fell sick and died in a wilderness and I was left as if I had been on the other side of the moon. Nobody in these historical countries, of course, has any idea of what the earth is like, or how a great lot of it might just as well be the moon. There seemed no more chance of getting across those infinities of futile soil patched with wattle, than of persuading a comet that had knocked you into space to take you back home again. I trudged along quite senselessly, till I saw something like a tall blue bush that wasn't one of the monotonous mass of blue-grey bushes, and I saw it was smoke. It's a good proverb, by God, that where there's smoke there's fire. It's a greater proverb, and one too near to God to be written often, that where there's fire there's man, and nobody knows which is the greater miracle. Well, I found somebody; he wasn't anybody in particular; I dare say you would have found all sorts of deficiencies in him if he'd been in the village or the club. But he was a magician all right; to me he had powers not given to beast or bird or tree, and he gave me some cooked food and set me on the right road to a settlement. At the settlement, a little outpost in the wilds, it was the same. They didn't

do much for me; they couldn't; but they did something and didn't
think it particularly unusual to be asked. The long and short of it was
that I got to a seaport at last and managed to make a bargain to work
my passage with the master of a small craft. He wasn't a particularly
nice man and I wasn't particularly comfortable; but it was not suicide
but a sea-wave that swept me off suddenly one night, early enough to
be seen and raise the cry of 'Man overboard!' That nasty little boat,
with its still more nasty little captain, coasted about for four hours
trying to pick me up, but it couldn't be done, and I was eventually
picked up by a sort of native canoe, rowed by a sort of half-native
lunatic who really and truly lived on a desert island. I hailed him as I
had just been vainly hailing the ship, and he gave me brandy and
shelter and the rest of it, as a matter of course. He was quite a
character, a white man, or whitish man, who had gone fantee and
wore nothing but a pair of spectacles and worshipped a god of his
own he had made out of an old umbrella. But he didn't think it odd
that I should ask him for help, and in his own way he gave it. Then
came the day when we sighted a ship, very far out, but passing the
island; and I hailed and hailed and waved long sheets and towels and
lit flares and all the rest. And eventually the ship did alter her course
and touched at the island to take us off; everybody was pretty dry and
official, but they did it as a regular matter of duty. And all this time,
and especially on that last stretch of homeward voyage, I was singing
to myself a song as old as the world: *Coelum non animam*—By the
waters of Babylon—or, in other words, of all things the worst is exile,
and it will be well with a man in his own home. After all my wild
hairbreadth escapes I stepped on to the dock in Liverpool, as a
schoolboy enters his father's house on the first day of the Christmas
holidays. I had forgotten that I had practically no money, and I asked
a man to give or lend me some. I was immediately arrested for begging
and began my career as a criminal by sleeping in jail.

"Now I suppose you see the point of the economic parable. I had
been in the ends of the earth, and among the scum of the earth; I had
been among all sorts of ragamuffins who had very little to give and
were often quite unwilling to give it. I had waved to passing ships and
hallooed to passing travellers and doubtless been heartily cursed for
doing so. But nobody ever thought it odd that I should *ask* for the
help. Nobody certainly thought it criminal that I should shriek at a
ship when I was drowning, or crawl towards a camp-fire when I was
dying. In all those wild seas and waste places people did assume that
they had to rescue the drowning and the dying. I was never actually

punished for being in want till I came to a civilized city. I was never called a criminal for *asking* for sympathy, till I returned to my own home.

"Well, if you have understood that parable of the New Prodigal Son, you may possibly understand why he thinks he found the Swine when he came home; a lot more Swine than Fatted Calves. The rest of the story consisted largely of assaults on the police, breaking and entering various premises and all the rest. My family has at last woken up to the fact that I might be reclaimed or my position regularized; chiefly, I imagine—in the case of some of them at least—because people like yourself and your aunt having been let into the secret is liable to be socially awkward. Anyhow, we are to meet here this afternoon and form a committee for turning me into a respectable character. But I don't think they quite realize the job they've taken on. I don't think they quite know what happens inside people like me; and it's because I rather want you to understand it, before they begin jabbering, that I've told you what I call the parable of the exile. Always remember that as long as he was among strangers, not to say scoundrels, he had a chance."

They had been sitting on a garden-seat during the conversation and Millicent rose from it, as she saw the black-clad group of the father and brothers approaching across the lawn.

Alan Nadoway remained seated with somewhat ostentatious languor, and its significance was sharpened when she realized that old Jacob Nadoway was walking well ahead of the others and that his brows were black as a thunderstorm in the sunshine. It was instantly apparent that something new and nasty had occurred.

"Perhaps it would be affectation to inform you," said the father with heavy bitterness, "that there has been another burglary in the neighbourhood."

"Another," said Alan raising his eyebrows. "That, when you come to think of it, is a rather curious word. And what is the other?"

"Mrs. Mowbray," said the father sternly, "went over yesterday to visit her friend, Lady Crayle. She was naturally disturbed about what had happened in our own house, and it seems that something happened about an hour earlier at the Crayles'."

"What did they lift off the Crayles'?" asked the young man, with patient interest. "How did they know there was a burglary?"

"The burglar was surprised and bolted," said Jacob Nadoway. "Unfortunately, he dropped something and left it behind in the haste of his flight."

"Unfortunately!" repeated Alan with an air of being mildly and conventionally shocked. "Unfortunately for whom?"

"Unfortunately for you," said his father.

There was a painful silence and John Nadoway broke into it in his blundering but unconquerably good-humoured way.

"Look here, Alan," he said. "If anybody is going to help you, these sorts of games have got to stop. We could pass it off as a practical joke of a sort, when you did it to us; but even then you frightened Miss Milton, and Mrs. Mowbray is all up in the air. But how the devil are we to keep you out of the police-court if you break into the neighbours' houses and leave your cigar-case with a card inside?"

"Careless—careless," said Alan in a vexed tone, rising with his hands in his pockets. "You must remember I am only at the beginning of my career as a burglar."

"You are at the end of your career as a burglar," said old Nadoway, "or else at the beginning of your career as a convict for five years in Dartmoor. With that case and card, Lady Crayle can convict you, and will if I give the word. I've only come here to offer you a last chance, when you've thrown away a thousand chances. Drop this thieving business, here and now, and I'll find you a job. Take it or leave it."

"Your father and I," said Norman Nadoway, in his detached and delicate accent, "have not always agreed about the treatment of hard cases. But he is obviously justified in this. I have a great deal of sympathy with you in many ways, but it is one thing to forgive a man thieving when he may be starving—it is quite another to forgive him, when he would rather go on starving, if only he may go on thieving."

"That's the point," assented the stolid John in fraternal admiration. "We're willing to recognize a brother who isn't any longer a burglar. The only other thing we could recognize would be a burglar who isn't any longer a brother. Are you just Alan, to whom father's ready to give a job, or a fellow out of the street whom we have simply to hand over to the police? But, by God, you can't be both."

Alan's eyes roamed round the family house and garden and rested for a moment on Millicent, with a certain expression of pathos. Then he sat down on the garden seat again, with his elbows on his knees and buried his head in his hands as if he were wrestling in prayer, or at least in perplexity of spirit. The three other men stood watching him with an awkward rigidity.

At last he threw up his head again, flinging back his black plume-like locks; and they all saw instantly that his pale face had a new expression.

"Well," said old Jacob, not without a new note of appeal; "won't you give up all this blackguard burglary business?"

Alan Nadoway rose. "Yes, father," he said gravely. "Now I come to look at it seriously, I see you have a right to my promise. I will give up the burglary business."

"Thank God for that," said his brother Norman, his hard delicate voice shaken for the first time. "I'm not going to moralize now, but you'll find there is one thing about any other job you get. It will be one in which a man need not hide."

"After all, it's a rotten job, burglary," said John with his jerky attempt at joviality and general reconciliation. "Must be a perfect nightmare always getting into the wrong house at the wrong end, something like putting on your trousers upside down. It'll pay you better really, and you'll get peace of mind."

"Yes," said Alan thoughtfully; "all that you say is true, and there is a sort of hampering complication about the life; learning the whereabouts of treasures and so on. No, I am going to turn over a new leaf. I am going to reform and go into a different line of life altogether. A simpler, more straightforward line. I am told that picking pockets is much more lucrative nowadays."

He continued to gaze thoughtfully at the distant palms, but all the other faces were turned towards him with an incredulous stare.

"A friend of mine down Lambeth way," said Alan, "does most frightfully well with people coming out of tube stations and so on. Of course, they're much poorer than the people who own all these safes and jewels and things, but then there are a lot of them, and it's wonderful what you can collect by the end of the day. My friend got fifteen shillings in sixpences and coppers off people coming out of the cinema; but then he's awfully nifty with his fingers. I reckon I can learn the knack."

There was a startled silence and then Norman said in a controlled voice:

"It would be of some importance to me to know that this is a joke. I will risk my reputation for humour."

"Joke," said Alan, with an absent-minded air. "Joke. . . . Oh, no, it isn't a joke. It's a job. And a jolly sight better job than any my father will offer me."

"Then you can follow it to jail!" said the old man, and his voice rang out in the garden like a gun announcing sunset. "Clear out of this place in three minutes and I will not call the policeman down the road."

And with that he turned his back and strode away followed by his other sons, and Alan remained standing alone by the garden seat, and he might have been a statue in the garden.

The garden indeed had grown more still, and in a manner grey and statuesque, with the creeping advance of twilight, and something of its too florid character was veiled by dusk and damp vapours beginning to rise from the surrounding meadows, though overhead the sky was clear and beginning to show the points of stars in the general greyness. The points brightened and the dusk sank deeper and deeper, and it did not seem for the moment that the two human statues left in the garden would move. Then the woman moved very swiftly, walking straight across the lawn to where the man stood by the garden seat, and in that greater gravity and stillness he became conscious of the last incongruity. Her face, which was commonly very grave, was puckered with derision, like that of an elf.

"Well," she said; "you've done it now."

"If you mean," he answered, "that I've done for my prospects here, I never thought I had any."

"No, I don't mean that," she said. "When I say you've done it, I mean you've overdone it."

"Overdone what?" he asked in the same stony style.

"Overdone the lie," she said, smiling steadily. "Overdressed the part, if you like. I don't understand what it all means, but it doesn't mean what it says, certainly not what you say. I could bring myself to believe that you were a burglar and broke into rich houses. But when you say you're a pickpocket who pinches sixpences off poor people coming out of the pictures, I simply know you're not, and there's an end of it. It's the last finishing touch that spoils a work of art."

"What do you suppose I am?" he asked harshly.

"Well, won't you tell me?" she inquired with a certain brightness.

After a strained silence he said with a curious intonation, "I would do anything for you."

"Well," she answered, "everybody knows that the curse of my sex is curiosity."

He buried his head in his hands and after a silence said with a great groan: *Amor Vincit Omnia.*

A moment or two later he lifted his head again and began to talk, and her eyes grew starry with astonishment as she stood and listened under the stars.

4

THE PROBLEMS OF
DETECTIVE PRICE

M R. PETER PRICE, the private inquiry agent, did not glow with that
historic appreciation of the type known as the English Lady
which was such a credit to the heads and hearts of Mr. Geoffrey
Chaucer and Mr. Alan Nadoway. The English Lady is a jewel of many
facets, or even a flower including some botanical variations. And Mr.
Price had seen, on many occasions, that face of the goddess which is
turned upon foreign waiters, discontented cabmen, people who want
windows shut or open at inappropriate times, and other manifest
enemies of human society. And he was just recovering from an
interview with a very pronounced specimen of the type, a certain Mrs.
Milton-Mowbray, who had talked to him in clear and decisive tones
for about three-quarters of an hour, without telling him anything of
which he could make any sort of sense.

So far as he could piece it out from his notes, it was something like
this. She was sure there had been a burglary in Mr. Nadoway's house,
where she and her niece were staying; and that they were keeping it
from her, so that she might not find out she had been robbed. She was
sure the burglary was at the Nadoways' house, because property
belonging to young Mr. Nadoway had been found after a burglary at
another house. The other house was Lady Crayle's house, and the
burglar must have gone there from the Nadoways', taking the
Nadoway things with him and then dropping them in his flight. As a
matter of fact, he must have dropped something at the Nadoways' too,

as she was sure her niece had picked up a sort of brooch thing, that nobody had seen before. But her niece wouldn't say anything about it; they were all keeping things from her—that is, from the indignant Mrs. Milton-Mowbray.

"He seems to be rather a careless burglar," Mr. Price had said, looking at the ceiling, "and not what you might call fortunate in his profession. First he steals something from somebody and leaves it at Mr. Nadoway's. Then he steals something from Mr. Nadoway and leaves it at Lady Crayle's. Did he actually steal anything from Lady Crayle? And at whose house did he leave that?"

He was a short, fat, baldish man whose features seemed to fold in on themselves so that it was impossible to say for certain whether he smiled, but the lady at any rate was neither of the temper nor in the mood to search his face for irony.

"That," she said triumphantly, "is just what I say! Nobody will tell me. Everybody is perfectly vague. Even Lady Crayle is vague. She says she supposes it must have been a burglary, or why should the man run away? And the Nadoways are vaguer still. I've told them again and again they needn't consider my feelings, I'm not going to faint, even if I have been robbed. But I really think I have a right to know."

"Perhaps it would assist them a little," said the private detective, "if you first of all told *them* whether you had been robbed. You see, this seems to me a rather puzzling business in a good many ways, but what I'm trying to get at is what has been taken from whom. We'll grant, for the sake of argument, that there were two robberies. And we'll grant, for the sake of argument, that there was only one robber. It's presumed he was a robber, because he leaves about in other people's houses, things you think cannot have belonged to him. But none of these things, so far as I understand, belonged to any of the people he was then in the act of robbing. None of these things, for instance, belonged to you."

"How can I tell?" she said with a sweeping gesture of agnosticism. "Nobody will tell me the truth. I am——"

"My dear madam," said Mr. Price with belated firmness, "you cannot require anybody to tell you the truth about yourself. Have you lost anything yourself? Have you missed anything yourself? For that matter, has Lady Crayle missed anything herself?"

"Lady Crayle wouldn't know whether she'd missed anything or not," said Mrs. Mowbray with sudden acrimony. "She's the very vaguest of the lot."

"I see," said Mr. Price, nodding thoughtfully. "Lady Crayle

wouldn't know whether she'd missed anything or not. And I rather gather that you yourself are in the same difficulty."

Then, before she could realize the affront sufficiently to reply he said rapidly: "I always thought Lady Crayle was supposed to be very capable, a great organizer and all that."

"Oh, she can organize meetings and movements and all that nonsense," said the Victorian lady scornfully. "Talk about her League Against Tobacco or her controversy about defining drugs, and she's all there. But she never notices anything that's lying about in her own house."

"Does she notice her husband, for instance?" inquired Mr. Price. "Is he left lying about in the house much? I always understood he was a very distinguished man in his day; and, of course, it's an awfully old family. I'm told Lord Crayle suffered badly when the Russian debt was beyond recovery, and I don't suppose his wife gets a salary for attacking tobacco. So they must be pretty poor, and would surely know whether they've lost anything of great value."

He was silent for a moment, ruminating and then said as suddenly as a pistol-shot:

"What was it exactly they picked up after the burglar bolted?"

"I believe it was nothing but cigars," replied Mrs. Mowbray shortly. "A whole big case stuffed with them. But as it had a card of one of the Nadoways, we presume the burglar had stolen it from their house."

"Quite so," he answered. "And now about the other things he had stolen from their house. I am sure you understand that, if I am to help you, I must be excused for assuming a more or less confidential position. I gather that your niece has become the secretary of Mr. Jacob Nadoway. I think I may infer that her taking such a position implies to some extent the necessity of working for her living."

"I was against her going to work for such people at all," said Mrs. Mowbray. "But when all these Socialistic Governments have taken away all our money, what can we do?"

"I know—I know," said the detective, nodding in an almost dreamy fashion, his eyes were again fixed on the ceiling and he seemed to be following a train of thought thousands of miles away. At last he said:

"We sometimes see these things in pictures that are quite impersonal. No personalities are intended. Let us suppose we are talking about nobody in particular. But the picture I see is that of a girl who once knew all about luxury and pretty things, who has accepted a duller and plainer life because there is nothing else to be done, and who earns her salary from a rather mean old man without expecting anything like a windfall. And then there's another curious picture. A man who's been an ordinary man of the world but driven to live the simple life, partly by poverty and partly by having a Puritanical wife with a fad against all his old luxuries and especially against tobacco. . . . Does that suggest anything to you?"

"No, it doesn't," said Mrs. Mowbray, rising and rustling. "I consider all this most unsatisfactory, and I don't know what you're talking about."

"He was really a very absent-minded house-breaker," said the detective. "If he had known what he was about, he would have dropped two brooches."

Ten minutes later Mrs. Mowbray had shaken the dust of the very dusty detective office off her feet and gone on to pour out her woes elsewhere; and Mr. Peter Price went to the telephone with a smile that he seemed to be hiding even from himself. He rang up a certain friend of his in the official police department, and their conversation was long and detailed. It largely concerned the prevalence of petty crime, especially larceny, in some of the very poorest districts of London. And yet, oddly enough, Mr. Price added the notes of this telephone conversation to his notes of the conversation with the aristocratic Mrs. Milton-Mowbray.

Then he once more leaned back in his chair and remained staring at the ceiling, plunged in profound thought and with an almost Napoleonic expression, for, after all, Napoleon also was short and in his later years fat; and in Mr. Peter Price also it is possible that there was more than met the eye.

The truth was that Mr. Peter Price was awaiting another arrival, in accordance with another appointment. The two were not unconnected, though it would have surprised Mrs. Mowbray very much if she had seen a figure so familiar as that of Mr. John Nadoway, of Nadoway and Son, enter the detective's office so soon after she had left. But many years before, the Junior Partner had been put to considerable difficulties in covering up some of the early exploits of the Senior Partner. Long after the elder Nadoway had become rich, and the younger Nadoway had so tardily decided that he should also become respectable, there were old scandals trailing behind the business like a tradition of blackmail, and malcontents whom it was still rather difficult to quash. Young John Nadoway had betaken himself to the private agency and practical experience of Mr. Price, who had paid off or scared off the malcontents so successfully that the new reputation of Nadoway's was fairly secure. To Mr. Price, therefore, young Nadoway once more betook himself, when faced with a family scandal on a far more ghastly and gigantic scale.

For Alan Nadoway, no longer acting anonymously or even like a thief in the night, but announcing his name even more plainly than when he left his visiting-card, had declared that it was his intention to pick pockets for a living in the neighbourhood of Lambeth; and that if he were put into the dock and the police news, it would not be under an alias. In the curious communication he had sent his brother, he gravely declared that while there was obviously nothing morally wrong about picking pockets, he could not reconcile it with his conscience (perhaps, he admitted, a too sensitive conscience) to deceive a kind policeman by giving a false name. He had tried three times, he pathetically declared, to call himself Nogglewop and in each case his voice had failed through emotion.

It was three or four days after the receipt of this letter that the thunderbolt fell. The Name of Nadoway, the subject of so many strivings, blazed in black-and-white in the headlines of all the evening papers; in a very different manner from that in which it blazed from so many of the parallel advertisements. Alan Nadoway, announcing himself as the eldest son of Sir Jacob Nadoway (for such was already the father's title), appeared in the police-court, charged with picking pockets not only once but regularly and successfully for several weeks.

The situation was the more sensationally insulting or exasperating, because the thief had not only robbed the poor in a most heartless and cynical fashion, but had selected the poor of the very district where his brother, the Rev. Norman Nadoway, had recently become a charitable and popular parish priest, abounding in every kind of good works.

"It seems incredible," said John Nadoway with heavy emphasis, "that any man could be so wicked."

"Yes," said Peter Price, a little sleepily; "it seems incredible." Then he got up with his hands in his pockets and looked out of the window and remarked: "You know, when you come to think of it, that's just the word for it. It seems incredible."

"And yet it's happened," said John with a groan.

Peter Price was silent so long that John suddenly jumped up as a man might on hearing a noise. "What the devil is the matter with you?" he asked. "Isn't it quite certain that it has happened?"

Price nodded and answered: "If you say it has happened, yes, I am quite certain. But if you ask what has happened, I am not certain at all. Only I begin to have a large general sort of suspicion."

Then after another silence he said abruptly: "Look here, I won't risk raising hopes or suspicions yet, but if you'll let me see the solicitor who's arranging the defence of your brother, I rather think I might have something to suggest to him."

John Nadoway left the offices of the detective with a slow gait and a puzzled expression, which he continued to wear all the way down to his country home, which he reached that evening, driving his own car with his usual competence, but without any shedding of his unusual perplexity and gloom. Everything had grown so puzzling, as well as so painful, that he found himself forced against the edges of existence, in a manner rare in the experience of men of his type. He would have said in all simplicity that he was not a thinker, and he would have seen nothing unnatural in the notion of a man walking through life to death, without stopping anywhere to think. But everything, down to the demeanour of that practical little private detective, was so damned mysterious. Even the dark trees before his father's house seemed to stand up in serpentine shapes like enormous notes of interrogation. The stars looked like those other stars called asterisks, which stand in the suppressed passages of a puzzle or a cipher. And the single window lighted in the dark bulk of the house was like a leering eye. He knew only too well that a cloud of shame and doom was on that house, like a thunder-cloud about to burst. It was the sort of doom he had tried to avert all his life, and now it had come he could hardly even pretend it was not deserved.

In the shadow of the veranda, with a sort of silent shock, he came upon Millicent, sitting in a garden-chair and gazing out into the dark. And in all that black and tragic house of riddles, perhaps her face was the darkest and most inscrutable riddle; for it was happy.

As she gazed, indeed, and became conscious of the sturdy figure of the business man blackening the faint shimmer of light on the lawn, a sort of misty change came across her eyes, that was not pain but had in it something of pathos. She felt a sort of sad friendship go out in a sympathetic wave towards this strong, successful and unfortunate man—as towards something deaf or blind. She could not analyse the softening, which was also a severing, until she remembered that she had nearly been in love with him when he was a boy in that garden. She did not know why she should feel so sharply and almost tragically that she was not in love with him now. That she could never, never, be in love with that kind of man now. That kind of man—well, he was the kind of thoroughly good man who thought that telling the truth was as right as cleaning the teeth. It would be like loving somebody quite flat—only in two dimensions.

For she felt that in herself a depth had opened like a new dimension, full of topsy-turvy stars and the inverted infinities of Einstein. She hardly looked into that abyss behind her, she hardly took in the positive novelty, but only the sharp negative, that she was not in love with John Nadoway.

All the more her cold compassion went out to him, without shyness, as to a brother. "I am so sorry," she cried, "for all you must be suffering just now. It must seem so dreadful to you."

"Thank you," he said, not without emotion. "We are having a trying time, of course—and sympathy from old friends does not hurt."

"I know how good you have been," she said, "and how hard you worked to keep off anything like discredit. And this must seem to you so discreditable."

The repetition of the one word "seem" at last penetrated his solid mind as a little queer.

"I'm afraid it doesn't only seem so," he said, "a Nadoway picking pockets is about the worst one could imagine."

"That is it," she said, nodding rather strangely. "Through the worst one could imagine comes the best one could not imagine."

"I'm afraid I don't follow," said the Junior Partner.

"You go through the worst to the best, as you go through the west to the east," she said; "and there really is a place, at the back of the world, where the east and the west are one. Can't you feel there is something so frightfully and frantically good that it *must* seem bad?"

He stared at her blankly, and she went on as if thinking aloud.

"A blaze in the sky makes a blot on the eyesight. And after all," she added, almost in a whisper, "the sun was blotted out, because one man was too good to live."

The Junior Partner resumed his plodding march with the new addition to his list of worries; that, among the inmates of the house, was a lady who was a lunatic.

5

THE THIEF ON TRIAL

THERE WAS AN extraordinary amount of fuss and delay about the hearing of the case of Alan Nadoway, considering that it was merely the trial of a common pickpocket. First of all, it was repeated everywhere, apparently on good authority, that the prisoner was going to plead Guilty. Then came all sorts of commotion in his original social circle, and a series of privileged interviews between the prisoner and members of his family. But it was not until his father, old Sir Jacob Nadoway, had sent his private secretary to the prison, apparently to conduct unprecedentedly long interviews with the prisoner, that the news went round that he was pleading Not Guilty after all. Then there was the same sort of rumour and dispute about his choice of a counsel, and finally it was announced that he had insisted on conducting his own defence.

He had been committed for trial after purely formal evidence, and in his earlier stages of silence and surrender. It was before a judge and jury that the case against him was fully opened; and the prosecuting counsel opened it in tones of stern regret. The prisoner was unfortunately the son of a great and distinguished family, the blot on the escutcheon of a noble, a generous and a philanthropic house. All were acquainted with the great reforms in the conditions of employment which would always be associated with the name of his elder brother, Mr. John Nadoway. Many who could not approve the ritualistic practices, or submit their intellects to the ecclesiastical dogmas upheld by his other brother, the Rev. Norman Nadoway, had none the less respect for the solid social work and active charity of that clergyman among the poor. But, however it might be in other countries, the English law was no respecter of persons and was bound to follow crime even to its most respectable retreats. This unfortunate man, Alan Nadoway, had always been a n'er-do-weel and a burden and disgrace to his family. He had been suspected, and indeed convicted, of attempts at burglary in the houses of his family and friends.

Here the judge intervened, saying: "That is a most improper remark. I find nothing about burglary in the indictment on which the prisoner is being tried." On this the prisoner remarked in a cheerful voice: "I don't mind, my lord." But nobody took the least notice of *him*, in the presence of a really improper legal procedure, and the judge and the barrister continued to look at each other with lugubrious countenances, until the barrister apologized and resumed. In any case, he said, there could be little doubt upon the charge of petty larceny, in face of the witnesses whom he intended to put in the box.

Police-constable Brindle was sworn and gave his evidence in one long rippling monotone, without any apparent punctuation, as if it were not only all one sentence but all one word.

"Acting on information received I followed the prisoner from the house of the Rev. Norman Nadoway towards the Yperion Cinema Theatre at about a hundred yards distant I saw the prisoner put his hand in the overcoat pocket of a man standing under a lamp-post after warning the man to examine his pockets I followed the prisoner who had joined the crowd outside the theatre a man in the crowd turned round and accused the prisoner of picking his pockets he offered to fight the prisoner and I came up to stop the fight I said do you charge this man and he said yes the prisoner said suppose I charge him with assault while I was questioning the other man the prisoner ran on and put his hand in the tail-coat pocket of a man in the queue. I then told this man to examine his pockets and took the prisoner into custody."

"Do you wish to cross-examine this witness?" asked the judge.

"I am sure your lordship will pardon me in the circumstances," said the prisoner, "if I am not well acquainted with the forms of this court. But may I at this stage ask whether the prosecution is going to call these three persons whom I am supposed to have robbed?"

"I have no objection to stating," said the prosecuting counsel, "that we are calling Harry Hamble, bookmaker's clerk, the man who is said to have threatened to fight the prisoner, and Isidor Green, music-teacher, the last man robbed by the prisoner before his arrest."

"And what about the first man?" asked the prisoner. "Why isn't he being called?"

"As a matter of fact, my lord," said the counsel, "the police have been unable to discover his name and address."

"May I ask the witness," said Alan Nadoway, "how this curious state of things came about?"

"Well," said the constable, "the fact is that as soon as I'd turned my back on him for a minute, he was gone."

"Do you mean to say," asked Nadoway, "that you told a man he was the victim of theft and might recover his money, and he instantly bolted without leaving his name, as if he were a thief himself?"

"Well, I don't understand it, and that's flat," said the policeman.

"Under your lordship's indulgence," said the prisoner, "there is another point. While two names figure as witnesses, only one name, that of Mr. Hamble, appears as prosecuting. It looks as if there was something vague about the third witness, too. Did you think so, constable?"

Outside the inhuman hurdy-gurdy of his official evidence, the policeman was a human being and capable of being amused.

"Well, I must say he was vague enough," he admitted with a faint grin. "He's one of these artistic musical chaps, and his notions of counting money is something chronic. I told him to look if he'd lost any and he added it up six times. And sometimes it was 2s. 8d. and sometimes it was 3s. 4d. and sometimes it got as far as 4s. So we thought he wasn't quite enough on the spot. . . ."

"This is most irregular," said the judge. "I understand that the witness, Isidor Green, is to give his own evidence later. The prosecution had better begin calling their witnesses as soon as possible."

Mr. Harry Hamble wore a very sporting tie and that expression of demure joviality which is seen in those who value their respectability even in the Saloon Bar. He was not incapable, however, of hearty outbursts, and he admitted that he had punched the head of the fellow who tried to pick his pocket. In answer to the prosecution, he told the story very much as the policeman had done, not without a gentle exaggeration of his own pugnacity. In answer to the prisoner, he admitted that he had immediately adjourned to the Pig and Whistle at the corner.

The prosecuting counsel, springing up with theatrical indignation, demanded the meaning of this insinuation.

"I imagine," said the judge somewhat severely, "that the prisoner implies that the witness did not know exactly what he had lost."

"Yes," said Alan Nadoway, and there was something odd and arresting in the roll of his deep voice; "I do mean to imply that he did not know exactly what he had lost."

Then, turning to the witness, he said briskly: "Did you go to the Pig and Whistle and stand drinks all round, in a regular festive style?"

"My lord," exploded the prosecuting counsel, "I must emphatically protest against the prisoner wantonly aspersing the character of the witness."

"Aspersing his character! Why, I am glorifying his character!" cried Nadoway warmly. "I am exalting and almost deifying his character! I am pointing out that he exercised on a noble scale the ancient virtue of hospitality. If I say you give very good dinners, am I aspersing your character? If you ask six other barristers to lunch, and do them well, do you conceal it like a crime? Are you ashamed of your handsome hospitality, Mr. Hamble? Are you a miser and a man-hater?"

"Oh, no, sir," said Mr. Hamble, who appeared slightly dazed.

"Are you an enemy of the human race, Mr. Hamble?"

"Well, no, sir," said Mr. Hamble almost modestly. "No, certainly not, sir," he added more firmly.

"You always, I take it," went on the prisoner, "feel friendly to your fellow-creatures, and especially your chosen companions. You would always do them a good turn or stand them a drink, if you could."

"I hope so, sir," said the virtuous bookmaker.

"You do not always do it, of course," went on Alan smoothly, "because you are not always in a position to do so. Why did you do so on this occasion?"

"Well," admitted Mr. Hamble, a little puzzled, "I suppose I must have been rather flush that evening."

"Immediately after being robbed?" said Nadoway. "Thank you, that is all I want to ask."

Mr. Isidor Green, professional teacher of the violin, with long stringy hair and a coat faded to bottle-green, was certainly as vague as the policeman had represented him. During the examination in chief, he got through well enough by saying that he certainly had a sort of feeling as if his pockets were being rifled; but even under Nadoway's comparatively gentle and sympathetic cross examination he became extraordinarily hazy. It seemed that he had eventually, with the assistance of two or three friends of superlative mathematical talent, reached the firm conclusion that he still possessed 3s. 7d. after he had been robbed. But the light thus thrown upon the robbery was a little dimmed by the fact that he had then realized, for the first time, that he had never had any notion of what he possessed before he was robbed.

"My thoughts are considerably concentrated on my artistic work," he said, with not a little dignity. "It is possible that my wife might know."

"An admirable idea, Mr. Green," said Alan Nadoway heartily. "As a matter of fact, I am calling your wife as a witness for the defence."

Everybody stared, but it was plain that Nadoway was serious; and with a gravity tinged with courtliness he proceeded to summon his own witnesses, who actually were no other than the two wives of the two witnesses for the prosecution.

The wife of the violinist was a straightforward and, save for one point, a simple bearer of testimony. She was a solid, jolly looking woman, like a superior cook; probably just the right woman to look after the unmathematical Mr. Green. She said in a comfortable voice that she knew all about Isidor's money—what there was of it; that he was a good husband with no extravagant tastes and had certainly had 2s. 8d. in his pocket that afternoon.

"In that case, Mrs. Green," said Alan, "it would seem that your husband's taste in mathematical friends is as eccentric as his taste in mathematics. He and his friends finally added it up and brought it out as 3s. 7d."

"Well, he's a genius," she said with some pride. "He could bring out anythink as anythink."

Mrs. Harry Hamble was a very different type; and, by comparison with Mr. Harry Hamble, a somewhat depressing one. She had the long sallow features and sour mouth not unknown in the wives of those who find refuge in the Pig and Whistle. Asked by Nadoway whether the date in question counted for anything in her domestic memories, she answered grimly: "It orter 'ave if 'e'd told me. 'E must 'ave 'ad a raise in wages and not told me."

"I understand," Nadoway asked, "that he treated several of his friends to drinks that afternoon?"

"Treated!" cried the amiable lady, in a withering voice. "Treated to drinks! Cadged for drinks, more likely! 'E got all the drinks 'e could for nothink, I dessay. But 'e didn't pay for nobody else's."

"And how do you know that?" asked the prisoner.

"'Cos he brought back his usual wages and a bit more," said Mrs. Hamble, as if this alone were a sufficient grievance.

"This is all very puzzling," said the judge and leaned back in his chair.

"I think I can explain it," said Alan Nadoway, "if your lordship will allow me to go into the box for two minutes, before I wind up for the defence."

There was no official difficulty, of course, about the prisoner appearing in both capacities.

Alan Nadoway took the oath and stood gazing at the prosecuting counsel with gloomy composure.

"Do you deny," asked the barrister, "that you were caught by the policeman with your hand in the pockets of these people?"

"No," said Nadoway, mournfully shaking his head. "Oh, no."

"This is very extraordinary," said the examiner. "I understood that you were pleading Not Guilty."

"Yes," said Nadoway sadly. "Oh, yes."

"What on earth does all this mean?" said the judge in sudden irritation.

"My lord," said Alan Nadoway, "I can put it all straight in five words. Only in this court one can't put things straight; one has to do what you call prove them. Well, it's all simple enough. I did put my hands in their pockets. Only I put money in their pockets, instead of taking it out. And if you look at it, you'll see that explains everything."

"But why in the world should you do such a crazy thing?" asked the judge.

"Ah," said Nadoway; "I'm afraid that would take longer to explain; and perhaps this isn't the best place to explain it."

The explanation of the practical problem was indeed set forth in further detail, in the final speech which the prisoner made in his own defence. He pointed out the obvious solution of the first problem; the abrupt disappearance of the first victim. He, that nameless economist, was a much shrewder person than the festive Mr. Hamble or the artistic Mr. Green. One glance at his pockets had shown him that he had got somebody else's money in addition to his own. A dark familiarity with the police led him to doubt strongly whether he would ultimately be allowed to keep it. He had therefore vanished with the presence of mind of a magician or a fairy. Mr. Hamble, in a hazier state of conviviality, had been mildly surprised at finding more and more pocket-money flowing from his pockets; and, to his everlasting credit, had dedicated it largely to the entertainment of his friends. But even after that, there was a little more than his normal salary left, to raise sinister doubts in the mind of his wife. Lastly, incredible as it may seem, Mr. Green and his friends did eventually arrive at a correct calculation of the number of coins in his pocket. And if it was in excess of his wife's estimate, it was for the simple reason that more coins had been added, since she sent him out, carefully brushed and buttoned up, in the morning. Everything, in fact, supported the prisoner's strange contention—that he had filled pockets and not emptied them.

Amid a dazed silence, the judge could only find it possible to charge the jury to acquit; and the jury acquitted. But Mr. Alan Nadoway made a very rapid dart out of the court, eluding journalists and friends and especially his family. For one thing, he had seen two pinch-faced men with spectacles, who looked as if they might be psychologists.

6

THE CLEANSING
OF THE NAME

THE TRIAL AND acquittal of Alan Nadoway in a court of law was only an epilogue to the real drama. He would perhaps have said that it was only a harlequinade at the end of the fairy play. The real concluding scene and curtain had taken place on that green stage of "The Lawns," which Millicent, oddly enough, had always felt to be like a sort of stage scenery, stiff and yet extravagant, with the jagged outlines of the foreign plants like the jaws of sharks and the low line of bow windows like the motor-goggles of a monster. With all its grotesqueness there had always mingled in her mind something almost operatic and yet genuine; something of real sentiment or passion that there was in the Victorian nineteenth century, despite all that is said of Victorian primness and restraint. It was that essentially innocent, that faulty but not cynical thing, the Romantic Movement. The man standing before her, with his quaint and foreign half-beard, had about him something indescribable that belonged to Alfred de Musset or to Chopin. She did not know in what sort of harmony these fanciful thoughts were mingling; but she knew that the music was like an old tune.

She had just said the words: "I cannot bear the silence, because it is unjust. It is unjust to you."

And he had answered: "It is because it is unjust to me that it is just. That is the whole story; though I suppose you would call it a strange story."

"I do not mind your talking in riddles," answered Millicent Milton steadily; "but I want you to understand something more. It is unjust to me."

After a silence he said in a low voice: "Yes; that is what has got me. That is what has broken me across. I've come up against something bigger than the whole plan I made for my life. Well, I suppose I shall have to tell you my story."

"I thought," she said with a faint smile, "that you had already told me your story."

"Yes," replied Alan; "I told you my story all right. All quite true, with nothing but the important things left out."

"Well," said Millicent, "I should certainly like to hear it with the important things put in."

"The difficulty is," he said, "that the important things can't be described. The words all go wrong when you describe such things. They were bigger than shipwrecks or desert islands; but they all happened inside my head."

After a silence he resumed, more slowly, like a man trying to find new words.

"When I was drowning in the Pacific, I think I had a Vision. I rose for the third time to the top of a great wave and I saw a Vision. I think that what I saw was Religion."

Something in the involuntary mental movements of the English Lady was halted and almost chilled. She felt faintly antagonistic to some associations, she hardly knew what. She was herself reverently, if rather vaguely, attached to a High Church tradition; but she only half realized the prejudice that had stirred in her. Men who come from the colonies and the ends of the earth, and say they have got religion, almost always mean that they have "found Jesus" or been to a revivalist meeting somewhere; and the whole thing seemed socially incongruous with his culture and hers. It was not in the least like Alfred de Musset.

With the uncanny clairvoyance of the mystic he seemed to seize on her passing doubt and said cheerfully:

"Oh, I don't mean that I met a Baptist missionary. There are two kinds of missionaries: the right kind and the wrong kind, and they're both wrong. At least they're both wrong as to the thing I am thinking about. The stupid missionaries say the savages grovel in the mud before mud idols, and will all go to hell for idolatry unless they turn teetotallers and wear billycock hats. The intelligent missionaries say the savages have great possibilities and often quite a high moral code, which is quite true, but isn't the point. What they don't see is that very often the savages have really got hold of religion, and that lots of people with a high moral code don't know what religion means. They would run screaming with terror, if they got so much as a glimpse of Religion. It's an awful thing.

"I learnt something about it from the lunatic with whom I lived on the desert island. I told you he had practically gone mad, as well as gone native. But there was something to learn from him, that can't be learnt from ethical societies and popular preachers. The poor fellow had floated to shore by hanging on to a queer old-fashioned umbrella, that happened to have the head carved in a grotesque face, and when he came raving out of his delirium, so far as he ever came out of it, he regarded the umbrella as the god that had saved him, and stuck it up in a sort of shrine and grovelled before it and offered it sacrifices. That's the point. . . . Sacrifices. When he was hungry, he would burn some of his food before it. When he was thirsty, he would still pour out some of the native beer that he brewed. I believe he might have sacrificed me to his idol. I'm sure he would have sacrificed himself. I don't mean . . ." he spoke more slowly still and very thoughtfully, "I don't exactly mean that the cannibals are right, or human sacrifice or all that. They're wrong—if you come to think of it—they're *really* wrong, because people don't want to be eaten. But if I *want* to be sacrificed who is going to stop me? Nobody, not God himself, will stop me, if I want to suffer injustice. To forbid me to suffer injustice would be the greatest injustice of all."

"You are rather disconnected," she said, "but I begin to have a glimmering of what you mean. I presume you don't mean that you saw from the top of the wave the vision of the divine umbrella."

"And do you think," he asked, "that what I saw was a picture of angels playing harps out of the Family Bible? What I saw, so far as I can be said to have merely *seen* anything, was my father sitting at the head of the table, in some great dinner or directors' meeting, and perhaps everybody drinking his health in champagne, while he sat gravely smiling, with his glass of water beside him, because he is a strict temperance man. Oh, my God!"

"Well," said Millicent, the smile rising slowly to the surface again; "it certainly seems rather different from heaven and the harps."

"But I," went on Alan, "was lost like loose seaweed and sinking like a stone, to be forgotten in the slime under the sea."

"It was horribly hard," she said in a trembling voice.

To her surprise he answered with a rather jarring laugh.

"Do you think I mean that I envied him?" he cried. "That would be a rum way of realizing religion. It was all the other way. From the top of the wave I looked down and saw him with a clear horror of pity. From the top of the wave I prayed, for one passionate instant, that my miserable death might avail to deliver him from that hell.

"Horrible hospitality, horrible courtesy, horrible compliments and congratulations, praise and publicity and popularity of the old firm, the old sound business traditions, and the sun of success high in heaven and glittering everywhere on one great ghastly whited sepulchre of human hypocrisy. And I knew that within it was full of dead men's bones, of men who had died of drink or starvation or despair, in prisons and workhouses and asylums, because this hateful thing had ruined a hundred businesses to build one. Horrible robbery, horrible tyranny, horrible triumph. And most horrible of all, to add to all the horrors, that I loved my father.

"He had been good to me when I was little, and when he was poorer and simpler, and as a boy I began by making hero-worship of his success. The first great coloured advertisements were to me what coloured toy-books are to other children. They were a fairy tale; but, alas, the one fairy tale one could not continue to believe. So there I was, feeling what I felt and yet knowing what I knew. You have to love as I loved and hate as I hated, before you see afar off the thing called Religion; and the other name of it is Human Sacrifice."

"But surely," said Millicent, "things are ever so much better with the business now."

"Yes," he said, "things are better and that is what makes it worse. That is the worst of all."

He paused a moment and went on in a lower key:

"Jack and Norman are good fellows, as good as they can be," he said; "they have done their best, but for what? Their best to make the best of it. To cover it up. To put a new coat of whitewash on the whited sepulchre. Things are to be forgotten, things are to be dropped out of conversation, things are to be *thought* better of—more charitably—after all it's an old story now. But that's nothing to do with what things *are,* in the world where things are, and always are; in the world of heaven and hell. Nobody has apologized. Nobody has confessed. Nobody has done penance. And in that moment, from the top of the wave, I cried to God that I might do penance, if it were only by dying in the sea. . . . Oh, don't you understand? Don't you understand how shallow all these moderns are, when they tell you there is no such thing as Atonement or Expiation, when that is the thing for which the whole heart is sick before the sins of the world? The whole universe was wrong, while the lie of my father flourished like the green bay-tree. It was not respectability that could redeem it. It was religion, expiation, sacrifice, suffering. Somebody must be terribly good, to balance what was so bad. Somebody must be *needlessly* good, to weigh down the scales of that judgment. He was cruel and got credit for it. Somebody else must be kind and get no credit for it. Don't you understand?''

"Yes, I begin to understand," she said. "I think you are rather incredible.''

"I swore in that moment," said Alan, "that I would be called everything that he ought to be called. I would have the name of a thief, because he deserved it. I would be despised and rejected and perhaps go to jail, because I chose after that fashion to *be* my father. Yes, I would inherit. I would be his heir.''

He spoke the last words upon a note that shook her out of her statuesque stillness, and she came towards him with an unconscious movement, crying:

"You are the most wonderful and amazing man in the world—to have done such a stupendously stupid thing.''

He caught her as she came forward, with an abrupt and crushing compression of the hands, and then answered:

"You are the most wonderful and amazing woman in the world, to have stopped me doing it.''

"And that seems terrible, too," she said. "I don't want to feel that I smashed such a magnificent mad thing; perhaps I was wrong after all. But don't you think yourself it was getting impossible—in other ways.''

He nodded gravely, continuing to gaze into her eyes, which no one now would have thought languid and proud. "You know the story from the inside by this time. I began as a burglar of the Santa Claus sort, breaking into houses and leaving presents in safes and cup-boards. I was sorry for old Crayle, whose confounded prig of a wife would not let him smoke, so I chucked him some cigars. But I'm not sure even there I may not have done more harm than good. Then I thought I was only sorry for you. I should be sorry for anybody who was secretary in our family.''

She laughed on a low and tremulous note. "And so you chucked me a silver clasp and chain to cheer me up.''

"But in that case," he said, "the clasp caught and held.''

"It also scratched my aunt a bit," she said. "And altogether, it did make complications, didn't it? And all that business of the poor people's pockets—well, somehow I couldn't help feeling it might get them as well as you into trouble."

"The poor people are always in trouble," he said gloomily. "They're all what you call known to the police. It was perfectly genuine, when I told you how it riles me that they aren't even allowed to beg, and that's why I started giving them alms before they started begging. But it's quite true that it couldn't have been kept up for long. And that has taught me another lesson as well, and I understand something in human life and history I never understood before. Why the people who do have those wild visions and vows, who want to expiate and to pray for this wicked world, can't really do it anyhow and all over the place. They have to live by rule. They have to go into monasteries and places; it's only fair on the rest of the world. But henceforward, when I see these great prisons of prayer and solitude, or have a glimpse of their cold corridors and bare cells, I shall understand. I shall know that in the heart of that rule and routine there is the wildest freedom of the will of man; a whirlwind of liberty."

"Alan, you frighten me again," she said, "as if you yourself were something strange and solitary, as if you also . . . ."

He shook his head, with a complete understanding. "No," he said; "I've found out all about myself as well. A good many people make that mistake about themselves when they're young. But a man is either of that sort or the other sort, and I'm the other sort. Do you remember when we first met and talked about Chaucer and the chain with *Amor Vincit?*"

And without moving his eyes or hands from where they rested, he repeated the opening words of Theseus in the Knight's Tale about the sacrament of marriage, and as he spoke those noble words as if they were a living language, I will so write them here, to the distress of literary commentators:

> ". . . The first Mover of the Cause above
> When he first made the fair chain of love
> Great was the effect and high was his intent:
> Well wist he why, and what thereof he meant."

And then he bent swiftly towards her; and she understood why that garden had always seemed to hold a secret and to be waiting for a surprise.

THE LOYAL
TRAITOR

1
THE MENACE OF
THE WORD

IT WILL BE best, both for the reader and the writer, not to bother about what particular country was the scene of this extraordinary incident. It may well be left vague, so long as it is firmly stipulated that it was not in the Balkans, where so many romancers have rushed to stake out claims ever since Mr. Anthony Hope effected his *coup d'état* in Ruritania. The Balkan kingdom is convenient because kings are killed and despotic governments overthrown with pleasing swiftness and frequency, and the crown may fall to any adventurer, good or bad. But meanwhile, in the same Balkan State, the farms remain in the same families, the plot of land, the orchard or the vineyard, descends from father to son; the rude equality of peasant proprietorship has never been greatly disturbed by large financial operations. In short, in the Balkan kingdom there is some safety and continuity for the Family, so long as it is not the Royal Family.

But with the kingdom in question here, how different! Whatever name we may give it, it was at least a highly-civilized and well-ordered society, in which the Royal Family continued serene and safe under police protection and constitutional limitations; in which all the public services were conducted with a regularity verging on tedium, and in which nobody was ever ruined or overthrown except the butcher, the baker, the candlestick-maker and the various types of tradesmen and common citizens who might happen to cross the path of large commercial operations. The country might well be one of the smaller German States that have been industrialized by dependence on mines and factories, or one of the former dependencies of the Austrian Empire. It does not matter; it is enough to secure the reader's respect and interest to know that it was a thoroughly modern and enlightened community, which had advanced in every science and perfected every social convenience until it was within reasonable distance of revolution; not a potty little palace revolution, in which a few princes are murdered, but a real, international, universal social revolution; probably beginning with a General Strike and probably ending with bankruptcy and famine.

It was all the more possible, because breezy events of this sort had already broken out in a neighbouring industrial state, and after some months of very bewildering civil war, had ended in the victory of one out of the six revolutionary generals fighting each other in the field; the victor being a certain General Casc, an able soldier who had originally come with the Colonial troops garrisoned in the neighbourhood, and who was credited in local gossip with being partly a negro; a fact which considerably consoled those who had been defeated by him. For our own territory, which we will call Pavonia, he was only of importance—as an unluckily lucky example.

The public crisis became acute in Pavonia with the appearance of the rather mysterious agitation about "The Word." To this day there are disputes about the nature of the movement. Some of the government agents and inquirers swore the ignorant populace did really believe that, with the discovery of a new Word, everything in the world would be explained. A wild pamphlet did actually appear, in which the writer argued with insane ingenuity that, as all modern publicity and popularization consist of concentrating a book into a paragraph, or a chapter into a sentence, so at last the whole truth about the present problem would be concentrated into a word. Crowds of impatient malcontents were adjured to Wait for The Word; and apocalyptic visions were provided, of the scenes of world-change that would follow, when once The Word was spoken. The Word would contain in itself, it was gravely asserted, a complete plan of operations and an explanation of the whole organized strategy of the revolt. Some said the whole fancy had originated with one Bohemian poet, who signed his poems, "Sebastian," and had certainly composed a lyric invocation full of allusions to The Word. Many repeated the lines which ran:

As Aaron's serpent swallowed snakes and rods,
As God alone is greater than the gods,
As all stars shrivel in the single sun,
The words are many, but The Word is one.

But nobody in office ever saw the revolutionary poet who tossed these little trifles at the government and the public; until he was identified one day in the street by the very last person who was likely to meet him.

The Princess Aurelia Augusta Augustina, etc. etc. (who had embedded somewhere in her stratified Christian names the name of Mary, by which she was called for convenience by her family), was the niece of the reigning monarch; and, having only just left school, did not as yet fully appreciate the difference between reigning and ruling. She was a vigorous young woman with red hair and a Roman nose; and having as yet learned more about Royalties in history than in politics, took their position with a certain simplicity and could even imagine (just as if she had really been in the Balkans) that they might be worth murdering or worth obeying. She had come back into the life of the Court and the capital, which she had left as a mere child, full of that irrepressible desire to be useful, which is so normal in women and so dangerous in great ladies, and she was at present making herself a nuisance by asking questions of everybody about everything. She naturally asked questions about the popular political riddle of The Word, and generally, as Mr. Edmund Burke would say, about the cause of the present discontents. She was all the more intrigued when nobody could tell her what The Word was and very few, in her world, what the row was all about. It was therefore with a considerable glow of superiority that she returned to her family one afternoon and announced that she had actually seen the seditious minstrel, who was apparently responsible for the somewhat obscure revolutionary rhyme and the somewhat mysterious revolutionary movement.

Her car was moving slowly down a quiet street, because she was on the look-out for a curio shop she had known in childhood and could not immediately locate. Just beyond the curio shop was a café, with a few tables outside it in the continental manner; and at one of these tables was seated in front of a green liqueur an odd-looking person with very long hair and a very high stock or cravat. I have said that historical and geographical identification matter little in this case;

and the reader may, if he likes, clothe this queer episode in any
outlandish or antiquated fashion of fantasies of costume; for indeed
the most recent fashion is full of quaint revivals and modes that might
be either very old or very new. The man with the stock might have
been some eccentric contemporary or creation of Balzac; he might
equally well have been an art student of to-day, with the most Futurist
views but the most Early Victorian whiskers. His mane of long hair
was of an incredible dark auburn that looked like dim crimson rather
than ordinary red; his forked or cloven beard was of the same
unnatural colour and was shown up by the high cravat which was of a
vivid sort of peacock-green. The colour of the cravat varied, however,
from day to day; sometimes it was of a brighter green when the spirit
of Spring inspired his songs; sometimes of purple when he was
lamenting the rich tragedy of his loves; sometimes completely black
when he had decided that the time had really come to destroy the
universe. He would explain to his friends that he followed without
faltering the clue of the mood and the sky of morning; but they never
recommended a necktie that did not contrast effectively with his
beard. For this was no other than the poet Sebastian, whose verses
counted for so much in the revolutionary movement of the moment.

The Princess, of course, was quite unaware of his identity; and
would have passed him with no particular comment beyond a
disapproval of his necktie. But he returned to her attention and
remained in it because of the curiously different conditions in which
she saw him only an hour or two later, when the shops and factories
had shut their doors and poured forth their populations. When she
came back again through the quiet street, it was no longer quiet. It
was especially the reverse of quiet in the neighbourhood of the café
where the stranger had been drinking the green liqueur; and if the car
moved slowly now, it was because of the difficulty of making its way
through an ever-thickening crowd. For the long-haired person in the
cravat was now standing on the café table and declaiming what
appeared to be alternate fragments of prose and verse, with some
modern intermediate types difficult to define. She came just in time,
however, to hear the end of the now familiar jingle or rhymed motto:

> "As God alone is greater than the gods,
> As all stars shrivel in the single sun,
> The words are many, but The Word is one.

"But The Word will not pass my lips, nor those of the Four Wardens of The Word who already know it, until the first part of the work has been accomplished. When the powerless have risen against the powerful, when the poor have risen above the rich, when the weak have risen and proved stronger than the strong, when——"

At this moment he and his hearers suddenly became conscious of the sober but elegant vehicle which was pushing its prow like a boat above the popular waves, and the somewhat haughty countenance that appeared above it, just behind the wooden countenance of the chauffeur. Most people present recognized the lady and there was a sudden stir and stoppage, as of embarrassment; but the poet standing on the table struck a new attitude of sublime impudence and cried aloud:

"But how hard it is for ugliness to rise against beauty. And we are an ugly lot!"

And the Princess drove on in a condition of towering rage.

2

THE PROCESSION OF
THE PLOTTERS

IT HAS ALREADY been explained that Pavonia was governed on
enlightened modern principles. That is to say, the King was
popular and powerless; the popularly elected Premier was unpopular
and moderately powerful; the head of the Secret Police was much
more powerful; and the quiet and intelligent little banker, to whom
they all owed money, was most powerful of all. But all four of them
were moderate in their respective rôles; none of them had ever pushed
matters to a rupture and all four of them were often in the habit of
discussing, at an informal Privy Council, the growing problems of
the State.

The King, whose historical title was Clovis the Third, was a lank
and rather melancholy man with yellow moustaches and imperial
and rather hollow eyes; well-bred enough to make his weariness
appear impersonal rather than personal in its application, but not
otherwise exciting company. The Prime Minister was short and
stout, and very vivacious for his stoutness; though a Pavonian of
bourgeois origin he was rather like a French politician, which is by
no means the same as being like an ordinary Frenchman. He had
pince-nez and a short beard and spoke to individuals in a guarded, but
to large crowds in a confidential tone of voice. His name was Valence
and he had been considered rather a Radical, until the new revolutionary movement had suddenly revealed him as a rather obstinate
capitalist; turning, as it were, his sturdy figure black against the red

glare. The Chief of Police was a big, bilious soldier named Grimm, whose yellow face told of fevers in many countries and whose tight mouth told very little of anything. He was the only person present who looked as if he would be in any way formidable in an hour of national peril; and he was always the most pessimistic of the four about his own hopes of dealing with it. The last was a slight, refined little figure with straight, grey hair and a hooked nose rather large for his attenuated features. He was dressed in dark grey so that his streaks of limbs seemed to repeat his streaks of hair; and only when he carefully fitted on a pair of tortoise-shell goggles, did his eyes seem suddenly to stand out and come to life; as if he were a monster who put his eyes on and off like a mask. This was Isidor Simon, the banker, and he had never taken any title though many had been offered to him.

The occasion of their special meeting was that the wild and hitherto rather vague movement called the Brotherhood of The Word had suddenly received support from a very unexpected quarter. The poet Sebastian was only a poor Bohemian free-lance, of obscure origin and apparently illegitimate birth. Even his surname was doubtful; it was easy for the newspapers to make fun of his real affectations and to underrate his real influence. But when it was actually announced that a man like Professor Phocus had declared himself a friend and follower of the poet, everybody felt that the whole social situation had changed. Phocus was quite another matter; he was the scientific world: the world of colleges and committees. He was a name, he was not indeed very well known personally, being much of a recluse; but his quaint figure with high and narrow top-hat, more like a pipe than a hat, and the green spectacles which he wore to protect his dim eyes from ordinary daylight, was a familiar enough object in certain places; especially the great National Museum, where he not only specialized in certain Palæo-Pavonian antiquities, but conducted select groups of students round to inspect the relics and sculptures which illustrated that branch of study. He was universally recognized as a man of vast learning and laborious accuracy; and when it was stated in cold print that he, Professor Phocus, had found prophecies concerning The Word in the prehistoric hieroglyphics of Pavonia, only two explanations seemed possible, both equally catastrophic. Either the great Phocus had suddenly gone mad; or there was really something in it.

For some time the banker had succeeded in allaying the fears of the Council, by what might seem a professional, but is in these days a practical argument. A popular poet might set all the crowds in the streets singing his songs; and a learned man of European reputation might induce all the dons in the world to read his book. But the salary of the learned man, for taking the tourists a tour of the hieroglyphics, was a little more than five guineas a week; and the salary of the poet was an unknown quantity that was frequently a minus quantity. You cannot make a modern revolution, or anything modern, without money. It was difficult to see how the poet and the professor managed to pay for the occasional leaflets they circulated or the printing of the poem about The Word; let alone for munitions or commissariat or soldiers' pay or anything that is necessary for the higher purposes of civil war. Mr. Simon, the financial adviser, therefore, had advised the King to disregard the movement until its backing was a little more financial. But to this Council the Chief of Police had brought news which seemed to alter everything.

"Of course," he said in his slow fashion, "I'd often seen the poet going into the pawnbroker's."

"The natural resort of poets, I suppose," said the Prime Minister; and rather missed the schoolgirl giggle with which his joke would have been greeted at a public meeting; for the King's face was blank and sad and the banker's careless and inattentive. No change ever appeared on Grimm's face, even on public platforms, and he went on steadily:

"Of course, any number of people go to the pawnbroker's— especially this pawnbroker; he is little Loeb, who calls himself Lobb and lives at the corner of the Old Market, in the poorest part of the town. He's a Jew, of course, but not so much disliked as some Jews of his trade; and such thousands of people do business with him that we were rather led to look into the matter. The result of our inquiries points to the man being quite incredibly rich, all the more because he lives like a poor man. The general belief is that he is a miser."

The banker had put on the goggles that made his eyes look twice as big; and as they peered across the table they were like gimlets.

"He isn't a miser," said Simon, "and if he's a millionaire, then my question is answered."

"Do you know him?" asked the King, speaking for the first time. "Why do you say he isn't a miser?"

"Because no Jew was ever a miser," answered the banker. "Avarice is not a Jewish vice; it's a peasant's vice, a vice of people who want to protect themselves with personal possessions in perpetuity. Greed is the Jewish vice: greed for luxury; greed for vulgarity; greed for gambling; greed for throwing away other people's money and their own on a harem or a theatre or a grand hotel or some harlotry—or possibly on a grand revolution. But not hoarding it. That is the madness of sane men; of men who have a soil."

"How do you know?" asked the King with mild curiosity. "How did you come to make a study of Jews?"

"Only by being one myself," replied the banker.

There was a short silence; and then the King went on with a reassuring smile:

"And so you think he may be spending his millions on financing a revolution."

"It would have to be that or a super-cinema or something," assented Simon, "and that would explain the pamphlets and printed songs, and may explain other things yet."

"The most difficult thing to explain," observed the King thoughtfully, "seems to be where any of these people actually are at any given moment. Professor Phocus is fairly regular in his round at the Museum, but I doubt if we any of us know his private address. My niece tells me that she has actually seen Sebastian, the poet, orating in the public streets; but I've never seen him, and nobody I know seems to have any idea of where he lives. And, from what I can gather, though any number of people go to Lobb's pawnshop, very few of them ever see Lobb. I was told he was dead: but that may be part of the plot, of course."

"It is exactly upon that point," said the Chief of Police gravely, "that I have a very important piece of further information to place before Your Majesty. Through a course of long and rather difficult inquiries, I have discovered that Lobb, the pawnbroker, did, about two years ago, purchase, under another name, a small but comfortable house in Peacock Crescent. I have set some of my men to watch it; and, according to their report, there is every reason to suppose that it is used, not regularly but intermittently, as a meeting-place for three or four persons who arrive very privately and generally after dark; dine there in comfort, but considerable secrecy, and do not appear to revisit it until the next little dinner of the kind. There seems to be no regular staff of servants, and the house is commonly shuttered and deserted; but a servant of one or other of these people generally goes out about an hour before dinner and gets in wine and provisions and presumably remains to wait at table. The tradesmen in the neighbourhood report that he appears to be catering for three or four people, but beyond that they profess to know nothing. The detective, one of my best men, whom I have set to watch the house, says that the guests always arrive about dusk and very much muffled up in cloaks and coats; but he says he could swear to three of them."

"Look here," said the banker after a grave silence, "the fewer people who know about this the better. I think it would be well if one or two of us went down personally, and posted ourselves in that particular street on one of these festive evenings. I don't mind going there myself, if you will give me the protection of your presence, Colonel Grimm. I know the professor and the pawnbroker by sight, and I dare say we might make a guess at the poet."

King Clovis, in a dry and rather reluctant voice, gave the details of the poet's purple and peacock-green appearance, as conveyed to him by his indignant niece.

"Well, that may be a guide, too, sir," said the banker briskly. And that was how it came about that the most powerful financier in Pavonia, and the officer in charge of the whole police system of that country, kicked their heels patiently or impatiently for several hours, a little way beyond the circle of light thrown by the last lamp-post in the silent and deserted Crescent.

Peacock Crescent was so called, not because its pallid and classical façade had ever been brightened by any peacocks, but out of compliment to the bird which was the royal cognizance of Pavonia, and presumably the origin of its name, and which was represented in very flat relief, with tail outspread, on a medallion at one end of the semicircle of houses. Round the whole semicircle there ran a row of classical pillars, in the manner of many terraces in Bath or old Brighton; the whole classic curve looked very cold and marmoreal in the moon which was rising over the clump of trees opposite, and it seemed to the watchers that every sound they made echoed and re-echoed as through a hollow silver shell.

Their vigil had already been a long one. They had seen, from about the time of twilight and onward, the routine of the preliminaries which the police had already noted as marking the rare re-awakenings of the house; the servant in his sober livery going out at the regular hour and returning with a basket containing bottles of wine and other provisions; the sudden lighting up of the dark house from within, or rather of the one room in it presumably reserved for the feast; the drawing down of the blind that the feast might be the more private; but none of the guests had as yet arrived. Closer inquiries of the local tradesmen had verified the fact that the servant had been making preparation for four diners; the actual number had slipped out in the course of his curt requests. The two distinguished spies in the street were not, of course, so completely isolated as they seemed. Other secret service men were within hail and the Chief of Police could without much difficulty put the constabulary machinery in action. Immediately in front of the crescent of houses was one of those picturesque but unmeaning scraps of ornamental shrubbery, with a railing round it, which are to be found in many city squares and secluded terraces. This clump of bushes threw a big shadow in the moonlight; and at one corner of the railing there lurked a plain-clothes officer with a motor-cycle, ready to start on any errand.

Suddenly, and in utter stillness, a small shadow seemed to detach itself from the big shadow and seemed to skim across the road as lightly as a dry leaf. Indeed it had something of the look of a dried leaf, for though the figure was not abnormally small, it was curled up as if shrunk or withered; the head was sunk so deep in high shoulders and a shabby waterproof that only a few hairy wisps wandered in the air, that might be beard or whiskers or even, as a wilder fancy prompted, eyebrows; the legs were rather long than otherwise but moving in a bent and crooked fashion like a grasshopper's. His passage across the road was so swift and surprising that the door of the house had opened to him and closed on him again before the watchers had fully recovered from their first surprise. Then Simon looked at Grimm and said, with a faint smile:

"The hurry is hospitality. That is the owner of the house."

"Yes, I suppose that is the pawnborker."

"That is the Revolution," observed the banker. "At least, that is the real basis of every revolution. They could do nothing without his money. They talk about a rising of the poor; but they cannot even rise so long as they are poor. Why, these four men would have nowhere to meet like this, if Lobb had not bought the house for them."

"I should be the last to deny that money is useful," answered Grimm, "but money alone won't make either a revolution or a realm."

"My dear Grimm," said Simon, "I know you are an officer and a gentleman; you can't help that, but really you are becoming romantic."

"Do I look romantic?" asked the bilious officer and gentleman. "No soldier is ever romantic—not about soldiering, anyhow. But what I say is horse-sense, for all that. There is no soldiering without soldiers; and money doesn't make soldiers. You can give a mob a mountain of munitions, and it's not good if they won't use them or can't use them."

"Well, I should say . . . . Look out, here's somebody else."

The other had already become conscious of a dull clang of sound for which he could not immediately account; and the next moment another shadow had passed across the scene of that shadow pantomime. This shadow had a sharply outlined and very high black hat like an elongated chimney-pot; and the moon gleamed for a moment on the green spectacles of Professor Phocus of the National Museum. He also disappeared rapidly into the hospitable house.

"That's the Professor," said Simon. "Perhaps, as he is so learned, he will lecture to them on munitions."

"Yes," replied Grimm, "I saw who it was. . . . But I'm bothered about something else. Did you hear a sort of iron creak and clang just before he appeared? It must have been the gate in that railing over there. I believe they must both have come out of that dingy little garden. What could they be doing there?"

"Nesting in the trees, perhaps; they look queer enough birds for anything," answered the other.

"Well, the railing isn't high," said the police chief at last. "They may simply have clambered in and out again to confuse the scent; but it's rum that my man over there didn't see them."

A long interval followed; and the two companions pacing up and down to pass the time, fell again into their discussion. "What I mean," said Grimm, "is that it's a bad blunder to reckon on material without moral. Money doesn't fight. Men fight. If the time comes when men won't fight, even money won't make them. And somebody has got to teach them how. How are your revolutionary armies going to be drilled? Will Mr. Sebastian drill them to recite poems? Will Mr. Lobb drill them to fill in pawn-tickets?"

"Well," said Simon, making a sign of warning, "here is Mr. Sebastian; so you had better ask him."

This time it was unmistakable that the newcomer threw open the gate of the little garden and crossed the road to the house. For Sebastian of the purple beard and peacock scarf walked with a certain swagger, even when a conspirator apparently alone under the moon; the gate closed behind him with a ringing clash and even the door of the house seemed to open and shut again with a shade of greater pomposity.

"Those are all we know of," said Simon thoughtfully. "The man said there were four," answered Grimm.

The intervals between these flitting appearances seemed to grow longer and wearier; and as the last was especially extended, the banker, having less of the professional patience of a policeman, began to grow more and more sceptical of the unknown guest, and to express a frank readiness for his own bed. But Grimm remained fixed in his theory of the quadrilateral council; and after a long interval, so long that they almost looked for dawn in the east, they heard the gate move once more and a tall figure approached the house. He was clad in a cape or cloak of grey that looked silvery in the moonshine; and as it fell apart showed a gleam, and almost a blaze, of more brilliant silver; for it seemed to be some sort of white and dazzling uniform, with stars and clasps. Then the man turned his face for a moment upwards to the moon; and the face was the final shock; for it was darker than the glittering garments. Under the moon it looked almost blue, or at least took on those varied tints of grey and violet that are the highlights on the African complexion; and Grimm knew that the man was General Casc, the Dictator from beyond the frontier.

3

THE PRINCESS INTERVENES

THE MOMENT THAT Colonel Grimm of the Pavonian Police saw that black face turned like a blue mask to the moon, he knew that the whole machinery of the State must act together like one mantrap to catch one man. He wanted to catch the other three men who were his fellow-conspirators, of course, and he thanked his stars for the chance of catching them all together in one room; but it was the fourth man whose presence made the huge and staggering difference. Before his companion could even speak, or do anything but stare, Grimm had sent his motor-cyclist down the street like a stone from a sling; and knew that police and soldiers were closing round and stopping the mouths of all the streets.

For Grimm had a special score to settle with the great General Casc. He had suspected months before that there might be movements on the frontier and attempts of the revolutionary foreign government to make signals to the discontented classes in Pavonia. He had repeatedly pressed diplomatic inquiries and demands through the Prime Minister and other accredited representatives of Pavonian interests, and the answer had always been soothing and had always been the same. General Casc gave his word of honour that he had not the faintest intention of meddling with the internal affairs of Pavonia. General Casc was a plain soldier and no politician. General Casc was getting on in years, and had every intention of retiring from the Presidency and from all public affairs. General Casc was seriously ill; and had practically already retired. All these diplomatic reassurances had been dispatched one after another, lulling to a large extent the listless amiability of the King, favourably impressing the fussy self-importance of the Prime Minister, and leaving only a very vague and dying doubt even in the more cynical mind of the Chief of Police. And now this was the sequel; and the secret of what was really going on. This was how the aged and more or less dying African retired into private life. General Casc was dangerously ill, but well enough to go out to dinner. By a curious coincidence, he was dining with the three men vowed to destroy the Government with which he professed to be at peace. The Chief of Police ground his teeth and looked down the street eagerly for the two or three files of gendarmes already advancing down it.

It was likely enough that there was little time to lose. The presence of the foreign military leader might mean all sorts of things. It might mean tons of dynamite under the street where they stood; it might at least mean dumps of munitions in every dark corner of the city, accessible to the leaders of the mob. At the worst, there was one thing that might save them yet. And that was the instant, sudden and simultaneous arrest of all the four men in that house, leaving the whole revolution without leaders. Grimm waited till his little troop of armed men had drawn up before the house and then cautiously advanced up the steps to the door. He had already made certain that similar groups were posted behind and on all sides of the row of houses, so that there could be no escape unless there was a subterranean exit. He had even put men with ladders further along the Crescent, in case there should be a stampede along the roof. Then, after a moment's hesitation, he struck once and heavily upon the door; and the light in the lighted dining-room instantly went out.

For some time there was no other response; then he hammered on the door again, calling out in his strong voice in the King's name and threatening that the door would be forced immediately. Then at last the door was opened by the pale servant in livery, who had evidently received orders to delay the entrance of the police by every exhibition of stupidity and helplessness. With almost inconceivable absence of humour, he said that his master and the company were engaged and could not see any visitors. But Grimm paid no attention to what he guessed to be an order repeated by rote. Without further ceremony he pushed the servant aside, merely saying to his subordinate behind, "Keep hold of this fellow; we may as well bag him with the rest."

Then he thrust his way down the dark passage and threw open the door of the dining-room.

It was undoubtedly the dining-room; for it offered a convincing picture of unfinished, or barely finished dinner. Of the four places laid, one at least was occupied by the paraphernalia of coffee; while others seemed to mark various stages of trifling with savouries and sweets. Beside the black coffee was a small and now empty bottle of champagne; opposite to it was a large and half-empty bottle of Burgundy; to the left of that, an even more formidable object, was a large and by no means untouched bottle of brandy; and opposite that, by a sort of meek fantasy of contrast, stood an untasted glass of milk.

Cigars and cigarettes of the best quality were placed on a small side table, so as to be immediately at hand; and there was every sign of a successful dinner-party, which had evidently been luxurious without being altogether conventional. At least, there was every sign of the successful dinner-party except the diners. Their chairs stood about the table, some of them thrust back a little way as if the occupants had risen in a natural and unhurried style; one at least was still drawn up to the table as if the diner was not so easily to be detached from his dinner. But he and all the rest had vanished; suddenly, silently and completely; as the light had vanished from the window with the first blow upon the door.

"Pretty quick work," said the Chief of Police, "but I suppose they're bolting for some other exit. Send the men down to the basement at once; and see that Hart is watching the house at the back. They can't be far off yet; this coffee is still quite hot and I think he was just going to help himself to sugar."

"Who was?" inquired Simon a little hazily. "Do you think they were all here?"

"Obviously they were," replied Grimm. "One doesn't need to be much of a detective to pick out the separate places of all four. Their very plates are like portraits; you can almost see them all sitting there. Look at that glass of milk; you don't suppose that mad poet or that nigger General drink milk, do you? But that's Professor Phocus to the life, if you can call it life. He's one of those dried up old dyspeptics who talk about nothing but health and get unhealthier every day by doing so. He's full of all sorts of food fads; and must be a most dismal person to dine with. However, the others have fortified themselves pretty well against dismalness. Our romantic Sebastian, who colours everything crimson and purple, even his hair—what else should he drink but Burgundy? But that hard-headed old savage Casc has gone

one better, you see. Brandy for heroes, as Doctor Johnson said. And yet the last is the most typical of all. How absolutely characteristic of the little Jew to have a little champagne, but very expensive; and to have black coffee, the proper digestive, after it. Ah, he understands health better than the health faddist does! But there's something blood-curdling about these cultured Jews, with their delicate and cautious art of pleasure. Some say it's because they don't believe in a future life.''

While he was talking thus, apparently at random, he was thoroughly ransacking the room, leaving to his subordinates the ransacking of the house, and his frown was heavy though his tone was light.

The ransacking of the room could for the present be only superficial, but so far as it went it was hardly hopeful. There were no curtains or cupboards, no book-cases; there was certainly no other door and it was preposterous to suppose that, under the eyes of all the gendarmes, four men could have escaped by the window. Grimm made a preliminary examination of the floor, which seemed quite solid, a sort of concrete, coloured with a dull, wavering pattern of an old-fashioned type. Of course, the four men might have gone out by the door of the room before their servant had opened the door of the house; but even so, it was not easy to say where they had gone to. For indeed the ransacking of the house had proved even more barren than the ransacking of the room; and they were considerably surprised to find that there was so little of the house to ransack. There was no basement; there was only one narrow back door; there was only one other small room, like a smoking-room, at the back of the dining-room and looking through open windows on to the street behind; there was a large and small bedroom of corresponding size on the floor above; and that was all. Grimm was somewhat surprised at this exiguous accommodation, as compared with the aristocratic stateliness of the façade. It sharpened a certain sense of the whole Crescent having something hollow about it; like a stone mask of some cold classical comedy. Perhaps the moon also made it look a little spectral; but he could not help entertaining for a flash of that pale light the absurd fancy that the street itself had been staged as a part of the plot or comedy, and that it was like a pasteboard palace in a pantomime. His common sense, returning, told him that the imposture was of an older and more ordinary sort; and bore witness only to the normal snobbishness of men who are content with small quarters so long as it is in a fashionable quarter. That row of showy and shallow mansions, with pillars and bow-windows, was probably only a row of men who liked to look richer than they were. Nevertheless, there was something queer about it considered as the headquarters of a vast conspiracy and the meeting-place of the four tribunes of a revolution. There was not much room to store dynamite or dump munitions *here*, anyhow. But another incongruous fancy flitted across his mind; they might well have been storing an entirely new sort of chemical gas, that made solid human bodies vanish like smoke or turn transparent like glass.

A searching and scientific examination, covering days and weeks, brought them no further than those first few observations of the first few moments. If there was any crack in the concrete floor, it followed no line or direction that they could discover; if anybody had escaped to anywhere, except into the bowels of the earth, he must have done it under a hundred staring eyes and the staring moon. The giant man-trap had closed with the most scientific precision and perfection; only the trap was empty. It was with this gloomy and even alarmist news that the Chief of Police and the financier, playing the amateur detective, went back to report to the Prime Minister and the King.

Despite the swiftness with which Colonel Grimm had darted out of the rear of the house after the fugitives, he was brought up all standing at the corner of the next street, by an exhibition that affected him like an explosion. The whole of the blank wall was plastered with new placards; so new that they might almost have been put there since the raid on the house; conceivably even flung behind as a last gesture of insolence by the runaway rebels, like the paper scattered by the hares in a paper chase. He put one finger to the paper-covered wall and found the paste on it still wet.

But it was the proclamations themselves that were most arresting. They were mostly scrawled in red paint or ink, which had even run here and there, perhaps with a melodramatic suggestion of blood. They all began with the word "Now" in gigantic letters; followed by the assertion "The Word will be spoken to-night." The brief paragraphs that followed were to the effect that all was now ready for the blow at the Government which had failed in its last desperate effort to capture the men who would to-morrow be the rulers of the city. It was notable that the people were adjured especially to "Look to the Frontiers" and it was not only impled that the mysterious "Word" was now to be spoken, but hinted that the thick and thunderous lips of the sinister African would speak it.

Passing up the Poplar Avenue towards the red-brick Georgian palace, they found the King of Pavonia in another room, in another suit of clothes and in another frame of mind. He was no longer in uniform, but in a light-grey lounge suit and very obviously lounging. King Clovis was a paradox in many ways; he hated formality and yet he was very formal, on formal occasions; in spite of the paradox, we might say that he hated formal occasions because they made him very formal. But in this more comfortable apartment, with tea-things on the table, he was in the bosom of his family, so far as the presence of a niece sitting on a sofa and staring out of a window constituted a bosom in the traditional sense. The Princess, whom the works of reference called Aurelia and whom her uncle called Mary, was rather distrait and silent; but the King had no objection to silence. The Prime Minister was not present; he always imparted a nameless nuance of fussiness; and the King had a great objection to fuss.

The Chief of Police told the story of his dramatic disappointment and the King listened to it with mild wonder but without any appearance of irritation.

"I suppose," he said, "that if that old Jew really bought the house specially for them, he must have fixed up some sort of trick in it."

"So I had supposed, sir," assented Grimm. "But we cannot as yet come on the faintest trace of the trick. And I can't help being a little troubled about what these four rascals may be doing. Their proclamations make it quite plain that they are preparing a big move."

"If you can't catch them," put in Simon, "can't you arrest anybody else? Surely the party must have some other leaders."

The Chief of Police shook his head. "That is the queerest thing about it," he said. "This is the most extraordinary movement I ever heard of, in the way in which it is disciplined and organized and, above all, silenced. There must be hundreds of them in it, but to hear them talk, or rather decline to talk, you would think there was nobody in it. It's called the Brotherhood of The Word, but it seems to me more like the Brotherhood of The Silence. They all stare you blindly in the face, and smile, or say a word about the weather; and there's no catching them by any cross-examination. That's evidently the policy of the whole business. The crowd is more invisible than the conspirators, so to speak. Only these four famous conspirators are paraded before us. Their private meetings are comparatively public; but the mind of the mob is still private and it melts at a touch. We can convict nobody but these four; and the only people we can convict are the only people we can't catch."

"Then we have actually nobody in custody," said Simon.

Grimm made a wry face. "We hung on to one stupid footman who opened the door to us," he said. "Not a very glorious bag to boast of when you are out gunning for General Casc."

"We must be thankful for small things," said the King. "What does the stupid footman say?"

"He doesn't say anything. It's possible he doesn't know anything. Indeed I think it's more than possible that the man is too stupid to know anything; a big lump of a fellow, probably chosen for his long legs; they say people choose flunkeys for their calves. Or he may have some dull idea of being loyal to his master."

The Princess turned her head for the first time and said: "Has anybody suggested the rather brighter idea of being loyal to his King?"

"I'm afraid," said Clovis, in a nervous and uneasy manner, "that the time has gone by for cavaliers and gallant courtiers, Mary. You can't solve modern political problems by telling people to be loyal to the King."

"Why do they tell them to be loyal to everything else except the King?" asked the young lady, with some warmth. "When there's a strike or something at the soap works, your newspaper tells them to be loyal to the soap-boilers, who are accused of being sweaters. The journalists tell them to be loyal to their Party and to their Trusted Leaders and all the rest. But if I talk of a leader who isn't a Party Leader, who's at least supposed to stand for the whole nation and all patriotic people, then you tell me I'm old-fashioned. Or else you tell me I'm young. It seems to be considered the same thing."

His Majesty the King of Pavonia stared at his niece with a sort of vague alarm, as if a kitten had turned into a tiger-cat on the hearth-rug. But she went on like one who is resolved to release an accumulation of impatience.

"Why must the King be the only private gentleman in Pavonia? All the others are extremely public gentlemen or public parodies of gentlemen. Why may any man talk to the mob except ourselves? Do you know what I really felt when I saw that purple-whiskered poet posturing on a table in the street? Of course, to start with, I had a sense of something horribly artificial; he was like some painted and gilded doll or mummy dancing. But what annoyed me most was that peacock-coloured scarf flapping round his neck; and making me remember the old peacock flag of the Pavonians, and how they say that the peacock fans were carried before the King even in battle. What business has he got to wear such colours, if we mayn't? We have got to be dull and genteel and die of good taste behind the drawn blinds of the palace. But the conspirators may be flamboyant. The republicans may be royal. That's why they appeal to the people; because they do exactly what kings used to do, when kings had any sense. Your papers and politicians talk about the dreadful growth of Red propaganda and wonder how it can be popular. Why, because it's Red, of course. Kings and cardinals and peers and judges used to be Red, when we weren't ashamed of having a little colour in our lives."

The constitutional monarch seemed more and more embarrassed. "Perhaps," he said, "we have wandered a little from the point. It was a small point we were mentioning at the moment, about the questioning of the footman and——"

"I have every intention of sticking to the point," said the Princess firmly. "I have every intention of sticking to the footman, too, and preventing any fool from letting him go. Don't you see he is just the sort of thing I mean? All the nonsense they talk against patriotism and militarism has just let the ordinary poor man slide and sink to be the servant of any rascally adventurer. He is put into a livery to be loyal to a conspirator, because we were afraid to put him into a uniform and ask him to be loyal to a king."

"Personally," said Grimm, "I have a great deal of sympathy with Your Royal Highness's view. But I'm afraid it's too late to do that now."

"How do you know?" demanded the lady with some heat. "Have you ever put the real point to a man like that? Have you ever asked him what he feels about his loyalties and his country and the king he heard about when he was a child? Not you; you've just badgered him like a barrister about details of time and place that no healthy human being ever remembers, and he's reduced to looking like the village-idiot, and I don't wonder. I should like to talk to him myself."

"My dear Mary——" began her uncle, now thrown thoroughly into disarray; and at the same moment he caught sight of the face that flashed on him over her shoulder, and his voice seemed to die away. Mr. Simon, the banker, had also begun to talk, after a tactful cough, and was saying:

"If Your Royal Highness will allow me to say so, we ought surely to preserve a sense of proportion. The footman is only a common fellow and, I imagine, quite illiterate; in that sense, as Her Royal Highness says, a man of the people—but only one man out of a very large people. As an experiment in social science, it might be very interesting to try these theories upon him; but he is only a sample of the social material all round. Meanwhile, we should surely lose no time in concentrating on the really great and dangerous public characters whom we are pursuing. The Professor is a man of world-wide reputation; the General is a military hero at the head of armies; and really to stand quarrelling over the ignorance of a chance lackey——"

As he spoke he found himself wavering between the door and the advancing Princess; and in his throat also the words seemed to dry up. For both men had suddenly seen the face of something that is intolerant and innocent and not altogether of this world; the completeness of that conviction in youth that as yet cannot believe in the complexity of living; and they fell back before her as the great princess demanded audience with a flunkey, as if there were something in her of that great peasant girl from Domrémy when she demanded audience of a King.

4

THE UNREASONABLENESS
OF WOMAN

W HEN THE GREAT police raid on Peacock Crescent had a conclusion *pour rire* in the bursting open of empty rooms and the pinching of a bewildered footman, the functionary was trailed along with the few other sticks of furniture that seemed faintly redolent of clues; and in the impersonal manner of men removing chairs and tables with a van. There was certainly nothing about him to indicate any significance beyond that of furniture. He was of the usual size and shape of fairly imposing flunkeys. His face had the sort of solid good looks, at once wooden and waxen, which went well with the powder of the old regime of flunkeydom; there was nothing notable except perhaps that, while his blank blue eyes expressed something more than even the fatuity required by his profession, the depressing regularity of his features was rather relieved by a length of chin that suggested some sort of obscure obstinacy. And, indeed, the police who had questioned and cross-questioned him came to the conclusion that they had to deal with a case of stubbornness as well as stupidity.

He had, of course, been bullied and badgered, and threatened with all sorts of entirely illegal things, according to the method which the police of all modern and civilized countries apply on principle to all servants, cabmen, costers and other persons supposed by their poverty to be an outlying province of the criminal classes; though every now and then those methods startle all Europe and are held up in flaming headlines of horror to the whole civilized world, when they happen to have been applied, by some fool or other, to a wealthy Jew or a heavily financed journalist. But the police had got nothing out of him that threw the least light on the meaning of his master's meetings and projects; and the weary investigators were beginning to attribute his silence to ignorance or idiocy. Only the Chief of Police himself, a man not altogether without sympathy and subtlety, still suspected that the taciturnity was tinged with fidelity.

Anyhow, the servant in his capacity of prisoner was drearily accustomed by this time to see the door of his cell open and some uniformed official come in with a note-book or a menacing fore-finger, trying to collect more facts from the barren soil of his speech. He was quite prepared for it to happen again and again, any number of times; but he was not prepared to see the same door open and introduce, not a policeman in uniform, but a beautiful lady in jewels and flaming fashionable colour scheme, who entered his prison as if it were the most natural thing in the world. Only dimly did he perceive the lowering and lumpish visage of a policeman in the shadows behind; and the lady herself seemed quite resolved that the policeman should be left in the shade. She shut the door behind her with a resolute clang and faced the astounded lackey with an equally resolute smile.

He knew who she was, of course; he had seen her in the illustrated papers and even driving about the city in her car. In reply to her first question he attempted some stumbling expressions of respect; but she waved them on one side with a direct familiarity that paralysed him even more.

"Don't let us worry about all that," she said. "We are both subjects of the King and patriots of Pavonia. At least I'm sure you must be really a patriot and I want to know why you don't behave like one."

There was a long silence, and then he said, looking at the floor and in a rather hang-dog fashion: "I don't want any misunderstandings, Your Highness. I don't set up to be much of a patriot; and these people were always good to me."

"Why, what did they do for you?" she demanded. "Gave you tips from time to time, I suppose. Paid you some sort of salary, probably much too small. What is that compared with what the country has done for us all? You can't eat bread without eating the corn of Pavonia; you can't drink water without drinking it from the rivers of your own land; you can't walk down the street in safety or liberty, without relying on the law that defends the citizens of the State."

He suddenly threw up his head, and the very blank emptiness of his blue eyes affected her with something dizzy and even dazzling.

"You see," he said, without a smile, "I am not walking in liberty down the street just now."

"I know," she said obstinately, "but it's your own fault, isn't it? I'm sure you know of something these men are doing, something that's hanging over all of us like a thundercloud; and you won't say a word to save us, by telling us where the bolt will fall."

He continued to stare in a vacant manner, and then repeated like an automaton: "The men were always good to me."

She wrung one hand with a gesture of exasperation, and said rather unreasonably: "I don't believe they did anything at all. I expect they treated you rottenly, really."

He seemed to meditate in his heavy way, and then said haltingly, but with an increasing suggestion of more instructed speech—as it were, working to the surface through the professional primness of his upper-servant intonation:

"You see, these things go a bit by comparison. At the only school I was ever sent to they had hardly any meals at all; my family never had any money and I was often hungry all night, and out in the cold as well. You see, it's all very well to talk about the State and patriotism and the rest. Suppose when I was freezing in the gutter I had gone down on my knees to the great statue of Pavonia Victrix in the Fountain Square and said, 'Pavonia, give me food,' I suppose the great statue would have stepped down from its pedestal at once and brought me a tray of hot cakes or a pile of ham-sandwiches. Suppose it began to snow when I had hardly a rag on my back; I suppose the Flag of Pavonia, flying on the top of the palace, would have come down off its pole to wrap me up like a blanket. At least, I suppose some people think it would. You have to have rather rum experiences to find out that it doesn't."

His figure remained heavy and motionless; but his voice took a new and rather indescribable turn or change.

"But I did get food at Peacock Crescent. Those horrible revolutionists, who you say are destroying the whole city, at least prevented me from being destroyed. Suppose, if you like, that they treated me like a dog; still, I was a stray dog and a starving dog; and they fed and sheltered me like a dog. You know what a dog would feel about turning on them or deserting them. Is thy servant less than a dog, that he should do this thing?"

Something in the lift of his voice on the Scriptural phrase startled her and made her stare at him with a new curiosity.

"What is your name?" she said.

"My name is John Conrad," he said quite readily. "I have no family now to speak of; but we were once rather better off in the world than we are at present. But I assure Your Royal Highness there's no particular mystery about that. Coming down in the world is common enough in these days. Commoner than coming up in the world, which is even worse."

She spoke in a lowered voice. "If you are really an educated man and a gentleman, you ought to be all the more ashamed to work with this gang of wreckers. It's all very well to talk about a dog; but it's not fair. A dog has only got a master, and naturally he sticks to the only duty required of him. A dog hasn't got a country or a cause or a religion or any general sense of right. But can you, as an educated man, reconcile it with any general sense of right to say you are a dog, and on that excuse fill the whole town with mad dogs?"

He gazed at her with a painful intensity; in some strange fashion the staring and startling social disparity between them had really faded away on the heat of intellectual incompatibility; just as she had tried to wave it away with a gesture when she first made her amazing entry to the prison. As he looked at her a slow and singular change seemed to pass over his face and he seemed to realize some meaning to the situation he had as yet been too stunned to see.

"It's beyond all possible goodness that you should trouble to talk to me like this," he said. "You, at least, are more generous to me than the men who only gave me food. You, I admit, have done more than they could ever have done for a man like me. But I don't recognize it about poor old Pavonia with its peacocks and palaces and police-courts; and I wouldn't give up an inch of my own scruples for them."

"If you like to put it so," she said quite steadily, "do it for me."

"I certainly wouldn't do it for the others," he said; "but, you see, that's just where my difficulty comes in. To obey you would be a pleasure; but I don't believe a bit of what you say about it being a duty. And what sort of a dog is it that won't do it for duty, but will do it for pleasure?"

"Oh, I hate that obstinate expression you've got!" she cried with a curious uncontrollable petulance. "I don't mind dogs; but I hate bull-dogs. They're always so ugly."

Then, suddenly altering her tone, the Princess added: "I don't see why you should be kept kicking your heels in this prison, all for your silly prejudices. They're bound to give you a long sentence for treason, if they do nothing else, if you will protect these devils who want to blow us all up to-morrow."

"Very well," he said in a hard voice. "Then I must make up my mind to be punished for treason because I will not be a traitor."

Something compact in his curt epigram seemed to savour almost of contempt; and her self-control suddenly gave way before a blaze of really royal anger.

"Very well, then," she cried, turning furiously towards the door, "you can lie and rot there for treason, because you won't listen to reason; it's all one to us, of course, except that your mad, sulky obstinacy may smash us all to smithereens in twenty-four hours. God knows, and I suppose you know, what these blasphemous brutes are going to do to us all. And perhaps God cares, but you don't. You don't care for anything or anybody but your own chin and your own brutal pride. I've done with you."

And she flung open the door, incongruously giving another glimpse of the pudding-faced policeman outside; then she vanished through the opening and the door clanged again and the prisoner was left alone in his cell.

He sat down on the plank-bed and put his head on his hands, remaining in this rigid ruminating posture for a long time. Then he rose with a sigh and approached the door once more, for he heard outside it the heavy movements to which he was already and too fully accustomed; and he knew that some other visitor, who would by no means be a beautiful lady, was coming to bother him once more. But on this occasion the official interview was somewhat longer than usual, and of a somewhat different character.

A few hours afterwards, when the Princess was declining, and the King accepting, a glass of Italian vermouth from a tray handed by a footman of a far less disturbing character, the Prime Minister, who was seated opposite in that private apartment of the palace, observed quite casually:

"So it looks as if they may be frustrated after all. I was jolly nervous up to an hour ago, for I swear they had got something big that was just going to burst; all their last proclamations were like the cocking of a rifle before the bang comes. But since this silly footman is going to tell us where they're hidden, I expect we shall be too quick for them after all. Grimm says——"

The Princess Aurelia Augusta, otherwise Mary, had risen to her feet as if she had received a personal insult.

"What's all this mean?" she cried. "The footman hasn't spoken. He refuses absolutely to speak."

"Your Royal Highness will pardon me," said the Prime Minister stiffly. "I have the news straight from the Chief of Police. The footman has certainly confessed the facts."

"It's not true!" said Her Royal Highness obstinately. "I don't believe it for a minute."

She seemed quite indignant about it; and indeed those who retain any capacity for surprise at the mystery of feminine psychology may be surprised to learn that, at her next interview with the prisoner, in the prison, she was very harsh and scornful towards him for having decided upon betraying all that she had told him to betray.

"So that's the end of all your heroics and stubbornness and sticking out your chin," she said. "You're going to save yourself after all, and give up all these poor deluded creatures that are in hiding."

He threw up his head in the rather startling fashion he had and stared at her with the blank but blazing blue eyes, that had always something about them of vertigo and the empty air, making the spectator dizzy.

"Well," he said, "I certainly didn't suppose you regarded them with so much sympathy."

"I regard them with great sympathy for having to do with you," she said, in a somewhat vicious manner. "Of course, I don't agree with them; but I'm quite sorry for them, being hunted and having to trust such people to hide them. I expect it was you who led them into mischief."

The last clause was perhaps an afterthought. She said it on those sound general feminine principles, which some masculine minds, in moments of annoyance, have thought slightly unprincipled. But she was never more surprised in her life than when he smiled and said:

"Yes, perhaps you are right. It was I who led them into mischief."

As she looked at him with a painful curiosity, he added: "But remember what you said. If I did them wrong, I did it for you."

An instant afterwards he burst out in a new and volcanic voice, that she had never heard before from him or from any man.

"Do you suppose I don't know that it's all utterly unfair? Why should you have that power, as well as all the other kinds? Why should you have the only unanswerable thing, the face that is unanswerable like God on the Judgment Day? We can call up ignorance against science and impotence against power; but who is going to raise up ugliness against beauty? Who——?"

He had taken a stride forward; but, what was much stranger, she had herself started and moved forward in response. She was staring into his face as if it had been blasted by a lightning-flash.

"Oh, my God!" she cried. "It can't be that!"

For she had in that instant become aware of an amazing possibility; and the rest of their interview was too wonderful to be believed.

5

THE TERMS OF
A TRAITOR

ONE SINGLE THOUGHT like a thundercloud brooded over Pavonia, its palace and principal city; the sort of concentration that commonly only possesses some ignorant village where a prophet or fanatic has predicted the instant end of the world. The last proclamations had had their effect; even the most careless were now convinced that at any moment a huge invasion on all the frontiers, or a horrible explosion in the heart of the city, would come at some signal they did not know, and by some gesture they could not arrest. The foreign invasion was felt perhaps as the more maddening of the two; but they were all the more bewildered because there had hung over all this mysterious movement the shadow or savour of something foreign. It was admitted that the reputation of Professor Phocus was even greater in other countries than in his own; men began to ask with some irritation where the wealthy pawnbroker had come from, and, with slightly greater hesitation, how he had made his wealth. But nobody doubted that these men had constructed some engine that was about to act with hideous energy. It was in the midst of all this tossing insecurity that the message came that the captive footman would speak. He had actually signed a grave document, which ran: "I can say The Word and stop the work of the Four Destroyers for ever and put them henceforth in your power. But I must name my conditions."

Whatever may have been the historical facts about the decayed family of John Conrad, there is no doubt that he entered on the scene

of a Committee of the State, which was also an audience with the
King, with the sort of dignity which does not generally appear in the
pomposity of footmen. He approached the small table in the palace,
round which were seated the four chief rulers of Pavonia, with a
proper gesture of respect but without the least appearance of
embarrassment or servility. He bowed to the King and accepted the
chair in which the King asked him to be seated; and it was the King
who was more embarrassed than the subject. Clovis of Pavonia
cleared his throat, looked down his nose reflectively for a moment and
then said:

"I hope it is unnecessary for me to add my personal word to any
arrangements that may have been made. But I am quite prepared to
add it, to avoid any misunderstanding. It is quite understood that you
have consented on certain conditions only to reveal what you know;
and I shall certainly see that those conditions are fulfilled. It is only
reasonable, in consideration of what you regard yourself as sacri-
ficing, that you should receive a really handsome equivalent."

"May I respectfully ask," inquired Conrad, "who is to decide
exactly what is an equivalent?"

"Your Majesty," interposed Colonel Grimm, "I do not believe in
beating about the bush. We have very little time to spare, if these
plotters are really about to spring a mine. I don't see how it can be
denied that the prisoner must be the judge of the equivalent. I have
tried to get the truth out of him by other methods which he may or
may not think he has a right to resent; in plain words, by
intimidation. It is only just to say that they have failed. It is also only
just to say that when intimidation fails, there is nothing else but
bribery. And the plain common sense of it is that he can name the
bribe."

The Prime Minister coughed and said a little huskily: "That is
rather a sweeping statement; but if Mr. Conrad would give us some
idea of what he would regard as a reasonable settlement . . . ."

"I shall require," said John Conrad, "nothing less than ten
thousand a year."

"Really," said the Prime Minister, in his rather flustered fashion,
"this sort of thing seems to me quite extravagant. You could do
anything you wanted to do, in your class of life, on much less."

"You are wrong," replied Conrad calmly. "My class of life is much
more exacting than you suppose. I do not see how I could keep up the
position of a Grand Duke of Pavonia on less."

"Of a Grand . . ." began Mr. Valence, and his voice seemed to fail
and fade away.

"Obviously," said Conrad in a reasonable tone. "It would be a gross disrespect to His Majesty, and to the lineage of one of the most ancient Royal Houses of Europe, to ask His Majesty to allow his own niece to be married to anybody under the rank of a Grand Duke of Pavonia."

The rest of the company regarded the affable footman much as the King and Court may have regarded Perseus when he turned them all to stone. But Grimm recovered his voice first with a good gross military oath, followed by a demand to know what the devil it was all about.

"I shall not ask for any formal political office in the government of the State," went on the footman thoughtfully. "But it is only reasonable to expect that a Grand Duke of Pavonia married to a Royal Princess will have a certain amount of influence on the policy of the country. I shall certainly insist on a number of essential reforms; especially directed to a juster treatment of the poor of this city. Your Majesty and gentlemen, if you are at this moment threatened by a thunderbolt from you know not where, and perhaps with the overthrow of your whole nation by foreign invasion and internal revolt, you have very largely yourselves to thank. I will give up to you these revolutionary leaders of whom you talk so much. I will help you to capture Doctor Phocus and Sebastian and Loeb and, if possible, even General Casc. I will give up my companions, but I will not give up my convictions. And when I come to occupy the high national position with which you will shortly honour me, I can promise you that though there will be no revolution, there will be a very drastic reform."

The Prime Minister rose to his feet in uncontrollable agitation; for professional reformers do not like to hear about drastic reform.

"These suggestions are intolerable," he cried. "They are fantastic. They are not to be listened to for a moment."

"They are my terms," said Conrad gravely. "I am quite ready to go back to prison if you will not accept them. I may say, in so far as I may touch upon such things, that the Lady chiefly involved has already accepted them. But I am quite ready for you to reject them; and I will go back and wait in my prison, and you will sit here and wait in your palace, for you know not what."

There was a long silence and then Colonel Grimm said very softly: "Oh, ten million howling devils in hell!"

The twilight was settling slowly over the long tapestried apartment, of which the ancient gold was sufficiently faded to have lost the mere glare of vainglory and to take on the grandeur of a rich but reflected flame; as if reflected from mirror to mirror down the endless memories of men. In the great sprawling tapestry covered with giants, which made the little group of modern men look so small at their feet, could be traced the mighty figure of Clovis the First going to his last great victory with the peacock fans carried before him and the Grand Dukes of Pavonia lifting behind him a forest of swords. There was nothing in that room that did not in some way recall the unreplaceable achievement of a special civilization; the busts of Pavonian poets, who could have written only in the Pavonian tongue, filled the niches and corners of the room; the dark glimmer of the bookcases told of a national literature not to be lightly lost or possibly replaced; and here and there a picture like a little window gave a glimpse of the distant but beloved landscapes of their native land. Even the dog that lay before the fire was of the breed of their own mountains; and there was not a man there so mean—no, not even the politician—as not to know that by all these things he lived and with all these things he would die. And under all these things, they fancied they could hear something like the steady ticking of a bomb and they waited for the catch that comes before the deafening death.

At length, in that silence as of the ages, Clovis the Third spoke for Pavonia and all his people, as it was in the days of old. He knew not whether it should be called a surrender or a stroke of victory; but he knew it was necessary and he spoke with a fullness and firmness of voice which had long been rare in him.

"The time is short," he said, "and there is no other course, I think, but to accept your terms. In return, I understand that you do seriously propose and promise to stop the activities of the man called Sebastian, of Professor Phocus, of Casc and Loeb, as enemies of this State, and to deliver them up to us, to deal with them as we will."

"I promise," said John Conrad; and the King rose suddenly to his feet, like one who dissolves an audience.

Nevertheless, most of the company that had formed the Council broke up in a curious condition of mystification and ill-ease. Oddly enough, perhaps, it had no reference to the elements in the case that were really extravagant and even absurd. The incredible parts of the story seemed to have stunned them all into a sort of sobriety, so that they could no longer feel them as incredible. It was not the notion of a lackey out of a villa in Peacock Crescent becoming a Grand Duke of Pavonia or marrying a Pavonian princess. It was not concerned with the contrast between his figure and his fate. Curiously enough, it was concerned with the very contrary. After sitting at the same table with the mysterious Mr. Conrad, none of them felt any longer any particular incongruity between him and such high ambitions. He gave rather the impression of a man familiar, not only with high ambitions, but with high aspirations. He moved with the indescribable poise of those who have never really lost their own social self-respect; and his manners seemed quite as fitted to a Court as those of the rough police officer or the rather prosaic politician. He had given his word very much as the King had given it, as if it were a word of some worth. And it was exactly there that the sediment of mystification remained in the mind of many of the company; and it was the same sort of doubt that had more deeply disturbed the mind of the Princess. It was not that the man did not seem like a Grand Duke, but that he did not seem like an informer. However conventional their ideas might be about the duties of a citizen, they could not, somehow, understand a man of this sort not retaining the darker virtues of a conspirator; or, in more popular phrase, the honour that is supposed to exist among thieves. Colonel Grimm was a policeman, but he was also a soldier; and there were elements in him that did not easily adapt themselves to a gentleman—especially when he was a gentleman—who turned King's Evidence. As he looked at the grave face and rather graceful figure of the ex-flunkey, he, who fancied himself a judge of men, thought that he could imagine Conrad more easily as a man blowing up the town with dynamite than as a man betraying his accomplices.

Nevertheless, the man's word was given, and Grimm felt certain that he would keep it; and heaved a huge sigh of relief on reflecting that they had probably seen the last of the power of Casc and Phocus and Sebastian over the people of that land. And though the worthy Colonel was in one sense wildly wrong about all his calculations in the case, he was, in fact, perfectly right in that one.

He joined John Conrad outside the palace and said to him with military brevity: "Well, I suppose we had better leave the next step to you."

The next step led them together down the long poplar avenue, past the outer gates of the palace, across the Fountain Square where stood (now somewhat symbolically) the statue of Pavonia the Victorious, down a number of genteel by-streets striking outward from the square, and finally into the familiar and stately curve of Peacock Crescent. By a coincidence, it was once more a night of broad moonshine and the pale façade of that terrace struck once more into him a certain chill of mystery, as of one looking at a marble mask. But it was not to the line

of the familiar houses, or to the door of the familiar house, that
Colonel Grimm was conducted by his guide. It was across the road to
the little plot of shrubbery, with the railing round it; and, passing
through the gate in the railing, they walked in the deep, dim grass and
under the shadow of the large shrubs. In a place where the grass was
shorter and smoother, immediately under the shadow of one of the
bushes, Conrad stooped down and seemed to be moving his finger
like one writing in the dust.

"Perhaps you do not know," he said, without lifting his head, "that
most of the proclamations and phrases in this revolution are jokes.
Almost what you might call practical jokes; certainly private jokes.
There is a sort of trap-door or lid that lifts in this place, and that
nobody ever found; because ordinary openings are roughly round or
square or oblong or triangular, or some such calculable shape. But
you cannot lift this until you have traced every curve in an extremely
complicated outline. Only it ought to be a familiar outline. Only it
isn't."

As he spoke, he appeared to jerk up a certain section of the turf,
which seemed to be in reality a board with grass growing on top of it;
like a large flat cap covered with green feathers. But when he held up
the green lid so that it was black against the moon, the other could
perceive that it was of a very elaborate outline, indented and
diversified as if with capes and bays.

"You ought to know that," he said. "You must have studied it often
enough in the Atlas; especially the military Atlas. That is the map of
Pavonia. And *that*, if you will excuse our little joke, is what we meant
when we said that we should look for safety to the frontiers."

Before the Chief of Police could reply, his informant had abruptly
disappeared with a sort of dive. The earth seemed to have swallowed
him up. But Grimm heard his reassuring voice coming out of the
newly-uncovered abyss, and saying cheerily: "Come along down.
There's quite an easy ladder. Just follow me; and you shall see the last
of the men you fear."

Colonel Grimm stood for a moment like a statue in the moonlight.
Then he plunged into the black well before him. And indeed, in
doing so, he rather deserved to have a statue, not merely in the
moonlight, but in the sun and the sight of men; like the statue of
Pavonia Victrix. For he had seldom done a braver thing in a life and
profession of no little courage. He was unarmed; he was alone; he had
really very inadequate reasons, when reasonably reviewed, for trust-
ing this mysterious mountebank and adventurer, or supposing that

such a man would keep his promise. But even if he did keep his promise, what after all, was his promise? That through this dark entry the solitary officer should be led into the very lair of the lion; into the presence of the invincible Casc, with his triumvirate of anarchs and the devil knew what array of military violence; all apparently established in a subterranean empire under the earth. It was hardly a metaphor to say that it was like descending into hell; and Grimm, though not given to sentiment, could hardly help feeling something sad and symbolic in the fact that the aperture above his head, growing smaller and smaller with distance, traced upon the dark the glimmering outline of his own country. The last dim light out of the sky looked down on him in the shape of Pavonia and then grew dark. It was almost as if he were falling through all-annihilating space, and Pavonia were a distant star. And indeed, when he came to look back on the unnatural wanderings of that night, he was haunted by a sort of contradiction in time and especially in space; by a sense that he had in fact travelled thousands of miles and covered continents and even worlds; combined with a logical certainty, like that of some mathematical fact apparently evaded in a mathematical puzzle, that he had really been operating over a comparatively small area and close to places that he knew; or (as he told himself somewhat bitterly) that he ought to have known. It was doubtless largely the result of his fatigue and the final perplexity with which he faced the final mystery; but it must be allowed for if we are to understand the dazed and almost drugged spirit of discipline in which he took the final phases of the affair. He had left something behind him in the upper air of the little garden; and he sometimes fancied afterwards that it was the power to laugh.

The light like a distant star above him disappeared; and he continued to descend the ladder, rung by rung, only very vaguely imagining what sort of perils or horrors might be below. But whatever he thought of it, it was nothing so extraordinary as what he found.

6
THE SPEAKING OF
THE WORD

COLONEL GRIMM OF the Pavonian Police was very exactly described as a hard-headed man; and one not easily divorced from reality. It was perhaps all the more strongly that he remembered that night as a nightmare. It really had the indescribable qualities of a dream; the repetitions and the inconsistencies; the scraps of past experience appearing like sudden pictures amid the chaos of the formless and unfamiliar; the general sense of having a double mind, one sane and the other mad. It was all the more so when his subterranean wanderings, beginning in the sunken shaft in the garden, did bring him back into what would normally have been called normal scenes. He did indeed revisit the glimpses of the moon; but it made him feel all the more like Hamlet's father's ghost. He could not help feeling that he was revisiting the glimpses of the other side of the moon and had come out on the other side of the world. He could not be certain that he had not found an outlet under some strange sky, with stars, and moons of its own, and yet presenting objects of a mocking familiarity. His first revelation, or rather menace of things yet unrevealed, came to him when, after groping through a level tunnel, he began to ascend what seemed to be a corresponding ladder in a corresponding chimney on the other side. When he was half-way up this vertical tunnel, the man ahead of him turned and said in a low and hoarse tone: "Stay where you are a moment. I will go on and look round; they won't be alarmed at me."

He remained hanging on the ladder and looking up at a pale disc of light like the moon itself, which showed the opening of the well. A moment after the disc was darkened, blotted out as by the cap that had covered the corresponding hole; but peering up through the dusk, he fancied there was something curious about this particular stopper. He flashed on his electric torch and nearly fell off the ladder. For the aperture was filled with a face peering down at him and grinning like a goblin; a turnip of a face with green spectacles which he recognized instantly as that of Professor Phocus. And Professor Phocus said, with the horrible distinctness with which things are sometimes said in a dream:

"You won't catch us so easily. We've only to say The Word and the world will be destroyed."

Then the grotesque stopper was taken out of the strange bottle; the disc of dull light reappeared; and after a few moments of bewildered waiting, he heard the voice of his guide whispering over the brink.

"He's gone," said Conrad. "You can come up now."

When he came up, it was to find himself once more in the moonlight and apparently somewhere in the back premises of Peacock Crescent. It expresses the dazed detachment from daily life which these experiences had somehow produced in him, that he was quite surprised to see the police, whom he had himself stationed to watch the place, standing round and composedly answering the rather conspiratorial signals of Conrad.

"You can go into the house in a minute," said Conrad in the same low voice. "I'll just nip in and see that everything's all right; but I'm sure they're all boxed up in there. Bring your men with you, of course."

He darted into the back of a house, which Grimm fancied was the house next door to the original scene of the raid; and for some little time the police and their Chief waited patiently outside. They had just begun to consider the advisability of following their solitary leader into the den of criminals, when they caught their breath and stood still, staring up at the house.

One of the window blinds was jerked up and there appeared at the window the unmistakable face and form which the Princess had beheld upon the café table. The poet, Sebastian, stood staring at the moon, in what is supposed to be the manner of poets; looking more than usually florid with his flaming red moustache and whiskers and a necktie of yet another glowing and romantic shade. Then he stretched out his arm to the moon, with a theatrical gesture, and

seemed to begin to sing, or at least to speak in a sing-song fashion. It
was impossible to conceive anything more operatic; in the sense in
which that word is almost synonymous with idiotic. But the words he
was chanting were familiar:

> "As Aaron's serpent swallowed snakes and rods,
> As God alone is greater than the gods,
> As all stars shrivel in the single sun,
> The words are many, but The Word is one."

Then he suddenly snapped the blind down and vanished, the room
behind him turning dark. They could hardly believe that the
incident, especially so senseless an incident, had really happened at
all.

The next moment they were conscious that their creepy friend the
conspirator had come close to them again in complete silence and was
whispering:

"You can go in now and nab them all."

Grimm, at the head of his stolid policemen, stumped up some stairs
and along one or two passages and arrived eventually in a large,
empty room. It was rather a curious room, having one table in the
middle, with four chairs and four pads of blotting paper, as if
arranged for a regular committee. But what was much more curious
was this: that in each of the four walls of the room there was let in a
door, with an old brass knocker, as if they were the four front doors of
separate houses. Each of them bore a notice in large letters; one being
inscribed "Professor Phocus," another "General Casc," a third "Mr.
Loeb," and a fourth simply "Sebastian," as with that magnificent
flourish with which foreign poets sign a single name.

"This is where they live," said John Conrad, "and I promise you
they shall not escape."

Then after a pause he added: "But before we seek them out in their
separate suites of apartments, I want to talk to you about something. I
want to talk to you about The Word."

"I suppose," said the official grimly, "that we are to be allowed to
hear The Word also; though somebody has just told me that it will
destroy the world."

"I do not think it will destroy the world," answered Conrad
gravely. "I hope it will rather recreate it."

"Then," said Grimm, "I may take it that when we do know The
Word, we shan't find that is a joke too."

"In one sense it's a joke," answered the other. "In one sense when you know it, you will know it's a joke. But the joke is that you know it already."

"I'm sure I don't know what you mean by saying so," said the other.

"You have heard The Word twenty times," said Conrad. "You heard it only ten minutes ago. We have shouted and bellowed The Word at you all the time; and made it as plain as a placard on the wall. The whole secret of this conspiracy is really in one word; only that we've never kept it a secret."

Grimm was looking at him with gleaming eyes under his heavy brows; and something like a suspicion was creeping into his face. Conrad repeated very seriously, with a slow and heavy enunciation the words:

"As all stars shrivel in the single sun . . ."

Grimm leapt to his feet with an oath and suddenly made a dash at the door labelled "Sebastian."

"Yes, you've got it," said Conrad with a smile. "It's only a question of which word you italicize. Or, if you like, of which word you begin with a big letter."

"The words are many," muttered Grimm, fumbling at the door.

"Yes," answered the other, "but the word is One."

Colonel Grimm flung open the door of the poet's suite of apartments and found it was a cupboard. It was quite an ordinary shallow cupboard with a few hat-pegs, and from these were hanging a red wig, a red artifical beard, a scarf of peacock colours and all the externals of the popular poet.

"All the history of the great revolution," went on John Conrad, in the calm tone of a lecturer, "the whole method by which it was enabled to spread and menace the great State of Pavonia is and always was to be summed up in a single word: a word I constantly repeated, but a word that you never guessed. It is the word One."

He stepped from the table to the door at right angles to the open one; the door inscribed with the name of the Professor; and throwing it open, revealed another cupboard, with a hat-peg supporting an unnaturally narrow, tall hat, a dilapidated waterproof and a bulbous mask bridged by a pair of green spectacles.

"These are the luxurious apartments of the celebrated Professor Phocus," he said. "Need I explain to you that there never was any Professor Phocus?—except myself, of course, who professed to be the

Professor. In the case of Loeb and Casc I ran rather a greater risk; for they were, or had been, real people."

He paused a moment, rubbing his long chin, and then said:

"But it's odd how you shrewd policemen blunder by not simply believing what you are told. You said that the Pavonian people must all be drilled in a wonderful conspiracy; simply because they denied that there was a conspiracy. They all agreed in that; so you thought that was conspiracy in itself. As a matter of fact they knew nothing; because there was nothing to know. It was the same with your international relations. Old General Casc told you again and again that he was old; that he was ill and in retirement. And so he is. He's in such complete retirement that he hasn't even heard that he is walking about the streets of the Pavonian capital in full uniform. But you wouldn't believe him, because you wouldn't believe anybody. The Princess herself said the poet looked all painted and artificial in his purple whiskers. And that would have told you the whole story, if you'd only listened to her. Then everybody said, even the King himself, that old Loeb the pawnbroker was dead, and so he was. He died years before I began to impersonate him with these trifling adornments."

And he threw open another cupboard, displaying a dusty interior festooned as if with cobwebs with the grey whiskers and shabby grey garments attributed to the miser.

"That was the beginning of the whole business. Old Loeb really did take this house privately, but for very private reasons; not exactly out of pure public spirit; no. I really was his servant, having come down to that sort of service; and the only thing I inherited from the old rascal's regime, the only thing I didn't invent myself, was the underground passage, which he had constructed for himself. As I say, there were no political ideals involved in that; odd sort of ladies used it and so on. He was not a nice old gentleman. Well, I don't know whether you will enter into the fine shade of my feelings; but, although I was starving and ready to be a scavenger, yet three years in the service of a sensual usurer left me in a rather revolutionary state of mind. It seemed to me that the world, as seen from that particular sewer, by that particular scavenger, was rather an ugly place. So I decided to have a revolution. Or rather, I decided to be a revolution. It was all very easy, really, if one did it slowly and with a little tact and imagination. I built up the characters of four quite different public men, two of them quite imaginary. You never saw any two of them at the same moment; and you never noticed it. When they were supposed to gather for their periodical dinner, I had only to put on one disguise after the other and go round behind the scenes, so to speak, in the underground passage, so that they only seemed to turn up one after another in a leisurely fashion. For the rest, you've no notion how easy it is to bamboozle a really enlightened, educated modern town, used to newspapers and all that. It was only necessary for each person to have a vast, vague reputation, more or less foreign. When Professor Phocus wrote learned letters to the papers, with half the alphabet after his name, nobody was going to admit they had never heard of the famous Professor Phocus. When Sebastian said he was the greatest poet in modern Europe, everybody felt that he ought to know. And if you get three or four names of that sort nowadays, you have got everything. There never was a time in history when the few counted for so much, and the many for so little. When the newspapers say 'The nation is behind Mr. Binks,' it means that about three newspaper proprietors are behind him. When the professors say 'The opinion of Europe has now accepted the Gollywog theory,' it means that about four professors in Germany have accepted it. The moment I'd got my millionaire and my man of science, I knew I was pretty safe; but the poet was a pleasing ornament and I knew the threat of the foreign general would throw you all into fits. By the way," he added apologetically, "I have not shown you the magnificent apartments of General Casc; but it's only the uniform. The rest consists chiefly of blacking."

"Quite so," said Colonel Grimm, politely. "I will excuse you from exhibiting the blacking. And now, what is to happen?"

The chief conspirator seemed to be still sunken in a sort of reverie. At last he said:

"I felt that all revolutions had failed through treason or disunion among the revolutionists. I resolved that the others should not betray me. I did not foresee that I might betray the others. But after all, this rebellion has also ended in betrayal. Colonel Grimm, I give up my confederates. The great poet Sebastian is captured and hanged; the great soldier Casc is captured and hanged; Phocus and Loeb are captured and hanged. You can see them hanging—on hat-pegs."

Then he added, with a bow of profound modesty:

"But their humble tool, John Conrad, has the pardon of the King."

Grimm once more sprang erect with a ringing curse which cracked and turned to a laugh. Then he said:

"John Conrad, you are a devil; but I shouldn't wonder if you brought it off after all. Clovis the Third may have forgotten that he is

still a king, but somewhere in his stale memories he remembers that
he is still a gentleman. Go on your way, Grand Duke of Pavonia; it is
possible that you know the way to go! After all, you have done what
you said you would do, and kept your own word in your own way."

"Yes," said Conrad, with a new sobriety, "it is the only thing worth
calling The Word."

It has been already explained that Pavonia possessed a modern and
enlightened Government; and in the light of this fact it may seem a
strain on the reader's credulity to say that it did actually keep its word
to the eccentric footman. The politicians and the financiers made
some difficulties, feeling that the keeping of promises must not
become a habit. But for once the King put his foot down, not without
a faint and far-off jingle of the ancient spurs and sword. He said it was
a point of purely personal honour, but there was a rumour that his
niece had a good deal to do with it.

EPILOGUE OF
THE PRESSMAN

THE THIEF, THE Quack, the Murderer and the Traitor had made their confessions of crime to Mr. Pinion of the *Comet* somewhat more briefly and personally than the same tales have been recorded here. Nevertheless, they took a tolerably long time from start to finish; and throughout the whole of that time Mr. Pinion had preserved an air of polite attention and had not interrupted by so much as a word.

When they were over, he coughed slightly and said: "Well, gentlemen, I'm sure I've been very much interested in your remarkable narratives. But I suppose most of us get misrepresented a bit from time to time. I hope you'll do me the honour, gentlemen, of allowing that I haven't pumped you, or prompted you, or stuck my oar in anyway; but have enjoyed your hospitality without taking advantage of it."

"I am sure," said the doctor heartily, "nobody could possibly have been more patient and considerate."

"I only ask," proceeded Mr. Pinion, in his gentle tones, "because in the newspaper world of my own country I am known as the Bloody Battering-Ram; also the Home-Wrecker, the Heart-Searcher and occasionally as Jack the Ripper, because of my unscrupulous ripping up of the most sacred secrets of private life. Headlines such as "Bull-Dog Pinion Pins President," or "Home-Wrecker Has Scalp of Screaming Secretary," are common on the brighter news-pages of my native state. The story is still told of how I hung on to Judge Grogan by one leg, when he was climbing into the aeroplane."

"Well," said the doctor, "I own I never should have guessed it of you. Nobody would think you'd ever done a thing like that."

"I never did," replied Mr. Pinion calmly. "Judge Grogan and I had a perfectly friendly conversation at his own country residence at his own request. But each of us has got to keep up his own professional reputation, whether it's as a Murderer, a Robber or a Reporter."

"Do you mean," asked the big man intervening, "that you didn't really batter or wreck or rip anything or anybody?"

"Well, not quite so much as you murdered anybody," answered the American in his guarded tone. "But I have to let on that I've been horribly rude to everybody, or I'd lose my professional prestige and perhaps my job. As a matter of fact, I generally find I can get anything I want by being polite. My experience is," he added mildly and gravely, "that most folks are only too ready to talk about themselves."

The four men around him looked at each other and then broke into a laugh.

"That's certainly one for us," said the doctor. "You've certainly got our stories out of us and done it by being perfectly polite. Do you really mean to say that if you publish them, you'd have to pretend you could only do it by being rude?"

"I guess so," said Mr. Pinion, nodding gravely. "If I published your story, I'd have to say I broke down the door of Dr. Judson's surgery as he was bandaging somebody with his throat cut, and just wouldn't let him finish till he'd told me his life-story. I'd have to pretend Mr. Nadoway was just off to his dying mother, when I boarded his car and got his views on Capital *versus* Labour. I'd be obliged to burgle the third gentleman's house or wreck the fourth gentleman's train, or do something to show my editor I'm a real live wire of a reporter. Of course you never need to do it really; you can do most things by decent manners and talking to people at appropriate times. Or rather," and he again suppressed a smile, "letting them talk to you."

"Do you think," asked the big man thoughtfully, "that that sort of sensationalism really impresses the public?"

"I don't know," said the journalist. "I should rather think not. It impresses the editor; and that's what I've got to think about."

"But, if you'll excuse me, don't you mind yourself," pursued the other. "Don't you mind everybody from Maine to Mexico calling you a Bloody Battering-Ram when you're really a perfectly normal and well-educated gentleman?"

"Well," said the journalist, "I suppose, as I say, that most of us are misunderstood one way or another."

There was a momentary silence at the table; and then Dr. Judson turned in his chair with a sort of jerk and said:

"Gentlemen, I beg to propose Mr. Lee Pinion as a member of the Club."

A CATALOG OF SELECTED
DOVER BOOKS
IN ALL FIELDS OF INTEREST

A CATALOG OF SELECTED DOVER
BOOKS IN ALL FIELDS OF INTEREST

CONCERNING THE SPIRITUAL IN ART, Wassily Kandinsky. Pioneering work by father of abstract art. Thoughts on color theory, nature of art. Analysis of earlier masters. 12 illustrations. 80pp. of text. 5⅜ × 8½.　23411-8 Pa. $3.95

ANIMALS: 1,419 Copyright-Free Illustrations of Mammals, Birds, Fish, Insects, etc., Jim Harter (ed.). Clear wood engravings present, in extremely lifelike poses, over 1,000 species of animals. One of the most extensive pictorial sourcebooks of its kind. Captions. Index. 284pp. 9 × 12.　23766-4 Pa. $11.95

CELTIC ART: The Methods of Construction, George Bain. Simple geometric techniques for making Celtic interlacements, spirals, Kells-type initials, animals, humans, etc. Over 500 illustrations. 160pp. 9 × 12. (USO)　22923-8 Pa. $9.95

AN ATLAS OF ANATOMY FOR ARTISTS, Fritz Schider. Most thorough reference work on art anatomy in the world. Hundreds of illustrations, including selections from works by Vesalius, Leonardo, Goya, Ingres, Michelangelo, others. 593 illustrations. 192pp. 7⅛ × 10¼.　20241-0 Pa. $8.95

CELTIC HAND STROKE-BY-STROKE (Irish Half-Uncial from "The Book of Kells"): An Arthur Baker Calligraphy Manual, Arthur Baker. Complete guide to creating each letter of the alphabet in distinctive Celtic manner. Covers hand position, strokes, pens, inks, paper, more. Illustrated. 48pp. 8¼ × 11.
24336-2 Pa. $3.95

EASY ORIGAMI, John Montroll. Charming collection of 32 projects (hat, cup, pelican, piano, swan, many more) specially designed for the novice origami hobbyist. Clearly illustrated easy-to-follow instructions insure that even beginning papercrafters will achieve successful results. 48pp. 8¼ × 11.　27298-2 Pa. $2.95

THE COMPLETE BOOK OF BIRDHOUSE CONSTRUCTION FOR WOOD-WORKERS, Scott D. Campbell. Detailed instructions, illustrations, tables. Also data on bird habitat and instinct patterns. Bibliography. 3 tables. 63 illustrations in 15 figures. 48pp. 5¼ × 8½.　24407-5 Pa. $1.95

BLOOMINGDALE'S ILLUSTRATED 1886 CATALOG: Fashions, Dry Goods and Housewares, Bloomingdale Brothers. Famed merchants' extremely rare catalog depicting about 1,700 products: clothing, housewares, firearms, dry goods, jewelry, more. Invaluable for dating, identifying vintage items. Also, copyright-free graphics for artists, designers. Co-published with Henry Ford Museum & Greenfield Village. 160pp. 8¼ × 11.　25780-0 Pa. $9.95

HISTORIC COSTUME IN PICTURES, Braun & Schneider. Over 1,450 costumed figures in clearly detailed engravings—from dawn of civilization to end of 19th century. Captions. Many folk costumes. 256pp. 8⅜ × 11¾.　23150-X Pa. $11.95

CATALOG OF DOVER BOOKS

STICKLEY CRAFTSMAN FURNITURE CATALOGS, Gustav Stickley and L. & J. G. Stickley. Beautiful, functional furniture in two authentic catalogs from 1910. 594 illustrations, including 277 photos, show settles, rockers, armchairs, reclining chairs, bookcases, desks, tables. 183pp. 6½ × 9¼. 23838-5 Pa. $8.95

AMERICAN LOCOMOTIVES IN HISTORIC PHOTOGRAPHS: 1858 to 1949, Ron Ziel (ed.). A rare collection of 126 meticulously detailed official photographs, called "builder portraits," of American locomotives that majestically chronicle the rise of steam locomotive power in America. Introduction. Detailed captions. xi + 129pp. 9 × 12. 27393-8 Pa. $12.95

AMERICA'S LIGHTHOUSES: An Illustrated History, Francis Ross Holland, Jr. Delightfully written, profusely illustrated fact-filled survey of over 200 American lighthouses since 1716. History, anecdotes, technological advances, more. 240pp. 8 × 10¾. 25576-X Pa. $11.95

TOWARDS A NEW ARCHITECTURE, Le Corbusier. Pioneering manifesto by founder of "International School." Technical and aesthetic theories, views of industry, economics, relation of form to function, "mass-production split" and much more. Profusely illustrated. 320pp. 6⅛ × 9¼. (USO) 25023-7 Pa. $8.95

HOW THE OTHER HALF LIVES, Jacob Riis. Famous journalistic record, exposing poverty and degradation of New York slums around 1900, by major social reformer. 100 striking and influential photographs. 233pp. 10 × 7⅞.
22012-5 Pa $10.95

FRUIT KEY AND TWIG KEY TO TREES AND SHRUBS, William M. Harlow. One of the handiest and most widely used identification aids. Fruit key covers 120 deciduous and evergreen species; twig key 160 deciduous species. Easily used. Over 300 photographs. 126pp. 5⅜ × 8½. 20511-8 Pa. $3.95

COMMON BIRD SONGS, Dr. Donald J. Borror. Songs of 60 most common U.S. birds: robins, sparrows, cardinals, bluejays, finches, more—arranged in order of increasing complexity. Up to 9 variations of songs of each species.
Cassette and manual 99911-4 $8.95

ORCHIDS AS HOUSE PLANTS, Rebecca Tyson Northen. Grow cattleyas and many other kinds of orchids—in a window, in a case, or under artificial light. 63 illustrations. 148pp. 5⅜ × 8½. 23261-1 Pa. $3.95

MONSTER MAZES, Dave Phillips. Masterful mazes at four levels of difficulty. Avoid deadly perils and evil creatures to find magical treasures. Solutions for all 32 exciting illustrated puzzles. 48pp. 8¼ × 11. 26005-4 Pa. $2.95

MOZART'S DON GIOVANNI (DOVER OPERA LIBRETTO SERIES), Wolfgang Amadeus Mozart. Introduced and translated by Ellen H. Bleiler. Standard Italian libretto, with complete English translation. Convenient and thoroughly portable—an ideal companion for reading along with a recording or the performance itself. Introduction. List of characters. Plot summary. 121pp. 5¼ × 8½.
24944-1 Pa. $2.95

TECHNICAL MANUAL AND DICTIONARY OF CLASSICAL BALLET, Gail Grant. Defines, explains, comments on steps, movements, poses and concepts. 15-page pictorial section. Basic book for student, viewer. 127pp. 5⅜ × 8½.
21843-0 Pa. $3.95

BRASS INSTRUMENTS: Their History and Development, Anthony Baines. Authoritative, updated survey of the evolution of trumpets, trombones, bugles, cornets, French horns, tubas and other brass wind instruments. Over 140 illustrations and 48 music examples. Corrected and updated by author. New preface. Bibliography. 320pp. 5⅜ × 8½. 27574-4 Pa. $9.95

HOLLYWOOD GLAMOR PORTRAITS, John Kobal (ed.). 145 photos from 1926–49. Harlow, Gable, Bogart, Bacall; 94 stars in all. Full background on photographers, technical aspects. 160pp. 8⅜ × 11¼. 23352-9 Pa. $11.95

MAX AND MORITZ, Wilhelm Busch. Great humor classic in both German and English. Also 10 other works: "Cat and Mouse," "Plisch and Plumm," etc. 216pp. 5⅜ × 8½. 20181-3 Pa. $5.95

THE RAVEN AND OTHER FAVORITE POEMS, Edgar Allan Poe. Over 40 of the author's most memorable poems: "The Bells," "Ulalume," "Israfel," "To Helen," "The Conqueror Worm," "Eldorado," "Annabel Lee," many more. Alphabetic lists of titles and first lines. 64pp. 5³⁄₁₆ × 8¼. 26685-0 Pa. $1.00

SEVEN SCIENCE FICTION NOVELS, H. G. Wells. The standard collection of the great novels. Complete, unabridged. First Men in the Moon, Island of Dr. Moreau, War of the Worlds, Food of the Gods, Invisible Man, Time Machine, In the Days of the Comet. Total of 1,015pp. 5⅜ × 8½. (USO) 20264-X Clothbd. $29.95

AMULETS AND SUPERSTITIONS, E. A. Wallis Budge. Comprehensive discourse on origin, powers of amulets in many ancient cultures: Arab, Persian, Babylonian, Assyrian, Egyptian, Gnostic, Hebrew, Phoenician, Syriac, etc. Covers cross, swastika, crucifix, seals, rings, stones, etc. 584pp. 5⅜ × 8½. 23573-4 Pa. $12.95

RUSSIAN STORIES/PYCCKNE PACCKA3bl: A Dual-Language Book, edited by Gleb Struve. Twelve tales by such masters as Chekhov, Tolstoy, Dostoevsky, Pushkin, others. Excellent word-for-word English translations on facing pages, plus teaching and study aids, Russian/English vocabulary, biographical/critical introductions, more. 416pp. 5⅜ × 8½. 26244-8 Pa. $8.95

PHILADELPHIA THEN AND NOW: 60 Sites Photographed in the Past and Present, Kenneth Finkel and Susan Oyama. Rare photographs of City Hall, Logan Square, Independence Hall, Betsy Ross House, other landmarks juxtaposed with contemporary views. Captures changing face of historic city. Introduction. Captions. 128pp. 8¼ × 11. 25790-8 Pa. $9.95

AIA ARCHITECTURAL GUIDE TO NASSAU AND SUFFOLK COUNTIES, LONG ISLAND, The American Institute of Architects, Long Island Chapter, and the Society for the Preservation of Long Island Antiquities. Comprehensive, well-researched and generously illustrated volume brings to life over three centuries of Long Island's great architectural heritage. More than 240 photographs with authoritative, extensively detailed captions. 176pp. 8¼ × 11. 26946-9 Pa. $14.95

NORTH AMERICAN INDIAN LIFE: Customs and Traditions of 23 Tribes, Elsie Clews Parsons (ed.). 27 fictionalized essays by noted anthropologists examine religion, customs, government, additional facets of life among the Winnebago, Crow, Zuni, Eskimo, other tribes. 480pp. 6⅛ × 9¼. 27377-6 Pa. $10.95

FRANK LLOYD WRIGHT'S HOLLYHOCK HOUSE, Donald Hoffmann. Lavishly illustrated, carefully documented study of one of Wright's most controversial residential designs. Over 120 photographs, floor plans, elevations, etc. Detailed perceptive text by noted Wright scholar. Index. 128pp. 9¼ × 10¾.
27133-1 Pa. $11.95

THE MALE AND FEMALE FIGURE IN MOTION: 60 Classic Photographic Sequences, Eadweard Muybridge. 60 true-action photographs of men and women walking, running, climbing, bending, turning, etc., reproduced from rare 19th-century masterpiece. vi + 121pp. 9 × 12.
24745-7 Pa. $10.95

1001 QUESTIONS ANSWERED ABOUT THE SEASHORE, N. J. Berrill and Jacquelyn Berrill. Queries answered about dolphins, sea snails, sponges, starfish, fishes, shore birds, many others. Covers appearance, breeding, growth, feeding, much more. 305pp. 5¼ × 8¼.
23366-9 Pa. $7.95

GUIDE TO OWL WATCHING IN NORTH AMERICA, Donald S. Heintzelman. Superb guide offers complete data and descriptions of 19 species: barn owl, screech owl, snowy owl, many more. Expert coverage of owl-watching equipment, conservation, migrations and invasions, etc. Guide to observing sites. 84 illustrations. xiii + 193pp. 5⅜ × 8½.
27344-X Pa. $7.95

MEDICINAL AND OTHER USES OF NORTH AMERICAN PLANTS: A Historical Survey with Special Reference to the Eastern Indian Tribes, Charlotte Erichsen-Brown. Chronological historical citations document 500 years of usage of plants, trees, shrubs native to eastern Canada, northeastern U.S. Also complete identifying information. 343 illustrations. 544pp. 6½ × 9¼.
25951-X Pa. $12.95

STORYBOOK MAZES, Dave Phillips. 23 stories and mazes on two-page spreads: Wizard of Oz, Treasure Island, Robin Hood, etc. Solutions. 64pp. 8¼ × 11.
23628-5 Pa. $2.95

NEGRO FOLK MUSIC, U.S.A., Harold Courlander. Noted folklorist's scholarly yet readable analysis of rich and varied musical tradition. Includes authentic versions of over 40 folk songs. Valuable bibliography and discography. xi + 324pp. 5⅜ × 8½.
27350-4 Pa. $7.95

MOVIE-STAR PORTRAITS OF THE FORTIES, John Kobal (ed.). 163 glamor, studio photos of 106 stars of the 1940s: Rita Hayworth, Ava Gardner, Marlon Brando, Clark Gable, many more. 176pp. 8⅜ × 11¼.
23546-7 Pa. $10.95

BENCHLEY LOST AND FOUND, Robert Benchley. Finest humor from early 30s, about pet peeves, child psychologists, post office and others. Mostly unavailable elsewhere. 73 illustrations by Peter Arno and others. 183pp. 5⅜ × 8½.
22410-4 Pa. $5.95

YEKL and THE IMPORTED BRIDEGROOM AND OTHER STORIES OF YIDDISH NEW YORK, Abraham Cahan. Film Hester Street based on Yekl (1896). Novel, other stories among first about Jewish immigrants on N.Y.'s East Side. 240pp. 5⅜ × 8½.
22427-9 Pa. $6.95

SELECTED POEMS, Walt Whitman. Generous sampling from *Leaves of Grass.* Twenty-four poems include "I Hear America Singing," "Song of the Open Road," "I Sing the Body Electric," "When Lilacs Last in the Dooryard Bloom'd," "O Captain! My Captain!"—all reprinted from an authoritative edition. Lists of titles and first lines. 128pp. 5³⁄₁₆ × 8¼.
26878-0 Pa. $1.00

THE BEST TALES OF HOFFMANN, E. T. A. Hoffmann. 10 of Hoffmann's most important stories: "Nutcracker and the King of Mice," "The Golden Flowerpot," etc. 458pp. 5⅜ × 8½. 21793-0 Pa. $8.95

FROM FETISH TO GOD IN ANCIENT EGYPT, E. A. Wallis Budge. Rich detailed survey of Egyptian conception of "God" and gods, magic, cult of animals, Osiris, more. Also, superb English translations of hymns and legends. 240 illustrations. 545pp. 5⅜ × 8½. 25803-3 Pa. $11.95

FRENCH STORIES/CONTES FRANÇAIS: A Dual-Language Book, Wallace Fowlie. Ten stories by French masters, Voltaire to Camus: "Micromegas" by Voltaire; "The Atheist's Mass" by Balzac; "Minuet" by de Maupassant; "The Guest" by Camus, six more. Excellent English translations on facing pages. Also French-English vocabulary list, exercises, more. 352pp. 5⅜ × 8½. 26443-2 Pa. $8.95

CHICAGO AT THE TURN OF THE CENTURY IN PHOTOGRAPHS: 122 Historic Views from the Collections of the Chicago Historical Society, Larry A. Viskochil. Rare large-format prints offer detailed views of City Hall, State Street, the Loop, Hull House, Union Station, many other landmarks, circa 1904-1913. Introduction. Captions. Maps. 144pp. 9⅜ × 12¼. 24656-6 Pa. $12.95

OLD BROOKLYN IN EARLY PHOTOGRAPHS, 1865-1929, William Lee Younger. Luna Park, Gravesend race track, construction of Grand Army Plaza, moving of Hotel Brighton, etc. 157 previously unpublished photographs. 165pp. 8⅞ × 11¾. 23587-4 Pa. $13.95

THE MYTHS OF THE NORTH AMERICAN INDIANS, Lewis Spence. Rich anthology of the myths and legends of the Algonquins, Iroquois, Pawnees and Sioux, prefaced by an extensive historical and ethnological commentary. 36 illustrations. 480pp. 5⅜ × 8½. 25967-6 Pa. $8.95

AN ENCYCLOPEDIA OF BATTLES: Accounts of Over 1,560 Battles from 1479 B.C. to the Present, David Eggenberger. Essential details of every major battle in recorded history from the first battle of Megiddo in 1479 B.C. to Grenada in 1984. List of Battle Maps. New Appendix covering the years 1967-1984. Index. 99 illustrations. 544pp. 6½ × 9¼. 24913-1 Pa. $14.95

SAILING ALONE AROUND THE WORLD, Captain Joshua Slocum. First man to sail around the world, alone, in small boat. One of great feats of seamanship told in delightful manner. 67 illustrations. 294pp. 5⅜ × 8½. 20326-3 Pa. $5.95

ANARCHISM AND OTHER ESSAYS, Emma Goldman. Powerful, penetrating, prophetic essays on direct action, role of minorities, prison reform, puritan hypocrisy, violence, etc. 271pp. 5⅜ × 8½. 22484-8 Pa. $5.95

MYTHS OF THE HINDUS AND BUDDHISTS, Ananda K. Coomaraswamy and Sister Nivedita. Great stories of the epics; deeds of Krishna, Shiva, taken from puranas, Vedas, folk tales; etc. 32 illustrations. 400pp. 5⅜ × 8½. 21759-0 Pa. $9.95

BEYOND PSYCHOLOGY, Otto Rank. Fear of death, desire of immortality, nature of sexuality, social organization, creativity, according to Rankian system. 291pp. 5⅜ × 8½. 20485-5 Pa. $7.95

A THEOLOGICO-POLITICAL TREATISE, Benedict Spinoza. Also contains unfinished Political Treatise. Great classic on religious liberty, theory of government on common consent. R. Elwes translation. Total of 421pp. 5⅜ × 8½. 20249-6 Pa. $8.95

MY BONDAGE AND MY FREEDOM, Frederick Douglass. Born a slave, Douglass became outspoken force in antislavery movement. The best of Douglass' autobiographies. Graphic description of slave life. 464pp. 5⅜ × 8½. 22457-0 Pa. $8.95

FOLLOWING THE EQUATOR: A Journey Around the World, Mark Twain. Fascinating humorous account of 1897 voyage to Hawaii, Australia, India, New Zealand, etc. Ironic, bemused reports on peoples, customs, climate, flora and fauna, politics, much more. 197 illustrations. 720pp. 5⅜ × 8½. 26113-1 Pa. $15.95

THE PEOPLE CALLED SHAKERS, Edward D. Andrews. Definitive study of Shakers: origins, beliefs, practices, dances, social organization, furniture and crafts, etc. 33 illustrations. 351pp. 5⅜ × 8½. 21081-2 Pa. $8.95

THE MYTHS OF GREECE AND ROME, H. A. Guerber. A classic of mythology, generously illustrated, long prized for its simple, graphic, accurate retelling of the principal myths of Greece and Rome, and for its commentary on their origins and significance. With 64 illustrations by Michelangelo, Raphael, Titian, Rubens, Canova, Bernini and others. 480pp. 5⅜ × 8½. 27584-1 Pa. $9.95

PSYCHOLOGY OF MUSIC, Carl E. Seashore. Classic work discusses music as a medium from psychological viewpoint. Clear treatment of physical acoustics, auditory apparatus, sound perception, development of musical skills, nature of musical feeling, host of other topics. 88 figures. 408pp. 5⅜ × 8½. 21851-1 Pa. $9.95

THE PHILOSOPHY OF HISTORY, Georg W. Hegel. Great classic of Western thought develops concept that history is not chance but rational process, the evolution of freedom. 457pp. 5⅜ × 8½. 20112-0 Pa. $9.95

THE BOOK OF TEA, Kakuzo Okakura. Minor classic of the Orient: entertaining, charming explanation, interpretation of traditional Japanese culture in terms of tea ceremony. 94pp. 5⅜ × 8½. 20070-1 Pa. $2.95

LIFE IN ANCIENT EGYPT, Adolf Erman. Fullest, most thorough, detailed older account with much not in more recent books, domestic life, religion, magic, medicine, commerce, much more. Many illustrations reproduce tomb paintings, carvings, hieroglyphs, etc. 597pp. 5⅜ × 8½. 22632-8 Pa. $10.95

SUNDIALS, Their Theory and Construction, Albert Waugh. Far and away the best, most thorough coverage of ideas, mathematics concerned, types, construction, adjusting anywhere. Simple, nontechnical treatment allows even children to build several of these dials. Over 100 illustrations. 230pp. 5⅜ × 8½. 22947-5 Pa. $7.95

DYNAMICS OF FLUIDS IN POROUS MEDIA, Jacob Bear. For advanced students of ground water hydrology, soil mechanics and physics, drainage and irrigation engineering, and more. 335 illustrations. Exercises, with answers. 784pp. 6⅛ × 9¼. 65675-6 Pa. $19.95

SONGS OF EXPERIENCE: Facsimile Reproduction with 26 Plates in Full Color, William Blake. 26 full-color plates from a rare 1826 edition. Includes "The Tyger," "London," "Holy Thursday," and other poems. Printed text of poems. 48pp. 5¼ × 7. 24636-1 Pa. $4.95

OLD-TIME VIGNETTES IN FULL COLOR, Carol Belanger Grafton (ed.). Over 390 charming, often sentimental illustrations, selected from archives of Victorian graphics—pretty women posing, children playing, food, flowers, kittens and puppies, smiling cherubs, birds and butterflies, much more. All copyright-free. 48pp. 9¼ × 12¼. 27269-9 Pa. $5.95

PERSPECTIVE FOR ARTISTS, Rex Vicat Cole. Depth, perspective of sky and sea, shadows, much more, not usually covered. 391 diagrams, 81 reproductions of drawings and paintings. 279pp. 5⅜ × 8½. 22487-2 Pa. $6.95

DRAWING THE LIVING FIGURE, Joseph Sheppard. Innovative approach to artistic anatomy focuses on specifics of surface anatomy, rather than muscles and bones. Over 170 drawings of live models in front, back and side views, and in widely varying poses. Accompanying diagrams. 177 illustrations. Introduction. Index. 144pp. 8⅜ × 11¼. 26723-7 Pa. $7.95

GOTHIC AND OLD ENGLISH ALPHABETS: 100 Complete Fonts, Dan X. Solo. Add power, elegance to posters, signs, other graphics with 100 stunning copyright-free alphabets: Blackstone, Dolbey, Germania, 97 more—including many lower-case, numerals, punctuation marks. 104pp. 8⅛ × 11. 24695-7 Pa. $7.95

HOW TO DO BEADWORK, Mary White. Fundamental book on craft from simple projects to five-bead chains and woven works. 106 illustrations. 142pp. 5⅜ × 8. 20697-1 Pa. $4.95

THE BOOK OF WOOD CARVING, Charles Marshall Sayers. Finest book for beginners discusses fundamentals and offers 34 designs. "Absolutely first rate . . . well thought out and well executed."—E. J. Tangerman. 118pp. 7¾ × 10⅝. 23654-4 Pa. $5.95

ILLUSTRATED CATALOG OF CIVIL WAR MILITARY GOODS: Union Army Weapons, Insignia, Uniform Accessories, and Other Equipment, Schuyler, Hartley, and Graham. Rare, profusely illustrated 1846 catalog includes Union Army uniform and dress regulations, arms and ammunition, coats, insignia, flags, swords, rifles, etc. 226 illustrations. 160pp. 9 × 12. 24939-5 Pa. $10.95

WOMEN'S FASHIONS OF THE EARLY 1900s: An Unabridged Republication of "New York Fashions, 1909," National Cloak & Suit Co. Rare catalog of mail-order fashions documents women's and children's clothing styles shortly after the turn of the century. Captions offer full descriptions, prices. Invaluable resource for fashion, costume historians. Approximately 725 illustrations. 128pp. 8⅜ × 11¼. 27276-1 Pa. $11.95

THE 1912 AND 1915 GUSTAV STICKLEY FURNITURE CATALOGS, Gustav Stickley. With over 200 detailed illustrations and descriptions, these two catalogs are essential reading and reference materials and identification guides for Stickley furniture. Captions cite materials, dimensions and prices. 112pp. 6½ × 9¼. 26676-1 Pa. $9.95

EARLY AMERICAN LOCOMOTIVES, John H. White, Jr. Finest locomotive engravings from early 19th century: historical (1804–74), main-line (after 1870), special, foreign, etc. 147 plates. 142pp. 11⅜ × 8¼. 22772-3 Pa. $8.95

THE TALL SHIPS OF TODAY IN PHOTOGRAPHS, Frank O. Braynard. Lavishly illustrated tribute to nearly 100 majestic contemporary sailing vessels: Amerigo Vespucci, Clearwater, Constitution, Eagle, Mayflower, Sea Cloud, Victory, many more. Authoritative captions provide statistics, background on each ship. 190 black-and-white photographs and illustrations. Introduction. 128pp. 8⅞ × 11¾. 27163-3 Pa. $13.95

EARLY NINETEENTH-CENTURY CRAFTS AND TRADES, Peter Stockham (ed.). Extremely rare 1807 volume describes to youngsters the crafts and trades of the day: brickmaker, weaver, dressmaker, bookbinder, ropemaker, saddler, many more. Quaint prose, charming illustrations for each craft. 20 black-and-white line illustrations. 192pp. 4⅝ × 6. 27293-1 Pa. $4.95

VICTORIAN FASHIONS AND COSTUMES FROM HARPER'S BAZAR, 1867–1898, Stella Blum (ed.). Day costumes, evening wear, sports clothes, shoes, hats, other accessories in over 1,000 detailed engravings. 320pp. 9⅜ × 12¼. 22990-4 Pa. $13.95

GUSTAV STICKLEY, THE CRAFTSMAN, Mary Ann Smith. Superb study surveys broad scope of Stickley's achievement, especially in architecture. Design philosophy, rise and fall of the Craftsman empire, descriptions and floor plans for many Craftsman houses, more. 86 black-and-white halftones. 31 line illustrations. Introduction. 208pp. 6½ × 9¼. 27210-9 Pa. $9.95

THE LONG ISLAND RAIL ROAD IN EARLY PHOTOGRAPHS, Ron Ziel. Over 220 rare photos, informative text document origin (1844) and development of rail service on Long Island. Vintage views of early trains, locomotives, stations, passengers, crews, much more. Captions. 8⅞ × 11¾. 26301-0 Pa. $13.95

THE BOOK OF OLD SHIPS: From Egyptian Galleys to Clipper Ships, Henry B. Culver. Superb, authoritative history of sailing vessels, with 80 magnificent line illustrations. Galley, bark, caravel, longship, whaler, many more. Detailed, informative text on each vessel by noted naval historian. Introduction. 256pp. 5⅜ × 8½. 27332-6 Pa. $6.95

TEN BOOKS ON ARCHITECTURE, Vitruvius. The most important book ever written on architecture. Early Roman aesthetics, technology, classical orders, site selection, all other aspects. Morgan translation. 331pp. 5⅜ × 8½. 20645-9 Pa. $8.95

THE HUMAN FIGURE IN MOTION, Eadweard Muybridge. More than 4,500 stopped-action photos, in action series, showing undraped men, women, children jumping, lying down, throwing, sitting, wrestling, carrying, etc. 390pp. 7⅞ × 10⅝. 20204-6 Clothbd. $24.95

TREES OF THE EASTERN AND CENTRAL UNITED STATES AND CANADA, William M. Harlow. Best one-volume guide to 140 trees. Full descriptions, woodlore, range, etc. Over 600 illustrations. Handy size. 288pp. 4½ × 6⅜. 20395-6 Pa. $5.95

SONGS OF WESTERN BIRDS, Dr. Donald J. Borror. Complete song and call repertoire of 60 western species, including flycatchers, juncoes, cactus wrens, many more—includes fully illustrated booklet. Cassette and manual 99913-0 $8.95

GROWING AND USING HERBS AND SPICES, Milo Miloradovich. Versatile handbook provides all the information needed for cultivation and use of all the herbs and spices available in North America. 4 illustrations. Index. Glossary. 236pp. 5⅜ × 8½. 25058-X Pa. $5.95

BIG BOOK OF MAZES AND LABYRINTHS, Walter Shepherd. 50 mazes and labyrinths in all—classical, solid, ripple, and more—in one great volume. Perfect inexpensive puzzler for clever youngsters. Full solutions. 112pp. 8⅛ × 11. 22951-3 Pa. $3.95

CATALOG OF DOVER BOOKS

PIANO TUNING, J. Cree Fischer. Clearest, best book for beginner, amateur. Simple repairs, raising dropped notes, tuning by easy method of flattened fifths. No previous skills needed. 4 illustrations. 201pp. 5⅜ × 8½. 23267-0 Pa. $5.95

A SOURCE BOOK IN THEATRICAL HISTORY, A. M. Nagler. Contemporary observers on acting, directing, make-up, costuming, stage props, machinery, scene design, from Ancient Greece to Chekhov. 611pp. 5⅜ × 8½. 20515-0 Pa. $11.95

THE COMPLETE NONSENSE OF EDWARD LEAR, Edward Lear. All nonsense limericks, zany alphabets, Owl and Pussycat, songs, nonsense botany, etc., illustrated by Lear. Total of 320pp. 5⅜ × 8½. (USO) 20167-8 Pa. $6.95

VICTORIAN PARLOUR POETRY: An Annotated Anthology, Michael R. Turner. 117 gems by Longfellow, Tennyson, Browning, many lesser-known poets. "The Village Blacksmith," "Curfew Must Not Ring Tonight," "Only a Baby Small," dozens more, often difficult to find elsewhere. Index of poets, titles, first lines. xxiii + 325pp. 5⅜ × 8¼. 27044-0 Pa. $8.95

DUBLINERS, James Joyce. Fifteen stories offer vivid, tightly focused observations of the lives of Dublin's poorer classes. At least one, "The Dead," is considered a masterpiece. Reprinted complete and unabridged from standard edition. 160pp. 5³⁄₁₆ × 8¼. 26870-5 Pa. $1.00

THE HAUNTED MONASTERY and THE CHINESE MAZE MURDERS, Robert van Gulik. Two full novels by van Gulik, set in 7th-century China, continue adventures of Judge Dee and his companions. An evil Taoist monastery, seemingly supernatural events; overgrown topiary maze hides strange crimes. 27 illustrations. 328pp. 5⅜ × 8½. 23502-5 Pa. $7.95

THE BOOK OF THE SACRED MAGIC OF ABRAMELIN THE MAGE, translated by S. MacGregor Mathers. Medieval manuscript of ceremonial magic. Basic document in Aleister Crowley, Golden Dawn groups. 268pp. 5⅜ × 8½. 23211-5 Pa. $8.95

NEW RUSSIAN-ENGLISH AND ENGLISH-RUSSIAN DICTIONARY, M. A. O'Brien. This is a remarkably handy Russian dictionary, containing a surprising amount of information, including over 70,000 entries. 366pp. 4½ × 6⅛. 20208-9 Pa. $9.95

HISTORIC HOMES OF THE AMERICAN PRESIDENTS, Second, Revised Edition, Irvin Haas. A traveler's guide to American Presidential homes, most open to the public, depicting and describing homes occupied by every American President from George Washington to George Bush. With visiting hours, admission charges, travel routes. 175 photographs. Index. 160pp. 8¼ × 11. 26751-2 Pa. $10.95

NEW YORK IN THE FORTIES, Andreas Feininger. 162 brilliant photographs by the well-known photographer, formerly with *Life* magazine. Commuters, shoppers, Times Square at night, much else from city at its peak. Captions by John von Hartz. 181pp. 9¼ × 10¾. 23585-8 Pa. $12.95

INDIAN SIGN LANGUAGE, William Tomkins. Over 525 signs developed by Sioux and other tribes. Written instructions and diagrams. Also 290 pictographs. 111pp. 6⅛ × 9¼. 22029-X Pa. $3.50

ANATOMY: A Complete Guide for Artists, Joseph Sheppard. A master of figure drawing shows artists how to render human anatomy convincingly. Over 460 illustrations. 224pp. 8⅜ × 11¼. 27279-6 Pa. $9.95

MEDIEVAL CALLIGRAPHY: Its History and Technique, Marc Drogin. Spirited history, comprehensive instruction manual covers 13 styles (ca. 4th century thru 15th). Excellent photographs; directions for duplicating medieval techniques with modern tools. 224pp. 8⅜ × 11¼. 26142-5 Pa. $11.95

DRIED FLOWERS: How to Prepare Them, Sarah Whitlock and Martha Rankin. Complete instructions on how to use silica gel, meal and borax, perlite aggregate, sand and borax, glycerine and water to create attractive permanent flower arrangements. 12 illustrations. 32pp. 5⅜ × 8½. 21802-3 Pa. $1.00

EASY-TO-MAKE BIRD FEEDERS FOR WOODWORKERS, Scott D. Campbell. Detailed, simple-to-use guide for designing, constructing, caring for and using feeders. Text, illustrations for 12 classic and contemporary designs. 96pp. 5⅜ × 8½. 25847-5 Pa. $2.95

OLD-TIME CRAFTS AND TRADES, Peter Stockham. An 1807 book created to teach children about crafts and trades open to them as future careers. It describes in detailed, nontechnical terms 24 different occupations, among them coachmaker, gardener, hairdresser, lacemaker, shoemaker, wheelwright, copper-plate printer, milliner, trunkmaker, merchant and brewer. Finely detailed engravings illustrate each occupation. 192pp. 4⅝ × 6. 27398-9 Pa. $4.95

THE HISTORY OF UNDERCLOTHES, C. Willett Cunnington and Phyllis Cunnington. Fascinating, well-documented survey covering six centuries of English undergarments, enhanced with over 100 illustrations: 12th-century laced-up bodice, footed long drawers (1795), 19th-century bustles, 19th-century corsets for men, Victorian "bust improvers," much more. 272pp. 5⅝ × 8¼. 27124-2 Pa. $9.95

ARTS AND CRAFTS FURNITURE: The Complete Brooks Catalog of 1912, Brooks Manufacturing Co. Photos and detailed descriptions of more than 150 now very collectible furniture designs from the Arts and Crafts movement depict davenports, settees, buffets, desks, tables, chairs, bedsteads, dressers and more, all built of solid, quarter-sawed oak. Invaluable for students and enthusiasts of antiques, Americana and the decorative arts. 80pp. 6½ × 9¼. 27471-3 Pa. $7.95

HOW WE INVENTED THE AIRPLANE: An Illustrated History, Orville Wright. Fascinating firsthand account covers early experiments, construction of planes and motors, first flights, much more. Introduction and commentary by Fred C. Kelly. 76 photographs. 96pp. 8¼ × 11. 25662-6 Pa. $8.95

THE ARTS OF THE SAILOR: Knotting, Splicing and Ropework, Hervey Garrett Smith. Indispensable shipboard reference covers tools, basic knots and useful hitches; handsewing and canvas work, more. Over 100 illustrations. Delightful reading for sea lovers. 256pp. 5⅜ × 8½. 26440-8 Pa. $7.95

FRANK LLOYD WRIGHT'S FALLINGWATER: The House and Its History, Second, Revised Edition, Donald Hoffmann. A total revision—both in text and illustrations—of the standard document on Fallingwater, the boldest, most personal architectural statement of Wright's mature years, updated with valuable new material from the recently opened Frank Lloyd Wright Archives. "Fascinating"—*The New York Times.* 116 illustrations. 128pp. 9¼ × 10¾. 27430-6 Pa. $10.95

PHOTOGRAPHIC SKETCHBOOK OF THE CIVIL WAR, Alexander Gardner. 100 photos taken on field during the Civil War. Famous shots of Manassas, Harper's Ferry, Lincoln, Richmond, slave pens, etc. 244pp. 10⅝ × 8¼.
22731-6 Pa. $9.95

FIVE ACRES AND INDEPENDENCE, Maurice G. Kains. Great back-to-the-land classic explains basics of self-sufficient farming. The one book to get. 95 illustrations. 397pp. 5⅜ × 8½. 20974-1 Pa. $7.95

SONGS OF EASTERN BIRDS, Dr. Donald J. Borror. Songs and calls of 60 species most common to eastern U.S.: warblers, woodpeckers, flycatchers, thrushes, larks, many more in high-quality recording. Cassette and manual 99912-2 $8.95

A MODERN HERBAL, Margaret Grieve. Much the fullest, most exact, most useful compilation of herbal material. Gigantic alphabetical encyclopedia, from aconite to zedoary, gives botanical information, medical properties, folklore, economic uses, much else. Indispensable to serious reader. 161 illustrations. 888pp. 6½ × 9¼. 2-vol. set. (USO) Vol. I: 22798-7 Pa. $9.95
Vol. II: 22799-5 Pa. $9.95

HIDDEN TREASURE MAZE BOOK, Dave Phillips. Solve 34 challenging mazes accompanied by heroic tales of adventure. Evil dragons, people-eating plants, bloodthirsty giants, many more dangerous adversaries lurk at every twist and turn. 34 mazes, stories, solutions. 48pp. 8¼ × 11. 24566-7 Pa. $2.95

LETTERS OF W. A. MOZART, Wolfgang A. Mozart. Remarkable letters show bawdy wit, humor, imagination, musical insights, contemporary musical world; includes some letters from Leopold Mozart. 276pp. 5⅜ × 8½. 22859-2 Pa. $6.95

BASIC PRINCIPLES OF CLASSICAL BALLET, Agrippina Vaganova. Great Russian theoretician, teacher explains methods for teaching classical ballet. 118 illustrations. 175pp. 5⅜ × 8½. 22036-2 Pa. $4.95

THE JUMPING FROG, Mark Twain. Revenge edition. The original story of The Celebrated Jumping Frog of Calaveras County, a hapless French translation, and Twain's hilarious "retranslation" from the French. 12 illustrations. 66pp. 5⅜ × 8½. 22686-7 Pa. $3.95

BEST REMEMBERED POEMS, Martin Gardner (ed.). The 126 poems in this superb collection of 19th- and 20th-century British and American verse range from Shelley's "To a Skylark" to the impassioned "Renascence" of Edna St. Vincent Millay and to Edward Lear's whimsical "The Owl and the Pussycat." 224pp. 5⅜ × 8½. 27165-X Pa. $4.95

COMPLETE SONNETS, William Shakespeare. Over 150 exquisite poems deal with love, friendship, the tyranny of time, beauty's evanescence, death and other themes in language of remarkable power, precision and beauty. Glossary of archaic terms. 80pp. 5³⁄₁₆ × 8¼. 26686-9 Pa. $1.00

BODIES IN A BOOKSHOP, R. T. Campbell. Challenging mystery of blackmail and murder with ingenious plot and superbly drawn characters. In the best tradition of British suspense fiction. 192pp. 5⅜ × 8½. 24720-1 Pa. $5.95

THE WIT AND HUMOR OF OSCAR WILDE, Alvin Redman (ed.). More than 1,000 ripostes, paradoxes, wisecracks: Work is the curse of the drinking classes; I can resist everything except temptation; etc. 258pp. 5⅜ × 8½. 20602-5 Pa. $5.95

SHAKESPEARE LEXICON AND QUOTATION DICTIONARY, Alexander Schmidt. Full definitions, locations, shades of meaning in every word in plays and poems. More than 50,000 exact quotations. 1,485pp. 6½ × 9¼. 2-vol. set.
Vol. 1: 22726-X Pa. $15.95
Vol. 2: 22727-8 Pa. $15.95

SELECTED POEMS, Emily Dickinson. Over 100 best-known, best-loved poems by one of America's foremost poets, reprinted from authoritative early editions. No comparable edition at this price. Index of first lines. 64pp. 5³⁄₁₆ × 8¼. 26466-1 Pa. $1.00

CELEBRATED CASES OF JUDGE DEE (DEE GOONG AN), translated by Robert van Gulik. Authentic 18th-century Chinese detective novel; Dee and associates solve three interlocked cases. Led to van Gulik's own stories with same characters. Extensive introduction. 9 illustrations. 237pp. 5⅜ × 8½. 23337-5 Pa. $6.95

THE MALLEUS MALEFICARUM OF KRAMER AND SPRENGER, translated by Montague Summers. Full text of most important witchhunter's "bible," used by both Catholics and Protestants. 278pp. 6⅝ × 10. 22802-9 Pa. $10.95

SPANISH STORIES/CUENTOS ESPAÑOLES: A Dual-Language Book, Angel Flores (ed.). Unique format offers 13 great stories in Spanish by Cervantes, Borges, others. Faithful English translations on facing pages. 352pp. 5⅜ × 8½. 25399-6 Pa. $8.95

THE CHICAGO WORLD'S FAIR OF 1893: A Photographic Record, Stanley Appelbaum (ed.). 128 rare photos show 200 buildings, Beaux-Arts architecture, Midway, original Ferris Wheel, Edison's kinetoscope, more. Architectural emphasis; full text. 116pp. 8¼ × 11. 23990-X Pa. $9.95

OLD QUEENS, N.Y., IN EARLY PHOTOGRAPHS, Vincent F. Seyfried and William Asadorian. Over 160 rare photographs of Maspeth, Jamaica, Jackson Heights, and other areas. Vintage views of DeWitt Clinton mansion, 1939 World's Fair and more. Captions. 192pp. 8⅞ × 11. 26358-4 Pa. $12.95

CAPTURED BY THE INDIANS: 15 Firsthand Accounts, 1750–1870, Frederick Drimmer. Astounding true historical accounts of grisly torture, bloody conflicts, relentless pursuits, miraculous escapes and more, by people who lived to tell the tale. 384pp. 5⅜ × 8½. 24901-8 Pa. $8.95

THE WORLD'S GREAT SPEECHES, Lewis Copeland and Lawrence W. Lamm (eds.). Vast collection of 278 speeches of Greeks to 1970. Powerful and effective models; unique look at history. 842pp. 5⅜ × 8½. 20468-5 Pa. $13.95

THE BOOK OF THE SWORD, Sir Richard F. Burton. Great Victorian scholar/adventurer's eloquent, erudite history of the "queen of weapons"—from prehistory to early Roman Empire. Evolution and development of early swords, variations (sabre, broadsword, cutlass, scimitar, etc.), much more. 336pp. 6⅛ × 9¼. 25434-8 Pa. $8.95

CATALOG OF DOVER BOOKS

AUTOBIOGRAPHY: The Story of My Experiments with Truth, Mohandas K. Gandhi. Boyhood, legal studies, purification, the growth of the Satyagraha (nonviolent protest) movement. Critical, inspiring work of the man responsible for the freedom of India. 480pp. 5⅜ × 8½. (USO)   24593-4 Pa. $7.95

CELTIC MYTHS AND LEGENDS, T. W. Rolleston. Masterful retelling of Irish and Welsh stories and tales. Cuchulain, King Arthur, Deirdre, the Grail, many more. First paperback edition. 58 full-page illustrations. 512pp. 5⅜ × 8½.
26507-2 Pa. $9.95

THE PRINCIPLES OF PSYCHOLOGY, William James. Famous long course complete, unabridged. Stream of thought, time perception, memory, experimental methods; great work decades ahead of its time. 94 figures. 1,391pp. 5⅜×8½. 2-vol. set.
Vol. I: 20381-6 Pa. $12.95
Vol. II: 20382-4 Pa. $12.95

THE WORLD AS WILL AND REPRESENTATION, Arthur Schopenhauer. Definitive English translation of Schopenhauer's life work, correcting more than 1,000 errors, omissions in earlier translations. Translated by E. F. J. Payne. Total of 1,269pp. 5⅜ × 8½. 2-vol. set.   Vol. 1: 21761-2 Pa. $11.95
Vol. 2: 21762-0 Pa. $11.95

MAGIC AND MYSTERY IN TIBET, Madame Alexandra David-Neel. Experiences among lamas, magicians, sages, sorcerers, Bonpa wizards. A true psychic discovery. 32 illustrations. 321pp. 5⅜ × 8½. (USO)   22682-4 Pa. $8.95

THE EGYPTIAN BOOK OF THE DEAD, E. A. Wallis Budge. Complete reproduction of Ani's papyrus, finest ever found. Full hieroglyphic text, interlinear transliteration, word-for-word translation, smooth translation. 533pp. 6½ × 9¼.
21866-X Pa. $9.95

MATHEMATICS FOR THE NONMATHEMATICIAN, Morris Kline. Detailed, college-level treatment of mathematics in cultural and historical context, with numerous exercises. Recommended Reading Lists. Tables. Numerous figures. 641pp. 5⅜ × 8½.   24823-2 Pa. $11.95

THEORY OF WING SECTIONS: Including a Summary of Airfoil Data, Ira H. Abbott and A. E. von Doenhoff. Concise compilation of subsonic aerodynamic characteristics of NACA wing sections, plus description of theory. 350pp. of tables. 693pp. 5⅜ × 8½.   60586-8 Pa. $13.95

THE RIME OF THE ANCIENT MARINER, Gustave Doré, S. T. Coleridge. Doré's finest work; 34 plates capture moods, subtleties of poem. Flawless full-size reproductions printed on facing pages with authoritative text of poem. "Beautiful. Simply beautiful."—*Publisher's Weekly.* 77pp. 9¼ × 12.   22305-1 Pa. $5.95

NORTH AMERICAN INDIAN DESIGNS FOR ARTISTS AND CRAFTS-PEOPLE, Eva Wilson. Over 360 authentic copyright-free designs adapted from Navajo blankets, Hopi pottery, Sioux buffalo hides, more. Geometrics, symbolic figures, plant and animal motifs, etc. 128pp. 8⅜ × 11. (EUK)   25341-4 Pa. $7.95

SCULPTURE: Principles and Practice, Louis Slobodkin. Step-by-step approach to clay, plaster, metals, stone; classical and modern. 253 drawings, photos. 255pp. 8⅛ × 11.   22960-2 Pa. $10.95

THE INFLUENCE OF SEA POWER UPON HISTORY, 1660–1783, A. T. Mahan. Influential classic of naval history and tactics still used as text in war colleges. First paperback edition. 4 maps. 24 battle plans. 640pp. 5⅜ × 8½.
25509-3 Pa. $12.95

THE STORY OF THE TITANIC AS TOLD BY ITS SURVIVORS, Jack Winocour (ed.). What it was really like. Panic, despair, shocking inefficiency, and a little heroism. More thrilling than any fictional account. 26 illustrations. 320pp. 5⅜ × 8½.
20610-6 Pa. $7.95

FAIRY AND FOLK TALES OF THE IRISH PEASANTRY, William Butler Yeats (ed.). Treasury of 64 tales from the twilight world of Celtic myth and legend: "The Soul Cages," "The Kildare Pooka," "King O'Toole and his Goose," many more. Introduction and Notes by W. B. Yeats. 352pp. 5⅜ × 8½.
26941-8 Pa. $8.95

BUDDHIST MAHAYANA TEXTS, E. B. Cowell and Others (eds.). Superb, accurate translations of basic documents in Mahayana Buddhism, highly important in history of religions. The Buddha-karita of Asvaghosha, Larger Sukhavativyuha, more. 448pp. 5⅜ × 8½. ,
25552-2 Pa. $9.95

ONE TWO THREE . . . INFINITY: Facts and Speculations of Science, George Gamow. Great physicist's fascinating, readable overview of contemporary science: number theory, relativity, fourth dimension, entropy, genes, atomic structure, much more. 128 illustrations. Index. 352pp. 5⅜ × 8½.
25664-2 Pa. $8.95

ENGINEERING IN HISTORY, Richard Shelton Kirby, et al. Broad, nontechnical survey of history's major technological advances: birth of Greek science, industrial revolution, electricity and applied science, 20th-century automation, much more. 181 illustrations. ". . . excellent . . ."—Isis. Bibliography. vii + 530pp. 5⅜ × 8¼.
26412-2 Pa. $14.95

Prices subject to change without notice.

Available at your book dealer or write for free catalog to Dept. GI, Dover Publications, Inc., 31 East 2nd St., Mineola, N.Y. 11501. Dover publishes more than 500 books each year on science, elementary and advanced mathematics, biology, music, art, literary history, social sciences and other areas.